Rainbow's End

Genaro González

Arte Publico Press
Houston
1988

This volume is made possible through grants from the National Endowment for the Arts, a federal agency, and the Texas Commission on the Arts.

Arte Publico Press
University of Houston
Houston, Texas 77004

Library of Congress-in-Publication Data
González, Genaro, 1949–
  Rainbow's end.

  I. Title.
PS3557.0474R35   1987   813'.54   87–18664
ISBN 0–934770–81–6 (pbk.)

Second Printing, 1991

Para mi madre, Dolores

Chapter 1

Over forty years ago, on a diluvian afternoon almost identical to the one he now contemplated, don Heraclio Cavazos had first stood on the Mexican bank of the Rio Grande and had seen U.S. soil. More precisely, he admitted, he had glimpsed American mud.

From inside the modest frame house where he lived with his daughter's family, a Spanish radio station issued updates on the hurricane's aftermath. A victim was relating her trauma on the air when Imelda called out from the living room, "Papá, can I switch to something less depressing?" Before don Heraclio could protest, his daughter tuned in a subdued report on estimated property losses and damage.

"I can't understand a word that gringo's saying."

"Believe me, papá, you're better off not knowing."

Four days earlier, with the hurricane season officially over, a tropical storm had been sighted in the Gulf of Mexico, on a possible collision course with the southern tip of Texas. A hurricane watch had become an alert, then a warning. Television newscasters commented that the Rio Grande Valley had not faced a storm of that magnitude since the late sixties, and for those who had not been around or who needed reminding, disaster footage of a decade ago had been resurrected.

Suddenly gale force winds had begun flinging large, serrated palm leaves, until even the stubborn don Heraclio had abandoned his post on the front porch. "Here it comes, Esteban. It's about to hit the fan."

His grandson, back from canceled classes at the community college, had agreed. "And we're smack in the middle."

But no sooner had they braced for the hurricane than it had veered south, slamming into Mexico. So while the Texas coast had weathered heavy rains and flooding, its southern neighbor had borne the brunt of the disaster. "Poor devils," was the phrase most often uttered that day. "As if they don't have enough problems already. But better them than us."

Barrio streets that overflowed after a normal rainfall were now a network of canals. "At least when it's this bad," don Heraclio told his daughter, "even the uptown rich get flooded."

But Imelda, inundated with housecleaning, barely heard the remark. Families evacuated from the worst-hit neighborhoods were being sheltered in classrooms, and for Imelda the school holiday only meant muddy tracks from nine-year-old Armandito, her adolescent Marina and Esteban. Fortunately her husband had reported to the packing shed for emergency repairs on the roof.

She felt so relieved when Armandito joined his friends in the flooded avenue that don Heraclio had to shout her usual warning: "Watch out for broken glass."

"Let him live a little," she said. "By Friday the mosquitoes will be sucking us dry. Anyway, I'm keeping an eye on him from here."

"A lot of good that'll do after he's cut."

She scanned the overcast. "The packing shed foreman who called Gilberto said the Rio Grande's overflowing. They've opened floodgates from here to Brownsville. The whole Valley's flooded. Imagine the migrants' faces when they come home next month."

Don Heraclio Cavazos noticed a sadistic satisfaction in her voice, but he let it pass. "As always, those with the least pay the most. The Bernal family and the Berensons have several fields down there. They weren't about to let their crops flood."

She cared little for her father's social concerns. Hypnotized by the monotonous flooding, she drawled her own observation: "Well, it'll keep back the tide of wetbacks. No more swimming across, at least for a few days."

"Let's hope not. Right now it's sheer suicide."

2

Chapter 2

Since leaving for the northern border, passengers on the Mexican bus had been plagued by delays and near-disasters from the hurricane rains. At first they had crowded around the adolescent driver, cringing whenever the bus entered a hairpin turn, groaning if it started to stall. Later, numbed by noise, fumes and a bone-jarring journey, they had turned into human cargo. But now, as they neared their border-town destination, there was much milling about and a revival of aspirations and fears. Even the pigs and poultry inside that ark on wheels grew more animated as they reached the end of the road.

The three young men who had shared the rearmost seat for most of the trip sat out the bottleneck at the door. They had met on the bus and, to while away the hours and to sidestep the thinnest one's silence over his real name, had decided to baptize each other with animal names. So the immense Mexican with windmill ears appropriately became the Elephant. Even his personality had a pachydermal air—placid and plodding, but with the latent temperament of a rogue elephant. The thinnest of the three, who guarded his past and kept his aliases in flux, had a fighting cock's spur tattooed on the web of his left thumb and forefinger. That, plus the tuft of hair which from a certain angle and with a little imagination resembled a cockscomb, earned him the name of the Rooster. The third became the Tomcat, an itinerant whose adventures included making love in every twisted alley of Guanajuato. But with each retelling his lovers switched identities and positions until the Elephant exclaimed, "Christ, those señoritas of yours change names more often than the Rooster!"

All three admitted one thing, though: they intended to cross the border without papers. For that reason the Rooster's comment as he rose from his seat took on an unintended but ominous tone. "Here's the end of the line."

They hobbled off the bus cracking spines and stomping the circulation into their legs. When the Rooster perched on the rear bumper, the Elephant asked, "What are you waiting for? A ride into Texas?"

"I'm resting for the swim."

"Are you crazy?! Right now the Rio Grande's swollen like a knocked-up sow."

The warning fell on deaf ears, and the Rooster looked around as if he had stepped off in another country. "What did you call that river?"

"The Rio Grande. We call it the Rio Bravo, gringos call it the Rio Grande River."

"Rio Grande River," said the Rooster. "And I thought only Mexicans loved to repeat themselves."

"Once you're across you can learn their double-talk. But for now . . ." The Elephant pointed to the Mexican flag flapping over the plaza. "See that eagle with a snake in its claws? Well, you'd better get used to seeing it for a few more days, even if you have to perch on a cactus and eat a snake or two. Better that than drowning."

For most of that afternoon they shared a park bench and watched the passers-by. Finally the Rooster grew impatient and approached a snowcone vendor. "Amigo, you must know these parts like the back of your hand. Let's say someone wanted to go for a swim . . ."

The vendor stopped shaving a block of ice to see if the Rooster was serious, then nodded. "A perfect day . . . to work on your drowned man's float."

Walking back, the Rooster had to face the Tomcat's kidding. "I could have told you that. Right now that river is both grande and bravo."

"He's probably too chicken to cross," said the Rooster.

The Elephant stared at him and shook his head. "Save that macho talk for when you're in Texas without papers."

He flexed his shoulders as though warming up. "It won't be long then."

"What a cocky little bastard! I'm waiting it out, and I'm twice as strong. But a lot less stupid." He sensed he had goaded his friend's pride. "Look, you're intelligent . . . quoting guys who died a million years ago. You're not some dumb beast like me. If anyone deserves to make it in . . ."

The Rooster started to protest when the Tomcat interrupted both. "All right, you've told us you're not going there to get rich. So what's the hurry? Listen to the Elephant. He finally made sense."

"Just wait a few days, Rooster. I'll even carry you across like St. Christopher with the baby Jesus."

But his mind was made up, and even as he worked up the will to lie he knew they would not believe him. "Christ, that trip turned the inside of my intestines into cement. I need to walk around a bit."

Nothing more was said. And although he alone was taking the risk, he felt he was compromising them as well. He pretended to follow some bills posted along a wall, then walked away without looking back.

Soon he reached the river, so turbulent it resembled flowing earth. Following the bank ridge, he took a narrow trail to the water's edge. There he crouched and contemplated the crossing, mulling over his plan until it became an obsession. Finally he convinced himself that its very boldness made it foolproof.

To begin with, the Border Patrol was not around, since no swimmer in his right mind would dare cross such a strong current. The site itself also seemed ideal: a sapling uprooted by the flood and lodged in midriver could serve as a rest stop. Part of the opposite bank had collapsed under the rains, leaving a caved-in gulley that would make climbing far easier than clawing up a steep, muddy bank. He was not a superstitious man, nor a religious one, but to turn his back on that cluster of omens seemed almost sinful. In the end it blinded him to the obvious . . . that an actual attempt was madness.

What he first mistook for a distant bridge became a pale, water-color rainbow, low and to his left. That meant a safer crossing within days, but with it a greater risk of being spotted.

Stripping to his rolled-up pants, he bundled his belongings inside his long-sleeved shirt, tied the cuffs and slung this across his back like a quiver. Then he waded in until the current tugged him off his feet.

He realized at once that he had stepped into something much deeper than he had bargained for, but he bridled his panic by stubbornly swimming farther out rather than back. He only hoped that the sapling had snagged deep enough into a sand bar to support him. What mattered now was keeping his head above water, although with every mouthful of air he drank an equal amount of river.

Soon his strokes turned into puny chops. The thought that he was striking an unfeeling enemy only enraged him further, and an untiring whirlpool sapped his strength until a breath of air felt as alien and painful as a gulp of water.

Then, for an instant and no longer, he promised himself, he stopped struggling and surrendered to a delicious defeat. I'm drowning, he thought with absolute indifference, and it felt as natural and effortless as breathing, suspended in an odd element that was neither air nor water.

His body still fought like some arrogant thing, a fitful infant succumbing to its mother's lullaby. Then he half-fathomed an ancient, cynical wisdom in the undercurrent: "A man never drowns in the same river twice."

Suddenly he was fighting for life again. He tore away from the undertow, and just when his left arm seemed incapable of another stroke he brushed against something solid and rough: bark. He grabbed at the sapling and gave a greedy, all-at-once gasp as single-minded and total as his first breath of life.

Shivering from exhaustion, he struggled to hold down the little nourishment left, but in the end he simply vomited a muddy trickle. "If those two could see me now," he said, then imitated the Elephant: "You're soaked and stranded, Rooster. I hope you're happy." He laughed and coughed, his thoughts utterly out of control. Finally he gave up and uncaged his mental bestiary, letting it spring out and animate his dying world.

One vision slowly devoured the rest: a snake, shimmering one color one moment, shedding it the next, swaying like a cloth in the breeze. Then his attention jelled: less than an arm's length away, coiled tightly around the sturdiest branch, a snake as thick as his forearm also waited out the flood.

It was a measure of his tenacity to live that he held his grip rather than plunge back into the river. Just then the snake flexed open its jaws in a shock of white.

He was as terrified of serpents as any man, and that bone-white mouth—the way a deep, fresh wound paled just before it bloodied—chilled him completely. My friend, he thought with an intensity transcending speech, we're in the same boat, but I'll be moving on soon. His telepathic chant was as much to convince himself as to charm the snake. We're both soaked to the bone, compadre, so let's live and let live.

The offer was accepted only too well. The water moccasin started its unhurried, hypnotic approach towards a thicker, more secure limb—its newfound friend's arm—slithering over in a side-winding way while seeming to twist in one spot. In spite of himself he instinctively backed away until he was down to a cluster of branches no thicker than his fingertips. Once more that sickening mouth pried open, and he gagged.

His thoughts turned into an exodus of trivial images, the way parasites abandoned a dying body and scuttled for a viable host. It was every idea for itself, without one thought staying for his survival. He had hoped that in the end the chaotic episodes of his life would cluster into a coherent pattern; now it seemed fitting that things should end on more of the same.

He tried to focus on the danger before him, but the serpentine twisting warped his sense of time, as when he stared too long at the dizzy, screwing turns of the barber pole back home. So he squeezed his eyes shut until they hurt, like the times he blocked out pain with another layer of pain, certain that if he opened them his courage would crumble into a scream. His temples started to pound from the strain of keeping his eyes closed, when a curious pressure skimmed his arm, subtle as a caress, but with an implied strength behind it. In the interval of an eyeblink he weighed the danger of keeping still against that of plunging back into the current. But by then he no longer had a choice: his arms, his entire body was paralyzed with fear.

Physically he was a prisoner, but through supreme self-discipline he managed to will his thoughts elsewhere. Yet even the memory in which he found refuge was not without its edge of irony: the morning the search party found his compadre Pánfilo's corpse crouched under a mesquite with a fistful of corncobs scattered about and with his pants still bunched around his ankles. He wore an embarrassed expression, as though the posthumous invasion of privacy was far worse than the bite. An old-timer in the group insisted that a viper pregnant with venom would actually hunt for human victims, and he offered some woodman's lore on surviving an attack. But the more absurd the circumstances surrounding one's death—and how much more ridiculous could one end up?—the more the rumor mongers hinted at murder. And since both compadres had thrown their lot against the local patrones and had ended up as underdogs, his own options had been clear: leave at once or tie his bowels into a knot. So he had fled, determined to reach the U.S. or die on the land he had fought for. And now he was stuck with a serpent on a winding no-man's river that was neither Mexico nor the U.S., in a limbo whose name neither side agreed upon.

He felt a persistent trembling along his arm, like the times his brothers had to prod him out of bed. He opened his eyes just wide enough to peek at the snake which was coiled cozily around his forearm. It lay utterly still, though; the twitching came from his own exhaustion, and the more he tried to bring the spasms under control, the stronger they became.

He stuttered through a hoarse lullaby, even though the serpent's blank stare gave no hint whether it was even asleep. Suddenly it abandoned his arm in a disoriented search, as if deciding in which direction to head. Before he even had a chance to react, it turned tail, slipped into the current and headed toward shore.

The spasms spread a new found strength along his limbs. He got his second wind, just in case the water moccasin decided to return.

Then he plunged into the current and did not pause until he reached the opposite bank.

But the moment he touched shore he sank hip-deep. "Shit!" he hissed as the earth sucked him in; "Shit!" as he imagined himself buried in mud just inched from a watery tomb; "shit!" determined that death would not cheat him back. He staggered and squelched up the slippery bank until he reached the first of several fields. His spastic movements gave him the eerie sense that someone else inhabited his body, but his momentum pushed him through occasional backslides.

He walked in a primeval and absolute silence, as though the rains had cleansed the earth of birds and insects. A fallow field bore waist-high weeds, and their wet lashing on his trousers was so hushed it seemed imagined. He hardened his steps into stomps to announce his presence in that mute world, but the spongy floor soaked up his pounding until he made his peace with the stillness.

A sudden downpour slackened his pace but did not stop him altogether. One of the furrows that followed a levee widened into a path, then opened into a dirt road. He pressed his stride until he saw an older man ahead waving his arms as if clearing the air of rain. The simple act of taking note broke both his pace and concentration. He meant to pause for a moment but had already left his last legs far behind.

The other man sprinted toward him, shouting in broken syllables. He stopped a few feet away and said something else, but his labored breathing scattered his speech and forced him to press a hand against his chest. He extended his other hand. "Samuel Ochoa."

The younger man simply stared. Everything about the stranger—his light skin, his indecipherable yelling, the very place he stood—had led him to expect an Anglo.

"Are you lost?" Samuel Ochoa asked in Spanish.

The weather-beaten young man looked all around. He remembered his last days on the run, convinced that his executioners were just footsteps away. He had covered his tracks so thoroughly that even his real name had the unfamiliar ring of an alias. But now, standing in the mud of a foreign field, his vigilance gave way to elation. He imagined his hunters helpless on the other side of that magical slash of geography, held back by political voodoo. But first he had to make certain. "Is this the United States?"

Samuel Ochoa smiled, certain that the young man was pulling his leg, like the other muchachos he lived with. He decided to humor him. "Yes. And you're in the year of our Lord, nineteen thir. . ."

"Then I'm not lost," he interrupted. "Heraclio Cavazos, at your service." He stretched out his hand and fell exhausted at the older man's feet.

Chapter 3

"Any mail for Heraclio Cavazos?" Imelda Menchaca asked the postman. Worried that the weather might delay delivery, she had joined her father on the porch to spot the mail jeep approaching. But after the check she was expecting for don Heraclio did not arrive, she waded back to the house with nothing but bills to show for her troubles.

The radio commercials were already being tailored to hurricane themes. Furniture damaged by rising waters was being offered "at unbelievable savings to the customer." Bernal's supermarket carried discounts on transistor radios, hurricane lamps and canned goods, keeping salient their near-brush with disaster: "We were lucky this time, but what about the next? Buy now, at incredible savings and be prepared."

"How odd," said Imelda. "Two days ago Bernal's checkers said they had to raise prices because of shortages. Now they're over-stocked."

"What's so odd about robbery?" asked don Heraclio. "They hoped to make a killing with the storm. Now they have to dump their surplus."

"Ay, papá. Next you'll say they publicize storms just to push stuff."

"For shopkeepers a disaster's no different than Christmas."

"Well, sometimes the t.v. people overdo it. If there's a water spout in the ocean their cameras are there to christen it. When the real thing comes along they've cried wolf too often."

Watching his grandson's antics as he splashed and screamed in the flooded street, don Heraclio felt a vague terror. Satisfied that Armandito was only playing, he told Imelda: "They had the boy terrified. Last night he asked if I had relatives in Mexico."

"What on earth for?!"

"He thought if we simply crossed the river we'd be out of danger."

"I really shouldn't laugh. I once thought that if Russia dropped the bomb we'd just cross the border and be safe. After all, who'd bother to bomb Mexico?"

Chapter 4

Heraclio Cavazos slowly recovered his walking legs while Samuel Ochoa surveyed the flood damage. "We'll be working these fields in a week," he said.

Heraclio seemed impressed. "You own them?"

Samuel smiled. "I'm just a field worker. The grower sent my crew boss to check the crops. But you know the saying: the dog sends the cat, and the cat sends the mouse. So now the mouse is up to his ass in mud while the cat's in the truck with his catnip." He thought for a moment and added, "Don Marcelo's a good man. But he drinks too much."

On their way to the truck Heraclio described his episode with the snake. Samuel picked up a battered cotton plant and opened a boll. "Did its mouth look like this?" Heraclio, who could not have made a better comparison, shivered in agreement. "A cottonmouth," said Samuel. "Good thing you took no chances. Most vipers won't swim after you, but a water moccasin will."

"I hope I don't run into one of his relatives."

"You won't. The floods brought this one down." He pointed to the fields. "Here we just worry about rattlesnakes."

"So this is where you work."

"Whenever I can get it. Times are hard, but don Marcelo prefers Mexicans, the wet kind. We're dirt cheap and don't make trouble."

"I know where that gets you."

"Maybe he can use an extra hand. You can room with me and pay our landlady from your first week's wages. The place is a zoo, though."

"After sharing a tree with a snake I'm ready for anything."

They rode into town in the back of don Marcelo's truck, drenched by renegade squalls. Since plunging into the river Heraclio had not known a moment's dryness, and he feared his appearance was a dead giveaway. But when they entered the town's flooded streets almost everyone was still drying out.

Samuel took him on a tour of the tenement house where he lived, with the rooms sounding more like cages than quarters. "The Porcupine and Greased Pig live here, along with the Possum twins. And over there. . ."

The dilapidated building was owned by doña Zoila Peña, who oversaw it from her spacious brick home next door. The tenement's upper floor was reached by a rickety stairway along each outside wall. Its ten spartan rooms housed some forty field workers, mostly undocumented transients. Doña Zoila called them "mis muchachos"—my boys—although some bachelors, like Samuel, were nearer her own age. The barrio knew the stag house as "la casa de los solos"; the neighbors across the alley, who had to tolerate an occasional Saturday night free-for-all, called it "la casa de los locos."

In fact most evenings there passed uneventfully, and the grinding routine was more menacing than the rare outbursts. Up before dawn, work until sunset, an evening poker game and then to bed. The monotony frazzled a few tenants into spurts of anarchy, and even the old-timers like Samuel kept a careful watch for the occasional solo who showed signs of going berserk.

Downstairs doña Zoila ran a general store where each muchacho had to buy something each week, even if only pork rinds or shoelaces. And while she called them boarders, no muchachos sat at her dining table. Both sides found the farce convenient: she was not about to feed forty-odd mouths, nor were her tenants eager to mind their manners in front of her educated son, who might one day be emperor of Texas, or whatever type of despot ruled the gringos.

That evening Heraclio met several muchachos, from the Poet to El Bruto, a monolith of a man who reminded him of the Elephant.

Even by the solos' standards, El Bruto was an isolate. Some said he was living proof of a missing link, but no one ever questioned his species to his face.

Besides, the resident zoologist was Father Adán, who had baptized the casa's fauna, and he had decided that an animal nickname for El Bruto was redundant. Decades of smoking marihuana had tinted Father Adán's eyes a permanent pink. Heraclio found him a likeable old man, despite an Old Testament intensity about him.

Heraclio spent the night with a few muchachos who sought news from the homeland or simply wanted to reminisce. Observing Samuel Ochoa, he sensed someone who had lived through a catastrophe and could not decide whether to lay bare his heart or close it forever. His subtle, feminine gestures seemed at odds with his large, farmworker's hands, giving the impression of an otherwise graceful woman trying to conceal a coarse feature but calling attention to it.

The other muchachos entertained him with dreams of saving their earnings, going back home and setting up modest enterprises. "What doña Zoila says is true," said one. "El vivo vive del pendejo"—the bright one lives off the dullard.

Another nodded. "Some day I'll open a drugstore back home, hire a pill pusher and rake in the pesos. There'll always be diseases in the world, and people to catch them."

A few preferred to stay. "I'm putting roots as a mesquite mechanic. A few tools and noonday shade are all I need. These gringos take better care of their cars than themselves."

When the Love Bandit's turn came up he cocked an elegant eyebrow, then confessed their ultimate fantasy. "Me?" he asked with a casual pose perfected in front of every mirror privileged to reflect his face. "I'm lazy but good-looking. Give me a rich, white widow like that lover boy Huero got . . . .Go ahead, laugh. One day you'll be picking my crops."

But their laughter was short-lived on hearing of their idol: Huero, whom none had met but whose name was a household word.

The truth behind the Huero legend was less glamorous. One sweltering afternoon, after taking a kidding for her rack of faded, peach shirts destined as moth excrement, doña Zoila had improvised an off-the-cuff pitch: "Call me sentimental, muchachos. That's the same style shirt Huero wore the day he landed that wealthy gringa." Their attention hooked, she added, "He was one of my first muchachos. The widow couldn't resist him in that peach guayabera. She even wanted their groomsmen in them, but Huero had to show who'd wear the pants in the house. Maybe he thought she'd fall for one of them. So I got stuck with twenty guayaberas gathering dust."

After that she could barely keep the shirts in stock, and picking out doña Zoila's muchachos in a crowd became child's play. On warm weekends they came out in full force and uniform: the antiseptic scent of Perro Consentido soap to exorcise mattress chiggers and insects within a ten-foot radius, brilliantined hair with two layers of Parrot pomade and a peach guayabera.

After Heraclio heard the muchachos out, he said, "I'm not here to marry any gringa. Not that they'd take me either. But I'd like to go north. San Antonio, maybe." When several eyes turned to his left he looked there too.

The Frog Prince returned his gaze. At first glance his nickname seemed incongruent: he had the Love Bandit's good looks with none of the vanity. Then he turned to show a deep crater on his left cheek. And when he said, "North, eh?", with a hoarseness that parched Heraclio's own throat, the metamorphosis was complete. "All I can say is good luck."

"What's there to it?" asked Heraclio. "You just follow your nose."

"You have to cross a huge ranch, the largest in the world, they say. It's brush country, and crossing on foot takes days. Full of rattlesnakes, wild boars and Rangers. Best way to sleep is in mesquite trees. Rest in the afternoon and move by moonlight, when it's cool. Your worst enemies are thirst and gringos. The windmills have water for cattle, but they could hide an ambush."

"By whom?"

"Anyone who can get away with killing a wetback. Even our own people, to make points. They say we poach."

"How do you know all this?"

The Frog Prince gave a tight smile, and his odd scar deepened. "The voice of experience. Years ago Samuel, myself and another muchacho tried our luck. Every mistake we could make we made— walking all afternoon, not bringing enough water. By the third day we were pissing in our canteens. When I finally worked up the nerve it stank."

"Nothing more bitter than cold urine," said Samuel.

"Tell me about it."

"Now he can't even stand beer," said the Love Bandit.

"Then, to my . . ." The Frog Prince closed his eyes and extended his arms. "To my right I saw windmill blades catching the sun. Seemed easy . . . leave the group, get water, then catch up.

"I caught two slugs for my troubles. Next thing I remember is choking on dust and Samuel telling me to keep still."

"Whoever shot him left him for the buzzards," said Samuel. "The other muchacho and I knew the bullet in his chest had to come out, so we dragged him under a huisache." Samuel contemplated his hands for a moment. "Don't ask what came over me. I'd never dug out anything worse than a mesquite thorn before. But in the end I took out the slug with a knife."

The Frog Prince caressed his cheek. "This one stayed as a souvenir."

"So long Hollywood," said a muchacho called Juanito. "He didn't even have to tell me how he got it. I figured it out myself the same week I came here."

For the rest of the evening Heraclio watched Juanito out of the corner of his eye. The next day he casually asked others about him, and everyone said the same thing: Juanito fantasized himself a detective. His room was littered with police gazettes, and through the years he had extracted public confessions from muchachos over past indiscretions. Each had later stole away in shame.

The others had struck an uneasy truce over his annoying habit of trailing them. They never caught him outright; he always "just happened to be there." Yet the minute he dropped his surveillance, each victim felt something like an invisible cage lifted from over him.

His other pastime, though, unnerved them. After stalking his prey's most private moves for several days, he would plot a foolproof plan to murder him. "In theory, of course," he assured them, but his target could only sit limply while Juanito ticked off his every intimate quirk and the how-to of the perfect homicide. After reducing him to a hypothetical corpse, he lost all interest.

As a result the Bald Eagle not only stopped lounging around the rooftop but grounded himself after suffering from fainting spells; after that he was the Dizzy Buzzard. The Love Bandit stopped brushing his teeth with baking soda after Juanito explained how easily a demented soul could substitute a lethal dose of pest poison. And the parasite-plagued Lalito El Malito began carrying his own newspaper to the outhouse, since the supply there might be cured with larvae from the "menudo" or "wrong-way" worm, starting a caravan through his bowels.

For Heraclio, Juanito was a natural enemy. By the second day he was glancing at the cock's spur tattoo of his clandestine group from back home. Juanito began with his typical obliqueness: "This casa is a den of thieves, you know."

"Don't leave out the sheep molesters," said Heraclio.

"I'm dead serious. The cops should surround the place with barbed wire and make everyone do ten years."

"Everyone?"

"Well, some of us have to stay outside, to sniff out the low life."

"Is it true what they say, about catching a thief? . . ."

Juanito replied by dropping the bombshell wrapped in ribbons. "What an original tattoo!" He spread Heraclio's thumb and forefinger. "Crude, but creative. And so mysterious. Don't tell me you're mixed up in some secret society."

Heraclio decided that to throw him off the scent he had to meet him head-on. "Now keep this to yourself," he said, nearly butting heads. "I was in the Mexican mafia. And anyone who sticks his nose in our business gets it sliced off. Now, I shouldn't talk, but you have quite a collector's item there, my friend."

Juanito's voice came close to cracking. "Now . . . be serious."

Heraclio lowered his own voice to a conspiratorial whisper. "Would I kid about this?"

Juanito primed his bobbing Adam's apple for an answer. But if any words were still there, he swallowed them back.

Chapter 5

Don Marcelo the crew boss drove up bleary eyed for their first day's work since the storm. He tapped his horn and Heraclio followed several muchachos down the casa's stairs.

"Good thing the fields are dry," Samuel told him, "or else he'd drink himself senseless."

Several men, women and children were already in the truck. Don Marcelo welcomed his new worker aboard while nursing his hangover. "Water everywhere," he said, squinting at the puddles, "and not a drop to drink."

Samuel offered him his canteen, but the Frog Prince said, "Might be piss."

"The way my mouth tastes, that's probably what I had last night."

He stopped at a friend's cantina in the country, left the engine running and sent his small son for a cold beer. "If he's out of cans with the horsey on the label," he added for the benefit of the crew in back, "then don't bother."

The boy returned empty-handed. "No more horsey!"

Don Marcelo gunned the truck's idle, torn between his hangover and his pride, until a mimic in back made the choice for him. "Bring back a mule, then! A zebra! Anything on four legs!"

The minute they reached the cotton field, the workers crowded the exit, anxious to make up for lost time. Heraclio watched them closely and soon coordinated his work into a swift, seamless rhythmn. But once the novelty wore off he settled into a more methodic pace.

When the crew came in for lunch he and Samuel joined the Poet under the truck. Heraclio rested against a tire and accepted some corn on the cob. He was so hungry that at first he overlooked the Anglo grower standing over him. Then he smiled, but the steely eyes stared through him as if he were one more cotton sack scattered about.

Heraclio held his stare until don Marcelo interrupted with his fermented breath. "This muchacho Mexican. He no speak English."

The grower slapped him on the back. "Hell, he ain't the only one!"

Heraclio let them move on before wondering aloud, "What planet's he from?"

"Your guess is as good as mine," said Samuel. "One day he showed up dirt poor, with nothing but his overalls. Our people felt sorry and fed him."

"Like a pet," said the Poet.

"That only opened his appetite. Sooner than you could say 'Chíngame' he started stealing land, mostly from our raza."

"How?" asked Heraclio.

"It helps if the law's on your side. I was working these fields long before he came, but I'm still the outsider."

"There's a lesson in all this," said the Poet. "Gringos help each other out while we stab each other in the back."

Heraclio shook his head. "What about all the help you've given me?"

"Gringos stick together against Mexicans," said Samuel.

"Otherwise they turn cannibal on their own kind. This friend from Guanajuato said gringo miners there killed each other over fool's gold."

"Well, we have our own cannibals," said the Poet. "Like don Luis Bernal."

Samuel rolled his eyes heavenward. "What this gringo doesn't own, don Luis does. He's also godfather to some of these men's children. But the old goat wants their wives, too. He says that way the men can call him compadre twice."

"At least this gringo doesn't follow women who go pee in the fields."

"Maybe he thinks he's too good for them," said Heraclio. "Don't forget, he's from another world."

"That's one thing I never forget," said Samuel. "And he makes sure I don't." He estimated the hour by the sun, then entered the field where the mud was packed. Heraclio took his sack and followed the older man's footsteps.

Chapter 6

One morning, riding to work in the rear of the truck, Heraclio pushed back a canvas flap and stuck his head above the side boards. He was letting the early chill clear his thoughts when another field truck zoomed by in the opposite direction, with a man waving wildly. Heraclio heard a shout cut short, but soon the other truck was tailgating and honking.

The moment don Marcelo pulled over, the other crew boss bolted from his cab. "This lunatic said he'd kill me unless I followed you. He made me do a Utah."

Don Marcelo deciphered his mangled English. "A u-turn? What for?"

Suddenly the Elephant jumped out on the shoulder, and the truck actually swayed. "Now get lost!" he told his crew boss. "Damn, I knew it was you, Rooster! Tell your boss to make room for two!"

The Tomcat sprang beside him. "Elefante, we still owe this man our picking sacks."

"Screw him. He was robbing us anyway. Now we're working for this guy."

Don Marcelo took the transfer in stride. If a crew of Venutians had flagged him down he would have hired them on the spot, provided they took alien wages. "I admire young men who know what they want," he said, then followed the Elephant on the side mirror as this one boosted himself up the scaffolding. The rickety frame, never intended for climbing, much less by someone that size, creaked dangerously. "There's a ladder if you gentlemen care to use it."

Heraclio was now wide awake, and the Elephant's enormous embrace squeezed out whatever sleep remained. "I never thought I'd see you again, amigo!" He seemed on the verge of tears.

The children in the truck milled about as if under a circus big top while the Elephant hoisted his friend against the canvas. "So there you were, like some gringo's dog sticking its head out the car window. Just hair and tongue whipping in the wind. So I pounded that bastard's roof till he turned round."

At noon Heraclio shared his lunch with the Tomcat, and several children fed the Elephant morsels; some even petted him and scampered away in amazed relief.

Later Heraclio took them to the casa. "We have to see Padre Adán."

"Who the Devil is he?" asked the Elephant. "A priest?"

For longer than anyone could remember, Father Adán had noted the comings and goings of the casa. He could give a complete history of each room's occupants, down to the most transient of tenants, as well as the circumstances surrounding their departures. He had also given nearly every muchacho an animal nickname; even those already baptized elsewhere sought his blessing.

For that reason Heraclio introduced him to the Tomcat. "El gato macho, eh?" asked Father Adán. "You'll need all nine lives with that look, like you swallowed the canary."

When he met the Elephant, though, his jaw went slack as if the name had been taken out of his mouth. He patted the new tenant's face and torso like a blind man and immediately demoted the current elephant-in-residence, who seemed a puny specimen by comparison.

The Poet had but one concern. "You can't leave the other poor creature nameless, Padre."

Father Adán faced a personal crisis. Except for the Possum twins, he could not allow identical animals to run around. People would think he had lost his touch. "Besides," he had once said, "this is no ark."

He toyed with the Mammoth as a substitute for the other muchacho, but his failure with prehistoric names made him reconsider. In the past he had spent so much time describing the beasts and then correcting the muchachos' pronunciation that he had concluded dinosaurs had become extinct for the same reason: who could remember such complicated names?

His eyes, already slits from a recent dose of marihuana, screened out the human world to better visualize his mental menagerie. He traced several species, then made his pronouncement: "Let the other be the Rhino!"

Pleased with his Solomonic judgment, he retired to his room to verify his choice in an illustrated animal book, already dog-eared and spineless.

Almost immediately the muchachos began calling the new tenant the Elephant, without the usual trial period for nicknames that captured less flattering features. Somehow his imposing dimensions never intimidated them. Perhaps he too had finally found an identity large enough to wear comfortably. For that reason he kept mum about his real name, saying only, "Then you'd really laugh out loud, and I'd have to crush a few bones."

The Tomcat, the only other one in the know, hinted vaguely, "Maybe your folks thought they could change your size that way, like magic."

"Maybe. It's made for some fragile little thing with chicken bones. Like Heraclio here." For those like Juanito, who pushed their curiosity too far, he offered a friendly warning: "Mess with an elephant and you get the tusks."

But his troubles soon began in another arena. Don Marcelo had several adjoining fields that would take over a week to pick, so the crew settled in for the monotonous scenery. The only entertainment was a daredevil pilot in a crop duster. At first his heart-stopping acrobatics delighted them, but by the third day they had escalated to sheer meanness. His favorite stunt was swooping over stragglers, forcing them to take a headfirst dive. Don Marcelo did not mind, though. "Keeps the lazy ones in line and the rest on their toes."

One afternoon, while the Elephant relieved himself in a corner of the field, the aviator strafed him twice. Unable to budge him, he finally flushed him out with a spray of pesticide. Choking, with his pants still unzipped, he stormed out, blind to everything but revenge.

"That gringo has the right idea!" yelled the Love Bandit. "Let's have him fumigate every time you use the outhouse."

Thus began a daily rivalry, the Elephant roaring oaths from atop the cotton trailer, the pilot diving so close that the Elephant swore he was bald. "One day I'll trick him into flying too low," he said, ramming his fist against his palm. His rage seemed so palpable that Heraclio imagined him plucking the spindly biplane in mid-air, like the gigantic gorilla in a poster outside the Anglo movie house. "Do what Pancho Villa did," said Heraclio. "He once tricked a pilot into landing by dressing his men in enemy uniforms."

When he failed to see the connection, Samuel spelled it out: "Dress up as a woman and flirt in some field until he comes down. He'll be like a buzzard with a broken wing then."

The Love Bandit insisted that no normal male would take him as bait.

On their last morning the barnstormer pulled out all the stops, but the Elephant was nowhere to be seen. The pilot was swooping in low and hard when a series of blinding flashes startled Heraclio. Expecting freak lightning, he glanced up the moment the plane clipped several rows, abruptly gained altitude and snagged in some power lines. For an eye blink it sputtered like a struggling fly snared in a cobweb; then the lines snapped and sizzled, and the plane somersaulted into an adjoining chicken farm and exploded.

The crew stood dumbfounded as the poultry farmer and his ranch hands threw buckets of dirt on the smoldering wreckage, trying to salvage any singed chickens that might have survived. The burnt feathers and pesticide stung everyone's eyes and prompted a female picker to weep at the sight of so much barbequed chicken going to waste. But since the farmer had already threatened to shoot on sight any trespassing Mexican as a chicken thief, the crew watched with folded arms and open mouths as his business went up in smoke.

Finally the Elephant arrived from the far end of the field, surveyed the disaster and said, "What lousy timing for my morning shit."

An albino muchacho who had infiltrated the chicken farm by posing as a deaf-mute Anglo returned with a terse report: "Ni plumas ni pelos"—neither feathers nor hairs. And while the spectators shuddered at the thought of burning even beyond a crisp, the Elephant had but one regret: "Now I'll never prove the bastard was bald."

Don Marcelo, eager to get them back to work, delivered a hasty eulogy: "He loved flying. Now's he's got a permanent pair of wings."

Heraclio kicked a large clod with his boot, and it crumbled into dust. "I don't think they hand those out where he's going. In fact, something tells me this roasting was just the beginning."

While no one mourned the pilot, his sudden and absurd end brought their own mortality closer to home. A metaphysical argument began circulating that the Elephant's rage had somehow jammed the controls. But it took Juanito's detective work to fit the pieces into a more prosaic puzzle.

He was already juggling two separate mysteries: the Elephant's absence just before the crash and the theft of The Love Bandit's shaving mirror that morning. The Love Bandit's vanity had even kept him in the casa rather than let the world see him in the stubble left from an unmagnified mirror.

Juanito pored over the events for days, until the epiphany struck him with a flash as blinding as the one Heraclio had described. He tracked down his key witness and found him holding down a muchacho's arm while another tattooed a Satan with angel wings.

"Those reflections right before the crash," Juanito blurted out, "where do you suppose they came from?"

"From the plane window, of course."

The other two muchachos seemed satisfied with the answer.

Juanito stared at each one. "No, no and no! Can't you see? El Elefante stole the mirror. Then he hid in the fields and blinded the pilot when he passed the power lines."

A shiver ran up Heraclio's spine, but he masked it as a shrug. "Maybe that flash was the pilot's bald head."

"Come on, Cavazos, don't act innocent. Not with your shady past."

By that evening the news had spread like wildfire. When the Elephant got wind of the rumors he waited for Juanito to collect his poker winnings, then calmly cornered him. "Look, if I ever kill a man I won't be as cute or clever as you say. But he'll be just as dead." He rested his forearm on Juanito's chest and pressed him to the wall. His victim turned three shades of ash but made no attempt to struggle free, and the Elephant discovered what Heraclio already knew: that the self-appointed avenger of crime was a coward.

The next day Juanito had changed his story and was telling anyone who would listen. "No reflection on your friend, Cavazos, but I doubt he could cook up such a scheme."

He put Juanito to the test. "You mean he's the blunt instrument type?"

"I mean he's not the type, period."

"I'm not so sure. I share a room with him, and now I keep El Bruto's revolver under the cot. I mean, the guy could crush you and claim he rolled over in his sleep."

Juanito pressed his temples as though the very thought pained him. "No, no, no. You're making things too difficult. He couldn't hurt a fly. Not even a human one."

Chapter 7

One Saturday evening Heraclio and the Poet were reminiscing about life back home when El Bruto barged into the room. "Up, you faggots! On your feet!"

It was the longest speech Heraclio had ever heard him utter, and that alone startled him. "Let's put out that fire!" he added, and left as suddenly as he had stormed in.

The one thing Heraclio feared more than drowning was suffering the pilot's fate. He jumped up to open a window when the Poet held him back.

"The man's in heat, Heraclio. He's inviting us to the red light district!"

El Bruto continued banging on locked doors, accusing the muchachos inside of self-abuse or worse. Hearing him, Heraclio wondered whether he had been reared by wolves; where he had learned those snorts and growls that passed for language and at times sounded like no other tongue was anyone's guess.

But what he lacked in the social graces he made up for with a contagion that had already infected The Poet: "Let's go, Heraclio! The night life!"

"And the women that go with it," said the Tomcat, who along with the Elephant and a few others had already gathered outside.

Even the Love Bandit was hiding bills in his socks. "I really don't have to go. I'm even getting paid as a stud next week . . ."

"By who?" asked the Tomcat. "Manolito Ramírez?"

"I didn't want to get personal, but actually it's your . . ."

The Poet stepped in between. "Lust waits for no man!"

Although Heraclio had spent too many nights cooped up in the casa, he still had his misgivings, and he turned to the Poet as his last hope. "But a minute ago you were talking about your sweet . . ."

"That was a minute ago, about someone I may never see again. Tonight we burn that candle God gave us!" And in truth no one else had more wax to melt than the Poet. For all of his bohemian rhetoric, he was the least experienced.

Heraclio peeled several bills from his wallet, and the rest cheered. "I didn't know we had a red light district," he said.

"We do in Mexico," said El Bruto.

"Mexico?! But how do we get there?"

"Easy," said the Elephant. "We'll walk across."

"And how do we get back?"

The Poet pushed him out the door. "We'll cross that bridge . . ."

Entering Mexico was in fact so easy that the memory of his own crossing seemed almost unreal. When a Mexican cop idly looked them over, Heraclio had trouble meeting his gaze with a clean conscience until he told himself: "What can he do? Deport me?"

He followed El Bruto into a cantina where the bar girls sensed that aura of men without women. A wisp of a brunette with very white teeth asked El Bruto if he had been drinking all day. She answered his incoherent reply with, "I knew it. No wonder I can barely understand you."

Several rounds later El Bruto seemed none the worse. "Let's see the stockyard."

Heraclio found himself weaving alongside, past sphinx-faced girls who aged decades when he turned for a second look. And he stumbled on the heels of El Bruto, through a village of women who pasted movie idols next to little corrals of plaster saints, who stripped bachelor love to its flesh-and-blood functions, who wrapped toilet paper around one hand like a boxer's bandage, and who paused from a cheap romance novel long enough to ask, "¿Ya, mi amor?"

And he staggered far behind El Bruto, who grabbed a woman's

crotch and asked, "What's that between your legs?" and was told, "Same thing your mother's got."

And although alcohol had numbed the Poet's tongue to where it felt like El Bruto's, he preached on the domestic virtues of whores, describing a certain artist's life with a prostitute. Afterwards El Bruto asked what hours the painter worked so he could pay her a call.

A moment later the Poet felt a saline aftertaste, fell to one knee and studied the fresh stain at his feet. "Look! The poet's disease!"

But El Bruto, whose fondest memories came from his days as a slaughterhouse stunner, needed no expertise in bloodshed to reach a diagnosis. "It's your own vomit, sissy."

By then Heraclio was also struggling against the hell spinning around him. Not the elaborate, abstract Hell where immortal poets slummed, but the shabby, third-rate hell on earth where dreamers threw up. The shanty-town hell where God had caroused as a Young Man, pockets stuffed with almighty dollars and testicles bursting with everlasting life; the open-all-night hell He frequented long enough to get the Devil out of His system and sow His lost tribes; the Mexico-never-sleeps hell He left behind when He crossed the river to a family and a job as a balding, tenured deity; the come-back-when-you-get-the-urge hell He meant to revisit but never got around to doing until He was impotent; the la-vida-no-vale-madre hell where His bastard sons and natural daughters venerated his portrait and mourned His death more than His own family because they had the most—and yet nothing—to lose; the Mexico-take-back-your-children hell where His illegitimate orphans paid legal fees in installments and waited with infinite patience for the promised inheritance forever being settled in celestial court.

Then he too fell to his knees, his last recollection El Bruto pushing the Poet's face closer to the ink blot of his vomit, trying to exorcise an incurable romantic. "This is life, goddamnit!"

The following morning they took turns recovering in the outhouse. Sufficiently revived, Heraclio asked how he had ever managed to swim back. "I carried you on my shoulders," said the Elephant. "All you needed was a halo to look like the baby Jesus."

The truth was just as incredible: "We walked across the bridge," said Samuel. "Right under immigration's nose."

"Actually," said the Tomcat, "the Elephant was on all fours."

"They let me through, though. I guess only americanos dare cross drunk."

Samuel patted Heraclio on the back. "We owe it all to you. You couldn't walk for beans either, but when they asked us the capital of Texas, you passed the test for all of us."

"What did I say?!"

"Who knows! But if not for you we'd be waking up with our underwear backwards in a Mexican jail."

Chapter 8

For many muchachos the trips to Mexican brothels became a frequent diversion. But with their hard-earned dollars and their air of marginal Mexicans, they were easy prey for shakedowns by federales. "Time was," said Samuel, "when a man could slip back to his motherland for a few hours in heaven. Now you have to watch your step there too."

Father Adán suggested another solution altogether. "Why throw away good money," he asked, eyeing doña Zoila's collie bitch, "when La Chula is there for the taking? No fleas, either. That's more than you can say for most whores." For whomever wondered if he were serious, he offered an invitation: "Go ahead. I have lots of vices, but jealousy's not one of them."

In time doña Zoila Peña worked out an agreement with the Mexican police who snared her muchachos in red light district dragnets. Whenever her Sunday flock turned up incomplete she sent out someone to search the bordertown jails for her missing black sheep. Dependable tenants were released under her custody and paid their fines in installments, of which she kept a portion.

Cat-house perfume or the more subtle scents of local dance partners were the souvenirs they brought back from the world, where girl friends spent their seasons grading vegetables in packing sheds or humming boleros over the roar of canning machines. The aromatic shirts provided a soothing antidote to the steady misogyny of the casa's radio, where mariachis never tired of warning the world of female treachery.

Without these pacifiers there was no telling what would possess them. On nights with a full moon some might open a window and howl in lunatic abandon or imitate the throaty moans of a woman in ecstacy.

On summer evenings doña Zoila listened to their antics with that patronizing amusement of the well-to-do. She cared for them in her own distant way, yet despite the prohibited pin-ups she let them nail to the walls, she was little more than an overworked surrogate. And no matter how many nomads she took under her wing and called "mi muchacho," she could never erase their indelible look of orphans.

So she sat outside as the sun hovered on the horizon with its last hydrogenous ounce of buoyancy, reminding her of a heavy-lidded child trying to stay up a bit longer. Barely rocking her chair, watching a muchacho hang his single, Saturday-night shirt out the window, she glanced at her own backyard where the maid was taking down her son's wardrobe that spanned the length of two clotheslines. And that businesswoman's brain that seemed to harden into annual layers—thin rings in lean years, thicker ones in prosperity—stopped spewing hog futures and plotting real estate killings to linger instead on that muchacho whose hopes for happiness hung with his peach guayabera, lofted like the rescue signal of some shipwrecked soul. But she quickly caught herself and came to her opportunistic senses with a falling back on cliches learned at her father's knee—better them than my own flesh and blood, and el vivo vive del pendejo. She knew full well that if her Pablito were tossed into that snake pit of poverty, he would not last a week.

Each year he resembled more his late father: the aloof gestures, the classic profile of a screen idol and more than a touch of vanity. Fortunately he lacked even a token feature from her own family. For in addition to inheriting her father's business acumen and connections, he had also bequeathed her a banker's no-frills face. What Pablo Peña saw in her, said the barrio wags, was the same face he worshipped on hundred-dollar bills.

Yet there had been no need to put an ear to the ground; she saw and heard for herself. On their honeymoon she caught him advising

33

her tenants to marry plain women. "Otherwise you'll see your own son overtake you each day." She weaved away while he told those future fathers that an adoring mother was nothing more than an unfaithful wife.

With his manhood on the line, though, he had finally consented to an heir. But as luck would have it, his vain streak ran more than skin-deep, as his conceited genes refused to mingle and regress such a flawless specimen.

And now, as doña Zoila's rhythmic rocking coaxed out a painful nostalgia, she remembered when, after going to countless specialists on male sterility on both sides of the border, they had finally consulted Malvina, the local healer. The first thing the curandera asked her was, "Why bring another parasite like him in the world?" The only reason they stayed was because they feared her supernatural wrath.

Along with her prescription Malvina whispered in his ear, "There isn't much time, so aim straight." He assumed she meant the potion's duration, but within weeks her words took on a meaning more macabre than anyone could have imagined: Pablo Peña had prostate cancer.

His last drop of optimism evaporated with the discovery that the disease had spread through his marrow. A hospital prognosis gave him as many months to live as the fingers on either hand. That very afternoon he confessed his long-standing affair with their nubile servant girl, a tropical nymph from Nayarit whose cool dark skin was its own antidote for the fever it provoked. On balmy summer evenings, and with an innocence which only added to lustful thoughts, she made the muchachos' mouths water like teething babes, as they hungered to nibble on her tropical mango flesh. For Pablo Peña that dream had become a reality every Thursday siesta for the past three years in the casa's extra room, where his wife stored mattresses for delousing.

Up to then Zoila had seen her husband's possessive attentions toward the girl as nothing more than paternal concern. She too would stop her periodically in front of the muchachos to inspect her perpetual hickeys. "If I ever catch the vaquero who's branding this heifer . . ." she once said while eyeing her muchachos, who were putting on a don't-look-at-me look.

The girl turned a deeper mouth-watering shade of brown. "I've told you, señora, it's a birth mark."

"It's more like the beauty mark on that Mexican movie actress. Gets lower each time she has her face stretched."

"My friend Chavela says there's a vampire loose in the barrio."

"Really. Now tell me about the pot of gold at the end of the rainbow."

"I swear." She unburied a crucifix from her moist bosom and kissed it. "This is all I wear at night. But some mornings I find it in . . ." She did not blush harder because her complexion was already saturated. "Chavela says they can't catch him because he takes his siestas in Mexico."

"That's all we need. Illegal vampires to come suck our blood. Well, if he pricks you any lower and knocks you up, he'd better take you to his coffin."

Pablo Peña's abrupt decision to make a clean breast of his sins left Zoila with a guilt-ridden rage. The confession at least explained his insistence on overseeing the girl's Thursday cleaning chores in the casa, ostensibly to protect her from stray solos. He chaperoned her so well that the gorgeous kitten was strictly off-limits to the muchachos, who chiseled a pragmatic commandment on their conscience: thou shalt not covet thy landlord's mistress. Instead they waited for the inevitable litter to pop out. "Protection from us? The only protection he gives her is those three-ply rubbers he uses," they would say.

The sex kitten, dismissed by the man she had made deliriously happy for the past three years, made the most of her misfortune by eloping on the first full moon with a tomcat tenant who later returned ten pounds thinner. Afterwards Zoila's recurring nightmare had been, Dear God, what if she went off pregnant? Pablo's days were dwindling, and she herself showed no sign of conceiving. Certain that her ex-servant had won the luck of the draw, she ignored his assurance that he had ended the affair before taking the potion.

She could not shake the feeling that the girl had gone back to her own kind, to spawn in that primordial swamp that bred her muchachos. And in her dream terrain Zoila saw herself waiting for Pablo's son to return to the casa of his conception, lost among the multitude. She would wait for the unwashed muchacho who had missed being her own flesh and blood by the span of a squirming, stubborn sperm. She would wait for his entrance one night, drawn like a moth into the room she had filled with stuffed animals for the rightful heir stolen long ago and far away in the belly of a gypsy kitten. She would wait surrounded by a rotting rag menagerie bought the same afternoon that something had told her, Today's the day; then later, with equal, cynical certainty, she had thought, Yes, Pablo's dice finally rolled the lucky number, but someone else had backed the winning bet.

So in her dreams she lay in bed tortured by invisible thorns of insomnia and corraled by an inanimate stuffed herd. Then she would turn to a flickering, silver-nitrate glow and see that young screen idol's face that no degree of poverty could ever emaciate, as their life force flowed into a union that missed its mark of incest by the breadth of a distant Thursday afternoon delight. Another chance, she prayed feverishly, Sweet Jesus, just one more chance! Then suddenly she would shudder awake sheened in the same sweat Pablo left on her after making love, except that tonight her husband lay prostrate in an adjoining room, an enervated stud sapped of his last siring, waiting impotently for the little death left.

It came on a Thursday afternoon as humid as those slippery, waking siestas when he prayed for heaven to claim him. A rosary for his soul was recited in the casa, with a captive chorus of muchachos who mumbled and went through the motions for nine consecutive nights.

The morning after the novena Zoila awoke to the first of those daily nauseas that left her drained yet vindicated. She no longer had time to dwell on the servant girl's fate, until the day she found herself surrounded by cold, gleaming chrome and the finest medical attention money could buy.

She went into prolonged labor. Little by little her cries and pleas took her senses to a filthy, ill-lit hovel where an ancient midwife chain-smoked cornhusk cigarettes and lectured sternly, "Stop that bitching, muchacha! You never complained all the times he put it in." She saw through her tears a sleeping mat and a pair of firm, dark legs, alien to her own spindly paleness. But after the blinding moment of birth she was back in the hospital's soothing hum.

She struggled against exhaustion to examine her newborn son, praying not for some shared feature to bond them but that he resemble his father. Her adoration of Pablito had none of the narcissism that passed for maternal worship; it was pure, unselfish love, as when she had worshipped his father.

Now, sitting in the evening breeze a few feet from the casa, serenaded by lunacies and fake orgasms, she thought about her son, destined for greatness. On coming of age he would find a worthy companion and elicit a torrent of love from a hundred other señoritas. He was already so removed from the rabble boarders that he would address them with an intuitive noblesse. He was so special that while she called each boarder "mi muchacho" she could never bring herself to call him that, because muchachos were snot-nosed brats in soiled diapers who tortured the family mongrel; they were hungover young men slurping menudo in the wee hours of some dirty diner. She could never call him something so affectionately commonplace. Her straight-walking son, who would never dream of coming home smelling of cheap liquor, much less of one-night-stand perfume.

Now, as she sat through the twilight, she lingered on the fate of Pablo's other son, the dark star that had once obsessed her. These days he rarely crossed her thoughts; an occasional dream was enough.

Looking out at the vast universe, wondering if other lives out there yearned to cross that void, she felt humbled but with a purpose. Why else would God have created so many aliens and so much stellar real estate? She thanked the heavens for her son's lucky star, stagnant and fixed in his family's constellation, while her muchachos howled and moaned at the passing moon.

Chapter 9

One daybreak a half-awake Heraclio boarded the truck and sought out a quiet corner. The night before, during an idle discussion, two muchachos not only discovered that the same woman was two-timing them, but each insisted he had taken her virginity. Their respective friends drew battle lines, but the brawl ended when El Bruto and the Elephant stepped in between. "You interrupted our beauty sleep," said the Elephant. Then, while El Bruto held them under each arm, he pulled down their pants and added, "First one to open his mouth again gets his cherry popped." And that had been the end of that.

Heraclio was burrowing deeper into a pile of cotton sacks when Samuel jabbed an elbow into his ribs. In his dream he was holding the winning hand for the largest poker pot in the casa's history, and in the instant that he startled awake, a sore loser drew a derringer and shot him point-blank in the chest. He shut his dream eyes in pain at the exact eyeblink when his real ones opened in stark terror, and for a few confused seconds he made sure he was not bleeding.

He found himself staring at a new family—five women—boarding single file. One, obviously the mother, mimicked his stupefied stare and muttered something to her brood. But it was her daughters who had caught Samuel's attention, and now his.

That was the first time he looked into the young woman's eyes and relived the paradoxical peace of drowning, the first time he saw the serenity that found its equilibrium between the flirting glances of the two younger sisters and the indifferent regard of the eldest, who acknowledged the crew as if she knew them for years.

The young woman with the tranquil eyes gazed at the workers as well, but cautiously, as though aware of their effect on men. So when she lingered on Heraclio, she startled him anew.

She wore a floppy work hat, its brim pushed far back and framing her face in a straw halo; she seemed to him a madonna who had come to toil among her worshippers. Sitting on the flat-bed floor beside her mother, she removed her hat, and a soft, black braid uncoiled down her shoulder. She stifled a slight yawn and gave a private yet self-conscious smile. At that instant she was more real to him than anything else.

"Pelado descarado!" said the mother, and he knew immediately he was the target of her insult. A burning embarrassment washed over him as if she had splashed him with a pail of scalding water. He looked away with an inside-out indignation, as though some other man had shown disrespect.

He spent the rest of the day doing his work and trying to piece together the jig-saw gossip about the new family. Her name was Graciela López; her family called her Chacha. Knowing that, he felt his universe shift: other faces became a blurred background for Graciela's features; and the voices of friends now had the irritating edge of cicada calls because they invaded the space where Chacha's words belonged.

He did his best to keep the turmoil inside, but that evening Samuel Ochoa knew that his friend was not the same man who had left the casa that morning. When asked what was wrong, Heraclio tried to mask his feelings with small talk, but his obsession slipped in on the oblique: "By the way, did you notice those sisters this morning?"

Samuel held his breath and nodded.

He steadied his voice. "There was one . . ."

Other than narrowing his eyes, his friend altered nothing.

"The quiet one with Indian cheekbones and skin so brown it even warms your eyes . . ."

Samuel exhaled and slapped him on the back. "Congratulations! We thought you'd lost interest in women."

He stepped behind Samuel and goosed him. "Can't a man stop going to brothels without being called queer?"

"Juanito saw a long hair on your shirt, but he thought you were putting the boots to doña Zoila's collie."

As the days passed, anything remotely connected to Graciela became a star in that splendid galaxy: the ripe milkweeds that scattered lacework in her wake, her floppy hat dangling like a cowgirl's round her neck, her cloth gloves cut off at the tips. Even the family lunch pail, pocked and galvanized, brightened his day, as did the voice of her battle-axe mother, simply because it signaled her daughter's nearness. And yet he could only stand anesthetized under her gaze, with no more insight into her soul than the intellect a lowly ant could muster. At the end of each working day he was left with nothing to fill her asphyxiating absense, nothing he could preface with "And she said to me . . ."

He faced an adversary determined to thwart him at every turn: himself. He became a man divided, at times telling himself, You're no Love Bandit, but they say the hog with the biggest snout gets the best ear of corn. Then he would wonder, So why are so many hogs running around hungry?

Neither did trying his best to be himself help. If she truly liked him then one muffed word would not ruin his chances. Because no matter how often he rehearsed his introduction, the thought of one mispronounced syllable sent him back to his autistic adolescence, when his family periodically asked him questions to make certain he still talked.

The other obstacle was her mother, who guarded her brood more jealously than a dozen brothers. Rumor had it that one day doña Lola's husband had simply stepped out for an afternoon refreshment and had never returned, taking only the clothes she had just starched and ironed for him. Later he had sent a note from Mexico, saying only that he had taken pity on a pubescent whore after receiving a sign from above. That explained her bitter attitude towards men, but Heraclio found it small consolation. "One guy walks out the door," he told Samuel, "and we're all locked out."

She especially protected Graciela, who could outpick anyone on the crew. Only Fela, the eldest, needed no shepherding. She transcended rebellion, as deaf to wolf whistles as to society's siren song. Heraclio once overheard doña Lola compare her two oldest daughters and realized that theirs was the difference between night and day. "Chacha's our bread and butter," she told another field woman, then glanced at Heraclio and another muchacho. "She can leave any of these jerks in her dust. But the minute I turn my back on Fela she goes into a trance." She squinted at the blazing sun. "God in his infinite wisdom gives, only to take away."

Cristina, the youngest sister, said, "Fela hears voices."

"Maybe she has a don," said the woman.

The other sister, Belia, asked, "Is that contagious?"

"It's a special power from God."

Doña Lola shrugged. "He should have given her common sense instead."

A man who loved to eavesdrop on women's conversations offered a theory: "Has she had dental work in Mexico? Sometimes the cheap fillings pick up signals from that radio station across the border."

"No. Her problem's a lazy body and an overactive imagination, and she inherited both from her father."

"She was papá's favorite," said Belia.

"He should have taken her with him," teased Cristina.

"She refused to eat for days, then did so only after we promised never to mention his name. That's about the time she cut her hair and started hearing voices. Right now she's an apprentice to a witch. Let's hope she's not spirited away like her father some day."

Doña Lola's four daughters, stooped in their labor, flanked her like pecking chicks. Graciela, who took two rows to match their slower stride, was bothered enough by her mother's favoritism to add that Fela's mentor, Malvina, was a healer, not a witch. But as far as Fela was concerned, her mother could have been showering her with accolades.

She was a strange one, thought Heraclio. While in many ways Graciela's opposite, she was in every way her equal. Her short hair, along with her visions and avocation, led to the muchachos dubbing her Joan of Arc. The same close-cropped style gave her eyes an unsettling strength. While Graciela's sloe-eyed look suggested an ancestral, Indian trace, Fela's hinted at a darker part of that alien world and reflected an intelligence at once innocent and sinister.

But if she failed to put him at ease, neither did she interfere. On odd occasions he would find both sisters working side by side without their mother to sour the moment, and as far as Fela was concerned he was just another of her tagalong spirits. Such opportunities took planning, though. Once he loafed around the scales until Graciela came in for a weighing, then he plotted which rows she would take next. The strategy was less than honorable, but the times called for unconventional tactics. He hurried ahead with his sack draped over his head to shield the meddlers' glances, feeling like a wolf in sheep's clothing out to waylay an innocent girl.

Knowing she always took two rows, he started a pair himself. In no time she closed the gap then stayed with his slower pace. He was rehearsing his opening line in his head when, as predictable a nuisance as the ant hills that plagued his rows, her mother called out: "Chacha! Where are you, child?"

She answered in that heart-quickening voice that made him startle as if an immediate reply were expected of him. "Right here! I've started two rows already!"

"Well, I need you here. Right now!"

Damn her mother! he thought.

She glanced at him, and it gave him the necessary courage. "Don't worry. I'll take over."

She smiled, as surprised as if a statue had sprouted speech, then promised, "I'll come help first chance I get." Then she was gone, but her voice, that unique, clean timbre he could have picked out in a mob, danced in the still air of the field.

Soon he realized the burden he had taken on: four rows to pick. The Tomcat and the Elephant offered to help, but he waved them away.

By then the crew had moved to another quadrant like a plague of methodical locusts.

"You'll be there all night!" hollered the Tomcat.

"And end up with one of your sissy nosebleeds!" said the Elephant.

He ignored them both. Finally, when the Elephant's prognosis seemed about to come true, she appeared at the opposite end and began helping him, advancing in that efficient and effortless way she had of passing through the world. When she was a few feet away his hands turned clammy, as if his turn had come to recite a poorly memorized poem.

Their bent heads just inches away, they picked the last plant, and when they reached for the same fluff of cotton and touched fingertips, they exchanged a strange static. They stood and laughed, relieved at being equally nervous. He glanced at the cotton in his hands, without any idea what it did there, then handed it to her so naturally that she took it without question.

"I didn't want to finish," he said, "so I could talk to you again."

He wanted only to observe his reflection in her eyes, to see her seeing him. His arms still tingled like the time El Bruto had dared him to try a street peddler's shock machine, and he had gripped the bars while the voltage was cranked up and his arms began to curl from the current, unable to let go. Then even his tongue had turned too thick to tell them to shut off the juice.

Her mother suddenly broke the spell. "Chacha! Get away from that idiot!"

He avoided doña Lola's path for several days. Not that he feared her: after the latest humiliation he was ready to do battle. But he also knew that if she prohibited her daughter from ever talking to him again, Graciela would obey.

Finally, on their way to work one morning, something told him he had to break the standoff. Don Marcelo was driving parallel to the field when a boy giving a crow's-nest account from atop a water barrel suddenly yelled, "We ran over a huge snake!"

But the serpent had merely sunk into the cultivated earth, and by the time the first observers popped their heads over the side boards, they only caught the swaying foliage.

When don Marcelo denied running over any reptile and accused the boy of inventing things to avoid working, one woman grumbled he could have hit a dinosaur and not noticed. He was sober enough to turn down a dare to enter the field himself. He did offer, however, to credit fifty pounds to whomever turned up the snake. "That's one reward that won't be collected alive," said doña Lola, who convinced the mothers to stay on board until the field was safe. The men kept quiet but were in no hurry to attack their work either.

Then Heraclio saw don Marcelo's tow chain coiled in a corner and felt the luck of the love-struck. Certainly he, the snake and the chain were all part of some grand design. "I'm going after it," he said with heroic calm, but when the commotion made him repeat himself, his fear squeaked through.

A prematurely toothless worker with a high-pitched voice did not help matters any. "That was no ordinary snake," he insisted. "That was a real monster, all right. An original, from when serpents walked upright. When I was a young goatherd I saw one swallow a kid whole. Whole! Hoofs and all! The men followed it to a cave and hacked it to pieces with machetes. Just remembering makes my ass pucker!"

Heraclio took advantage of the man's histrionics to beg Samuel's help. Samuel, hoping to impress a young woman of his own, came to his aid. Praying that their quaking arms would not set the chain rattling, they went to where the serpent had disappeared. Two men armed with a ladder for the cotton trailer joined them. The rest stayed on the truck and offered advice.

They began flogging a small radius at a time, sprinting away in case they flushed out the snake. Finally they hurled out the chain as far as possible and were almost yanked along by the momentum. They were dragging it back in, remarking how terror made everything heavier, when their back-up men yelled that they had a monster in its links.

Even those in the truck panicked. When one of the men on the ground propped the ladder against the truck, the mob screamed that any serpent able to hitch a ride on a chain could easily climb a ladder. The stranded fellow heard that the serpent was already following him, and his efforts turned frantic. By now the snake had slithered into the field, but the mob threw the man overboard, ladder and all. When Heraclio and Samuel helped him up from behind, he must have imagined the snake's coils, for he gave a weak bleat and fainted.

It was then that Fela López parted a path through the crowd and into the field. Unlike the other women, she wore no superflous skirt over her work pants, and Heraclio almost mistook her for a man. Samuel, though, recognized her at once and helped quiet enough of the mob to let her speak.

"The serpent is going to cross into the levee," she said in that reedy, windborne voice that doña Lola recognized from her daughter's trances. "It'll stay there until we leave."

The entire crew waited and watched on the treadmill of an eternal present; waited with the awesome terror of newborns entering another world; watched until the serpent, more monstrous than anyone had imagined, crawled out of the field, under the truck and into the levee.

Someone finally found his voice: "A-ask if there's any more like it in the field."

For the rest of the day the camp stood divided: some swore that the interval between the young witch's pronouncement and the serpent's retreat had been too brief for coincidence; others simply said they had lost a good half-hour waiting for a cheap magician's trick. But no one dared ask Fela herself, who went on with her day's work as if picking flowers in the countryside. She even disappeared behind the levee, returned with a bright yellow shrub and attended to the man suffering from nervous exhaustion.

Perhaps it was Heraclio's recklessness that still resonated through him; or the eerie afterglow of Fela's conjuring, leaving faint, mysterious pinpoints like the first fireflies at dusk. Regardless, he laughed aloud at his fractured heroics, and when Graciela glanced his way he yelled across several rows: "I caused a riot back there!"

"What if that thing had swallowed you whole?"

"Your sister could have pulled me out, like a rabbit from a hat."

Samuel, working closer to her, gestured him to trade rows. "I'll keep the older sister occupied," he murmured as they crossed furrows.

"There's no . . ." But at that moment Fela smiled at his friend, and Heraclio's own happiness grew.

Something like rarified air rushed into his lungs, and he seemed invincible. Being next to Graciela felt so right that even her mother kept her distance.

"I'm Graciela López."

He suddenly realized they had not introduced each other.

"Heraclio Cavazos. I'm one of . . ."

"Doña Zoila's muchachos?"

"Yes. Are you from . . .?"

"Mexico? Oh, no. My family's lived here since Santa Anna lost this very land to the gringos."

He studied her for a moment. "Are you like . . . your sister? Like a mind reader?"

She made a quizzical face, then laughed. "Oh, no! It's just that . . ."

It was his turn: "You already knew what I was about to say."

He persuaded her to talk about her daily routines, some of which he already knew from heresay but which took on a special meaning coming from her. He also coaxed out some minor intimacies:

"I have no patience for cooking. I'd rather work with a field hoe than slice my fingers with a kitchen knife. In some ways I'm worse of a tomboy than Fela. At least she boils potions and remedies . . . ."

"What else? Let's see . . . I love gardening. It's a shame our yard is so tiny. Plus our puppy digs up everything . . . ."

"My favorite flower? The hibiscus, any color. No fragrance, nothing frilly. It's only there to make your eyes glad."

By the end of the afternoon he felt his valor shrinking back into shyness, so he pressed his luck while there was still time. "Would you wear a hibiscus in your hair for me? Any color?"

She blushed as if he had read her thoughts again, but held his gaze. "I was going to wear one this week, but now I feel you'll tease me. Some other time," she promised, "when you least expect it."

Chapter 10

On Saturday afternoons he began standing catercorner to her house under a gnarled mesquite, biding his time for hours on end. Graciela, flattered yet worried, protested during a conversation in the fields: "You make mamá nervous. This morning she even woke up and thought you were in our living room."

"Then she should let us meet like two adults."

"She's threatened to call the Border Patrol."

"She can call in the Texas Rangers, for all I care."

"But you're too obvious. Next you'll be wearing a sign on your back."

"That worked for us in Mexico. At least for a while."

"She even calls you my guardian angel."

He heard Samuel's whistle that meant her mother was approaching. "I'd say she deserves that honor herself."

He would have been less amused by the other nickname doña Lola had tagged on him. "There's that scabby lizard again," she once said after looking out her living room window for the third consecutive Saturday and seeing his lovesick pose. "Clinging to his favorite tree. The Mexican variety, if I'm not mistaken." She pretended to observe more closely. "Um-hm. Its back's still wet."

Suspecting that Graciela shared the blame, she glanced at the former apple of her eye, now corrupted by the worm of romance. She touched on Fela's good points, such as they were. "One good thing about my witch. She's crazy but not stupid. She visits the casa but won't let those barnyard animals follow her home."

Neither daughter contradicted her, and Fela's alleged indifference was convenient for both. Indeed, serving as a go-between on her daily trips to the casa kept alive Fela's own hopes of running into Samuel Ochoa.

Even the fact that Fela was letting her hair long failed to raise doña Lola's suspicions; she assumed her daughter was keeping a religious promise of some sort.

One autumn afternoon a sudden norther upset the cycle of balmy Saturdays. The chilling wind made hostile noises outside the López house but added a snugness inside. Doña Lola went to the window with a ready remark about how nice it would be to get an uncluttered view out front when she saw, gnarled to his tree, Graciela's constant admirer. For one awful heartbeat she had the chilling certainty he had frozen to death in his short-sleeved shirt.

In fact he was huddled against the south side of the trunk, shielding himself from the drizzle. Even after she saw he was alive and shivering and not just a carcass with hair flapping in the wind, her heart went out to the poor idiot rubbing against the rough bark for warmth.

Dammit, she warned herself, don't let him melt your heart, nobody's forcing him to stay out there. She retired to the coziness of the kitchen, hoping he had the good sense to give up and go home. But the rattling window panes tattooed a stark image of chattering teeth, until she murmured, "Ask him in." Graciela, warming her bare toes by the oven, leaped to her feet. Whether she had spied him while covering her hibiscus plants with cardboards or whether some intuition had alerted her, she rushed outside barefoot.

"Muchacha loca! Why bring him in if you catch your own death of cold?!"

His incessant chattering teeth announced his entrance. Offered coffee, he clacked his spoon until it seemed the cup might chip, and he kept a conversation going to keep his trembling jaws preoccupied. "Thank you for your kindness, señora."

Doña Lola, convinced that the slightest pampering turned men into despots, shrugged. "I couldn't let you freeze solid. Then I'd have your corpse out there every day, like a scarecrow."

"Strange," said Fela. "I thought lizards were cold-blooded."

All four sisters exploded in laughter, and on seeing their mother turn livid, they suffered a second outburst. Graciela apologized between gasps. "You must think this is a madhouse."

He smiled back. "I can tell you've never visited the casa."

He walked home that night completely happy, in a serape improvised from one of Graciela's crazy quilts. His promise to return it provided an excuse for another visit.

Even the air smelled cold, but for now he was content to remain wrapped inside his cocoon. Any other time the icy drizzle would have turned his face into a pincushion, but tonight it only made him more ecstatically alive.

Chapter 11

With the harvest season almost over, Graciela and Cristina took advantage of an early afternoon off to buy groceries at Bernal's market. Several helpers in back were unloading produce from the family truck. Their supervisor kept staring at the two women, and at the first opportunity Cristina pulled her older sister behind a pyramid of cans. "Imagine who's giving us the eye! Luisito Bernal, don Luis' son!"

Graciela took a carrot from her basket and worked up some enthusiasm for her sister's sake. "At least he knows we're more than just farm animals."

When they were ready to leave, Cristina paused by the register and pretended to recount her change. He quickly approached, still carrying a burlap sack. "Don't leave with the wrong impression, ladies." Graciela expected an apology for his rude staring and got instead: "I'm not some poor worker giving you the eye."

Graciela nibbled her carrot to hide her irritation. "So what if you are? There's no shame in working with your hands."

"Oh, I work," he said, pointing to don Luis' office. "But papá insists I learn the business from the bottom up."

When Cristina gave a fawning sigh he shifted his axis more in line with Graciela's. "I hear you're engaged to one of the muchachos."

For a moment she thought she had misjudged him. "Heraclio Cavazos," she said, and waited for his best wishes. "Do you know him?"

He sniffed. "Not really. I hear he works in my father's fields."

"That's where we met."

"I'm don Luis' son, Luisito," he added in case she had any doubts.

"You don't say." She cracked her carrot in one bite, took her kid sister's arm and left him holding his sack.

A month of Sundays later, Luisito parked the produce truck across the street from the casa. In the rear sat his usual sidekicks and hangers-on. Father Adán called them the hyena pack after Luisito boasted that once he tired of a woman he threw them his leftovers.

His reputation as war lord of the local women was common knowledge among the older muchachos who spotted his truck when they stepped outside. Sniffing danger, they bolted up the side stairs again.

This went on for several hours until a new muchacho asked about the standoff. Father Adán explained: "He's worse than his old man. When it comes to women, Luisito can't stand competition, not even from a compadre."

"What do you mean, 'a compadre'?"

The Love Bandit said, "That's when two men sleep with the same woman. Like your father and me."

Luisito's stalking presence soon turned the casa into a henhouse under siege. Juanito reviewed his soul for moral breaches and decided to organize an early poker game, while the Love Bandit simply stayed in bed with a beer and a bag of pork rinds.

Around two in the afternoon Heraclio stepped out into the street. Already late for his movie matinee with Graciela, he overlooked the Bernal truck. Luisito would have missed him too, had not one of his men interrupted his nap.

"Cavazos," he called out in that slurred tone he used to hand out workers' wages. But when Heraclio walked to the truck without hesitation, Luisito was taken aback. He assumed Graciela had already complained of his attentions. "Cavazos, you've been sticking your nose in my love life."

Heraclio, close enough to smell the liquor on Luisito's breath, held his stare for a few unbelieving seconds, wondering if Luisito was pulling his leg. Convinced it was a matter of mistaken identity, he said, "I'm not seeing one of your women, Luisito. I have a fiance."

Luisito slowly got out of the truck and tugged at his crotch. "She's the one I'm talking about, stupid."

Someone from Luisito's pack yelped to warn that things were about to get interesting. The rest circled him, and suddenly Heraclio understood the social call. He also knew he had to act before his reason or Luisito's men could subdue him.

In the adrenaline's blur his first punch only wobbled his opponent off balance, but the next wallop connected solidly on the jaw. Then a flurry of blows hit him from all sides, and for a stinging instant he relived the time he had stirred up a hornet's nest as a child.

Several muchachos came to his aid but held back the moment they saw Luisito. Instead they began lunging at the henchmen, just enough to keep them from ganging up completely. Their guerrilla tactics ended the instant El Bruto left the outhouse: soon he was back to his old profession, single-handedly dispatching meat on the hoof.

Samuel and the Elephant were staggering back from an overnight trip to the red light district when they rounded the alley and stumbled into the arena. By then only the original rivals were fighting, with Luisito on the losing end. El Bruto had cowed everyone else into a single, terrified herd. Then one of Luisito's men tore away in a final effort to turn the tide. Samuel had no time to recognize him, much less figure out the fracas, when he stepped in between and braced for the impact that never came. Instead, the thug stopped less than an arm's length away and sank a field knife into his abdomen.

In the first baffling moments he felt only a queer repulsion, like the queasy flip-flop his stomach made when don Marcelo took a dip in the road too fast. He fumbled with his shirt buttons until a more immediate instinct short-circuited his etiquette. Tearing open his shirt, he felt an odd protrusion, and when he dared look down, a slippery intestine coiled through his open fingers like some blind, gestating monster. The tingling in his gut evaporated into an eerie warmth, then even that sensation died. As the numbness traveled down his legs and he fell at the foot of the stairs, certain he was dying, he thought of Fela López.

Chapter 12

For the past half-hour Fela had been fighting to keep Samuel Ochoa from her thoughts. The more he intruded, the more impatient she became. Her back-and-forth pacing only added to Graciela's own anxiety. "What the Devil's eating you, Fela? Look, I don't know what's keeping Heraclio, but just go on ahead and meet us in the lobby. Mamá won't mind."

"I think we'd better go for him instead."

Graciela no longer dismissed her sister's moods as mere menstrual cramps. She asked what was wrong, but Fela threw the whole thing back at her. "Has anyone ever told you biting your braid drives people up the wall? No? Well, you're like our puppy worrying a bone." She added another excuse: "Besides, I promised a muchacho a love potion."

"You're going to the casa again?! How many times this week?"

"Who's counting? But as long as there's lovesick idiots I won't starve. This one wants the goods before the second feature starts."

"You mean he's slipping it in some poor girl's soft drink?"

She found the idea amusing. "I guess so."

"Fela! Shame on you! You probably think you're above it all . . ."

"He's really a nice muchacho. The girl just doesn't know it yet."

"Oh, really. Would you marry him?"

"Well, he's better than . . ." She faked a forgetting spell. "Heraclio's old friend."

"Samuel?" But Graciela was already back to her own concerns, and she neither pursued the matter nor noticed how her sister avoided her eyes.

Fela wrapped an amber vial in newsprint. "So are you going or not?"

Graciela thought twice. As long as she still lived under her mother's roof, her warnings against entering the casa were in force. Only Fela, with her devil-may-care temperament, was exempt. "All right. But I'll wait outside."

A short distance from the casa a gatekeeper of the latest gossip intercepted them as they neared the crowd: "They nailed a muchacho!" He was almost grinning from the excitement. "The other man had a machete! There's blood and guts all over the place!"

"Don't add to the story," said someone else. "It was only a knife."

They pushed through the shifting curtain of bystanders and almost stumbled over Heraclio, crouched on the sidewalk. Graciela tried to say something but only uttered a cry, and Fela felt a perverse, tongue-biting relief that Samuel had been spared. Then she spotted the fresh trail of blood up the steps.

"Heraclio's all right," she managed to tell her sister. She embraced her partly to give herself courage, then hurried up the side stairs while she still had the strength.

She hurried down the familiar hallway where she routinely delivered herbs and potions, to the door she had often passed hoping to find open. This time her wish came true.

Samuel was conscious and moaning in his cot. His wound was partly exposed, and every time his intestine peeked out, the Elephant bellowed for help. He was not bleeding profusely, but the compress El Bruto had improvised needed replacing. She took over the nursing and turned to a gawking muchacho. "Bring me webs to clot the blood. Lots of them."

He made a squeamish gesture. "What if there's spiders?"

"Use a stick, stupid." Then, without looking up, she asked, "Who did it?"

The muchacho squirmed. "What's the difference? What's done is done."

"I asked his name, not your philosophy of life."

Aware of her reputation as a witch, he knew his answer was the same as signing the man's execution order. But when he sought compassion in those unforgiving eyes, he knew it came down to the assailant or himself. "They call him Tata. Don Luis handpicked him as his son's bodyguard. He's Luisito's guardian angel, always has a weapon under his wing."

Samuel stifled a groan, and she tenderly pressed his hand: "Don't be such a macho or you'll bust another gut."

"Will he need a doctor?" asked the Elephant.

She hesitated. Although he would pull through, he still needed shots and sutures. The dilemna was in the town doctor, a crotchety, Old World eccentric who would just as soon turn him in as treat him. She gestured the Elephant to wait while she made sure the intestine was not perforated. Then she unwrapped the amber vial and put several drops on Samuel's lips. "It won't mend your insides." She smiled. "It might even break your heart. But for now you'll feel no pain."

He nodded, trusting her completely, knowing that no matter what happened, she was at his side.

The muchacho returned holding a branch furred with cobwebs. Taking it, she remembered the night of the spring carnival, when she had run into Samuel and he had offered her cotton candy. She had already accepted when a friend teased, "The poor man hardly eats for thinking of you, and now you take the little supper he has from his hands." She had brushed away a wisp of spun sugar from her lips and had vanished among the lovers and loners.

She applied a gauze of webs, and he responded with a feverish, incoherent confession that she suppressed with her fingertips. She was undoing his remaining shirt button when she noticed a streak on his sleeve as red as rouge. She told herself it was blood, leaned over for a closer look and caught the rancid whiff of last night's perfume.

It was as if Tata's knife had gutted her own insides. She felt a shivering terror as harrowing as any journey into the supernatural and bit her fist to clench her emotions. She had always bragged of being immune to that common cold others called love, and now she found herself stricken without cure, lost like a child in its dark side. She heard the Elephant's voice, tiny and insignificant against the roar of her blood, but could not tell whether he asked, "Is he all right?" or "Are you all right?"

Somehow she managed an answer: "Get the doctor." She too sounded timid and forlorn, as if talking through an inverted megaphone.

"But a while ago you said . . ."

"That was then. This is now."

"But that old German goat . . ."

"Everything has its risks. Like sleeping with whores." She held his stare, certain that if she blinked, her tears would never stop.

Fortunately he glanced away. "I could bring this doctor from across the border. A veterinarian, actually. He treats us when the girls . . ."

"Fine." She headed for the door without looking back, sparing him embarrassment and herself further grief. "He can kill two birds with one stone."

She hurried home and threw the latch on her door, far from Graciela's compulsive retelling of the afternoon's events. While her family offered prayers and promises for Samuel's recovery, she lit the blood-red candles her mentor had never dared use. Then she recited the ritual to avenge Samuel while her feelings for him remained.

All of that night and into the dawn she racked her soul for an antidote against love, refusing to believe that chants and potions could enhance but never destroy it. Her fanatical will vowed to exhaust every spell under the sun, and to overturn the wisdom of her ancient teacher, Malvina: "Love is as frightening as the supernatural. Believe once and it becomes forever real."

Chapter 13

On seeing his only son stagger into the house under Tata's wing, don Luis Bernal immediately asked how Luisito's opponent had fared. "He walked away on his own," said one of the workers, and don Luis felt the defeat in his own bones.

Another remark made the humiliation complete: "Our poor patroncito even took a beating under his tongue. By a wetback, at that!"

Don Luis considered tipping off the Border Patrol to haul away the whole lot of muchachos. But many were his own workers and customers. Besides, he maintained an uneasy truce with doña Zoila, and she was certain to retaliate.

Tata offered to revisit Heraclio. "I'll use hot lead instead of cold steel." He stitched the sign of the cross on his body. "This time it's tas! tas! tas! tas!" When his boss failed to warm up to the idea, he added, "Or I can bring the girl here . . . show her whose chicharrones crack loudest."

Don Luis dismissed that idea as well, but it inspired his own. "Sometimes a priest works better than a pistolero, especially when a woman's involved. There's no quicker way to a woman's skirt than through another skirt."

So he called in some pending favors from Father Coronado, who suddenly found himself a pawn on the Bernal side of the board, alongside hoodlums and hired guns. The aged priest hung on don

Luis' words as if they came from above, telling himself that the plan was in Graciela's best interests. He crafted a heart-to-heart argument with the care of an Easter sermon and arranged for a private talk.

Graciela, oblivious to the pastor's hidden agenda, heard out his homily on a woman's supreme Christian duty: finding the best father for her future children. She replied with a few cliches of her own until he finally broached the subject: "I'm aware you plan to marry one of the muchachos. I also know he never attends church. On the other hand there's Luisito, another of your suitors. He never misses a Sunday, and you won't find a better provider. His family's donated more statues of saints than we can name."

She stopped listening and instead looked at the frescoes for an anchor of faith or divine guidance. But suddenly the saints had the faces of common men, and every statue feet of clay. "With all due respect, Father, we both know what Luisito's after. The only thing he'll provide me with is what he gave that girl who left a foundling on your parish steps." By now she could barely mask her rage. "And when he showed up drunk at the casa, was that before or after Mass?"

"Now, Chacha, I've never condoned violence. But don't his actions speak for his feelings?"

"Yes. He's a coward who lets others do his fighting."

His experience with the López women told him to forsake the argument.

Graciela kept the incident to herself until her mother suggested she see Father Coronado about a church wedding. On hearing what had happened, doña Lola stood speechless. Fela, though, put on her war paint. She set aside the lemon grass tea she was brewing and cinched the waistband she wore for serious matters. "That old priest is just a puppet. Don Luis' paw is pulling the strings, and he won't stop until he feels cold steel."

Don Luis Bernal was sitting on his front porch, paring his hoof-hard toenails the old-fashioned way, when he spied three women cross his ranch gate. His first thought was that a small mob had come to complain about his infested grain, then he remembered it was still stored in his warehouse. But when his German shepherd circled one of them and shied away as if she had smeared wolf fat on her dress, he left his knife unclasped and under his chair, just to be on the safe side.

The women were some distance away, but from his son's descriptions the young lady with the confident stride had to be Graciela. He even smiled at the irony: earlier that year, without even knowing her name, he had tried to corner her in the fields, but her mother had stepped in like a she-wolf. In the end it had been Tata's remark that had dissuaded him. "Leave a few good mangoes for your own son, don Luis."

He noticed a family resemblance in the other young woman, but it was not until the trio came closer that the hair on his nape bristled like cat fur: Fela la curandera!

Just last month a sinister incident had thrust her into notoriety. Tata, his right-hand man and Luisito's guardian angel, had been out in back, fixing a field shredder, when suddenly he had stumbled into the kitchen, mute with horror and holding a mangled arm. It was a freak accident that quite simply should never have occurred, and nothing but witchcraft could explain it. At first the barrio had suspected old Malvina. But she lacked the raw cruelty of youth that had powered the act, so all eyes had turned to her apprentice. "If she can chase out serpents from the fields," they had said, "she could crush Tata's wing."

Doña Lola stopped at the porch steps. "Forgive our dropping by unannounced, don Luis . . ."

"Sandra!" he barked through the screen door. "Coffee for our guests!"

Graciela dispensed with the amenities. "We didn't come here to gossip like comadres," she said loud enough for the maid to hear, then added in a more private tone, "We're here to set your son straight."

He looked her over once more, slowly and part by part, admiring his son's taste. Judging her purely on breeding potential, she seemed excellent stock: attractive, healthy and spirited. Her background made little difference; indeed, he felt that women rescued from poverty made more manageable wives. She should even feel flattered by his son's attentions, he thought, and it was only her sister's sorcery that kept him from saying so. "Any business you have with my son, say it to his face. We live separate lives."

Fela climbed the porch steps without asking permission and addressed him with the familiar "tú". "Liar. You do everything but change his underwear. But I'll do as you say. I'm going straight to the mistress who's wiping his snot this instant . . ."

"Please get this straight, señorita. Whoever he wants for his wife . . ."

All three interrupted him at once, but Graciela prevailed. "What that brat needs is a wet nurse."

Once more the memory of Tata's crippling checked his pride. "I'll ask him to leave you in peace, then." For once he spoke sincerely, but kept his motives to himself: the fear that the supernatural strain in the López family might turn up in his grandchildren. He babbled through several euphemisms until Fela said for him:

"Tell him you'll leave out little werewolves from your will. Just make sure he stops sniffing at Chacha's scent, or he'll be howling at the next full moon."

He watched them cross the gravel road, where Fela paused to pick leaves from a shrub and then began to walk barefoot. He started rubbing his exhausted eyes when a woman's voice—so close that her whisper thundered—gave him the fright of his life. "Listen well, old man!" Her cool breath of wild spearmint would have excited him any other time, but now it only chilled him further. "See those two over there?" He nodded but did not dare open his eyes. "They care, even about things like you. But I'd just as soon see your hide nailed to the wall." Something slammed close to his groin and nearly made him lose control of his bladder.

He thought he felt her footfall down the wooden steps but found it impossible to filter out his own trembling from other vibrations. Taking a deep breath to steady his pounding heart, he held it until he had to exhale, then looked up.

She was walking just behind her family, sandals in hand, as though she had never left their side.

It never happened, he told himself, it was all in my mind. He repeated it several times until he was able to stop shaking. Then he glanced down and saw his knife, buried a hand's breadth from his crotch.

Chapter 14

Graciela and Heraclio were married without incident in a civil ceremony with Samuel Ochoa as witness. The groom wondered why doña Lola had decided against a church wedding but did not press his luck by asking.

He agreed to move in with the López family for the time being. Life with women was as different as he could get from life at the casa. The serene gathering of dinner scraps for their puppies, the seven-o'clock radio soap opera—all of these rituals took as much getting used to as the world of the muchachos.

Only the eccentric Fela was excused from following the clock-work of the household. She made it clear that her thoughts ticked to a different metronome, and while her younger sisters complained she never did her share of housework, neither one protested to her face.

Only Graciela dared to take her on. One Sunday afternoon, while Heraclio helped with the gardening, the two sisters locked horns with him in the middle. The argument centered around a bed of dried geraniums: Graciela wanted to plant new flowers in their place; Fela had been eying the strip for an herb patch.

"Just what we need," said Graciela. "More weeds."

"At least herbs cure people. Flowers are only good for putting on graves."

"Fela, our pup almost died from nibbling those plants you have out back."

"I brought him around with other herbs, didn't I?" The neighbors turned down their radio to snoop, and Fela played up to them "Look, if you dare . . ."

"You'll do what, you witch?! Curse your own flesh and blood? Why not shrivel up my husband as well?"

Heraclio braced himself with a deep breath.

"Don't tempt me, Chacha!"

"Go ahead!" By now the neighbors were standing by their screens. "And take anyone else who can hear you!"

Suddenly doors and windows began banging shut. Both sisters looked at each other, then burst out laughing.

Fortunately for Heraclio such moments were rare and helped him appreciate the placid evenings after the soap opera went off the air and the women gathered to discuss their day. It made no difference that they had spent the entire time together; each account was given polite attention. The consensus on the day's events gave him the impression that all was well with the world.

They began asking him about life in the casa. At first his roughhouse slang stood out against their euphemisms, but soon the two youngest started repeating phrases that passed their mother's censorship.

They especially asked about this or that muchacho, until one day he wondered aloud why they never mentioned Samuel. "I know my compadre's older, but . . ."

"That's easy," Belia interrupted with her feet-first candor. "That beau belongs to Fela, but she's not saying. She's like those pups that don't eat but won't let the others eat either. She was just as jealous with papá"

Suddenly she looked back as if Fela's stare had singed her neck. She waited in terror for some internal organ to explode. It never came, but she turned mute for the rest of that evening.

The following day he mentioned the incident to Samuel. "Watch out, compadre, there's no running from a sorceress."

Samuel glanced down and stammered like a schoolboy confessing a crush to his best friend. "Then my only defense is running into her arms." And his thoughts took him back to that morning on don Marcelo's truck when he had jabbed Heraclio's ribs without meaning to, any more than a man shot in the chest could keep his arms from flinging. Seeing her that first time, he had felt himself felled as surely as those beasts El Bruto had dispatched as a slaughterhouse stunner.

The reply caught Heraclio off guard, until finally he understood the sadness that followed his compadre like a curse. Then the volatile alchemy that simmered between Samuel and his sister-in-law seemed as impossible yet as natural as his own love for Graciela.

Although Samuel's confession was news to Heraclio, the other muchachos had long suspected as much. And while the older man was not one to wear his heart on his sleeve, neither was he an able dissimulator; his infamous losing streaks at the casa's poker table attested to that. It was during one such loss that the Elephant raked in Samuel's last earnings along with the winning pot and left his condolences. "Uy, 'mano, you'd think the Man upstairs would at least let you get lucky at cards. It's the least He could do after putting Heraclio's sister-in-law in your path."

Samuel said nothing but felt relieved that his sentiments were now public.

"Is it true she's a sorceress?" someone asked. "They say if you marry one you're a slave for life."

The Frog Prince corrected him: "That's true no matter who you marry."

Father Adán said, "At least a witch can have you believe you're loving every minute."

The Elephant felt responsible for Samuel's silence. "Listen, I'm treating at the red light district Saturday night." He quickly added over the hoopla, "Only for Samuel! He needs it. You'd think he'd fallen for a faithfully married woman."

"Worse," said the Love Bandit. "Father Coronado says she struck a pact with Satan. And that's forever, you know. Even her afterlife is sold."

"Father Coronado's full of shit," said Samuel, "even if it's been blessed by the Pope."

Several nominal Catholics in the group took offense, even though they spent more time in whorehouses than in church. The

Elephant added, "Father Coronado's jealous because her prayers cure people."

"They're chants to the Devil," said the Love Bandit. Of all the odd champions of the Church, he seemed the least likely: his sole devotion consisted of forbidding any woman he got pregnant from seeking an abortion.

Samuel sized him up. "Since when are you Father Coronado's altar boy?"

The Tomcat quickly came between their tempers. "Samuel's got his work cut out for him, though. She's a harder nut to crack than a nun who take vows."

"How dare you compare her to a nun?!" said the Love Bandit. "Witches are the Devil's own whores."

The Elephant moved in before Samuel could. He hooked the Bandit's neck in the crook of his elbow, uprooted him from his chair, then dragged him out of the room and harm's way. "You know," he mused in a one-sided conversation, "for someone called the Love Bandit, you sure have a lot of hate in that little dark heart."

Chapter 15

On a suffocating morning like many others that monotonous August, Samuel waited at the top of the stairs for don Marcelo's honk. Even the Tomcat's kidding did nothing for his despair, and the humidity stuck to his clothes like field dew. So when he boarded the truck and doña Lola extended the first of several dinner invitations, he could not believe his luck. That day he worked like muchachos half his age.

In time even Fela looked forward to his visits, since his dropping by kept alive doña Lola's hopes of finding her a husband. And as long as her mother was happy, she had one less problem to clutter up her life. Besides, with Samuel she could vent the tomboy side she had never outgrown and that had remained stifled in that household; because contrary to her expectations, Heraclio's presence had only made the others act even more ladylike.

Samuel, though, obliged her in the physical contact that always left him emotionally ragged but ready for more. Each Sunday afternoon, before the others could pamper him with courtesies, she took him to her room whose sole concession to decoration was pictures of folk saints and charismatics. "I'm practicing rituals," she would say to scare away snooping souls.

Doña Lola suspected she was enchanting him into falling in love. By doing nothing she gave her implicit consent, since love allowed an unlimited arsenal. And Fela, secluded with him in a room that no one dared enter, instigating good-natured wrestling bouts, could have made love under her mother's nose had she wished. But in time doña Lola understood, in a way Samuel never could, that she had nothing to fear.

Meanwhile, Fela's other would-be suitors invented conflicting excuses for keeping a healthy distance. So while one muchacho saw her as a woman bristling with personal problems, his roommate offered the opposite view: "Really? She seems rather simple-minded to me."

Even the Love Bandit, who found challenges an aphrodisiac, passed up the chance, saying she seemed too vulnerable. The Tomcat almost choked on his potatoes that time. "Since when have you worried about a woman's feelings?"

The Bandit caricatured that regal, unnerving gaze that could numb a man's libido on the spot. "She acts like her piggy bank slot is lined with velvet."

"Maybe it is," said the Frog Prince. "But you'll never make a deposit to find out."

All agreed on one thing, though: Fela López was a must to avoid. Not that she minded in the least. It kept away those immature pups who thought themselves wolves. "They're like that little mutt Cristina had as a child. The more she banged him around, the more he came back for more." As for the occasional macho who took her indifference as a personal affront, "What he really wants is a woman to put him in his place. But why turn men into bigger babies?"

So when Samuel Ochoa came around with his quiet courtship, she was totally unprepared. She began teaching him how to heal muscles and bones—an art she had learned from Malvina—because something about Samuel suggested a natural talent.

During one session that went late into the evening, she showed him a kneading technique above his sternum, then continued stroking his chest with the absent-minded familiarity of a lover. "The nerve of that old Malvina! She says your motives for becoming a bone healer are less than honorable." Her distracted caress left a burning shiver which he was certain betrayed him. "Imagine! I hope I don't end up that sentimental in my old age, where I'm seeing love in everything."

He looked away from those eyes that magnified his every insecurity. "If you do, and if I'm still around, we can share all the love that's left."

For a moment she was no longer an otherworldly sorceress, but a timid girl unable to let go her grasp. Desperate to dominate her feelings, she nervously rubbed his chest as if erasing his heart. "You sound like an old man already."

He gazed at the chiffonier mirror she rarely bothered to use. Incense and candles had clouded it, but even his fogged reflection could not hide his graying hair. "I am an old man."

She retrieved her self-control and with a steady hand traced the scar on his abdomen. "Then all the more reason to take these lessons seriously. There's nothing sorrier than an old bachelor complaining about aches and pains."

The following night brought an opportunity to apply the teachings. During a game of draw poker, the Love Bandit turned testy. Perhaps his losing three consecutive hands to Samuel's amateur tactics did the trick; or possibly he resented his rival's headway, however slight, against Fela's armor, while he had yet to make the tiniest dent. At any rate the provocations were not long in coming. "So how are your classes with Joan of Arc?"

"They're coming along."

"Maybe I'll ask her for a massage next time she's in the casa. An aching bone down here won't give me a moment's rest." He winked at the others. "Sometimes it even wakes me up in the middle of the night."

Samuel, sitting directly across, simply shrugged at first. Then, with a roughhouse kick that could have passed for horseplay, he knocked over the Bandit's crate seat and pinned his forearm on the box, like a lever on a fulcrum. He brought down the weight of his upper body, and the ulna cracked with a sickening snap that passed through everyone's bones. For a moment the Bandit studied the unnatural rearrangement of his Greek-god physique, as though the trauma touched him no closer than a statue's shattered arm. All at once his face blanched with awareness, and he fainted.

Samuel stood and pocketed his cash. "Tonight was too good to last."

That was the only time they saw him raise a hand in anger. That same night his victim became his first patient. After Samuel improvised a special sling to allow the Love Bandit to pick cotton, the Love Bandit milked his infirmity around mothering women to the maximum. He also scammed a dinner invitation from doña Zoila after hinting he had tripped on the casa's rickety stairs.

Don Marcelo, boasting the world's only one-armed cotton picker, offered him an occasional beer, while the muchachos, either out of pity or the novelty of aiding an oddity, began piling small mounds of cotton along his rows, like superstitious offerings against a similar fate.

The Elephant quickly put a stop to that practice. "Don't pamper the bastard with handouts," he warned them, "or he'll keep playing on people's sympathies." With the Bandit within earshot, he told Samuel, "Next time just snap his neck. That way he'll suffocate with his head up his ass."

Chapter 16

Besides Samuel, the only other tenant who visited Graciela and Heraclio was the Elephant. For reasons no one could fathom, he fascinated their newborn Imelda. The bond was mutual: he fussed over her health like a nanny. During Imelda's lengthy colic spells, which Fela said foretold her niece's adult stubbornness, he would drop by and share in the all-night vigil, even if he only got his mammoth frame in the way.

So when Father Coronado suggested they find her a baptismal godfather, he was their hands-down choice. When the priest stipulated he had to take Holy Communion first, the muchachos kidded him about reserving a spot in heaven. "They'll never finds wings large enough to lift you," said Samuel. "They'll have to hoist you up with pulleys."

"Or put propellers on you," said Juanito.

"Even if you get up there," said the Tomcat, "you'll send heaven crashing down."

He ignored them with a saintly patience that paid off when he left the confessional booth feeling two tons lighter. On his way to a rear pew he bumped into Juanito, panting and out of breath, who "just happened to be there." He was hiding a watch to clock the Elephant's penance; for only minutes before, another muchacho had remarked on the confession: "It's the moment of truth. If he did kill that pilot, it's good for a million Hail Marys."

Just then Father Coronado emerged from his booth like a gambler on a roll, in that crusading mood his parish had learned to avoid. He collared Juanito, the first available sinner, for a spiritual cleansing. "No scrubbing or pounding on the river rocks," promised the priest. "You young souls need less ablution than Pablito Peña's shirts."

But by the time the laundering met the Father's standards, Juanito felt lucky to leave with a shred of redeemable soul. He sneaked off to a dark corner of the church with the naked gratitude of a sinner in a fig leaf. By then the Elephant had left, and by the time he mumbled through his own penance, the casa poker game was almost over. He arrived with a sour-grapes expression that convinced no one, and when they invited him for the last hand, he said, "Father Coronado says gambling's immoral."

The Frog Prince gave him a knowing look. "Got your ass too, eh? My first and last time in that coffin he made me confess things I never even suspected were sins. Gave me ideas for later, though."

"So gambling's a sin, Juanito. What about his own bingo games?"

"That's for a good cause . . ." He paused as if reciting by rote. "We throw our sweat and our sacred seed on women of the night."

"Pearls before swine, eh? Well, I'd rather throw my money on whores than spend it on life-sized statues."

Juanito gave a sheepish grin, bleated a soft laugh, then moved closer to the fold. "If you want to know the truth, those madonnas look pretty sexy. Too bad you can't look up the skirts of statues."

On the day of Imelda's baptism the Elephant descended the church aisle with the stark terror of a cornered animal. Cupped in his gigantic hand, tiny Imelda appeared as helpless as a newborn marsupial.

Throughout the ceremony Graciela glanced up at him with the same dizziness she got looking up at the town's water tower. Seeing him sway ever so slightly, she thought, My God, what if he topples over? The hypnotic, Latin rites droned on as she waited to snatch Imelda the second he tilted a degree too far. But he weathered his vertigo and clammy hands to the end.

Afterwards Samuel consoled Heraclio. "You may have lost a daughter to the Church, but you've gained an elephant for a compadre."

At Doña Lola's back-yard dinner crammed with relatives and friends, Graciela and Heraclio accepted Father Coronado's apology. "And to think I tried to stand in the way of this lovely child."

The Elephant chuckled. "Padre Adán is working on her second baptism."

"She's just a baby!" said Graciela. "A nickname at her age is downright mean." She turned to Father Coronado for support, but he had disappeared among the guests.

For the past hour the priest had followed Father Adán's trail after hearing he had baptized a muchacho last Sunday. He took the matter seriously: either this Father Adán was an outright imposter or, worse, a defrocked man of the cloth still passing as a crucifix-carrying member.

Each inquiry on his whereabouts sent the priest down a more depraved spiral that finally ended in the alley behind the house. A seedy muchacho, the kind whose soul he simply wrote off as a bad debt, pointed to a tight knot of misfits who had skipped the church service. "He's wearing the orange shirt, next to the guy in lime slacks."

As Father Coronado approached, someone in the group cleared his throat. Father Adán, assuming that no upright citizen would join them, casually turned and offered a joint burnt to his fingertips. "The last puffs are the best," he said. But the priest, paralyzed by those impossibly red eyes that almost glowed like live coals, found it impossible to focus. Suddenly the recurring adolescent nightmare that had pushed him into the priesthood sprang to life: being face to fearsome face with the Devil incarnate.

Father Adán moistened his fingertips, sizzled out the toke and swallowed it. "Forgive me, your holiness. For a second I thought I was at a costume party."

The priest gripped his crucifix until his blood circulated from his heels up to his head again. But by then the furnace of Father Adán's imagination was fully stoked, and it spewed a rambling thesis that boiled down to this: was it possible the original Adán had pinned such difficult names on the first species that he unknowingly spelled their extinction?

Father Coronado replied he knew of no ecclesiastical evidence on the matter, but promised to ask the Vatican.

The white lie only raised the discussion to a more altered state. Father Adán, awed by the priest's high connections, made a more pragmatic proposal: would the Church consider baptizing people with animal names? "I thought of going to the Protestants with the idea, since they're more open to new things. But it's time we Catholics came up with more innovations of our own than just a saint every century, don't you think? Hell, some people already call their animals Pancho or Pepe or any other saint's name."

Another muchacho with that lost look of sheep gone eternally astray added, "Samuel just bought Fela a parrot named Cuco."

"There you are. For instance, your holiness, what's your Christian name?"

Father Coronado, still groping in an unreal terrain, went blank. "It's been so long . . ." Someone snickered that the smoke had stoned him. Finally he strung the rosary beads of his reason. "Uh . . . José!"

"There you have it, José! It's so ordinary you even forgot. That's my point! The last thing this world needs is another José. Everybody's brother is named José. I even have two: José and José José. Now what do all these Josés running around have in common except a very common name? I've known hundreds of Josés, but I never would have guessed you were one more. On the other hand, with two guys named Greased Pig . . ."

A stoned muchacho slurred out, "Tell him about your plan to dress priests in peach guayaberas and marry them off to Anglo widows."

Father Adán plucked an unlit joint from his fingers. "No more for you. Seriously, Father. The Pope can send me snapshots of his cardinals and compadres. I name them and he takes it from there. I already have a good one for him, but he'll have to wait to find out."

Father Coronado thanked him, then left them with a hasty mass blessing more fitting for a flock of vampires.

Back at the house he looked for Heraclio and was relieved to find him sober. It was necessary for what he had to discuss. "To be honest," he told him in private, "I had my doubts about you, being one of the muchachos. But you're a hard worker. From northern Mexico, I'll bet." Heraclio did not answer one way or the other. "What bothers me is that most muchachos come here, uh . . ."

"A little wet behind the ears? Look, Father, if a man's worst sin is walking around without the right papers, then I'd say he's doing fine."

"I agree. But this country's still going through hard times, my son, and the fewer mouths to feed, the better. This government's been sending many of our people back to Mexico."

"You mean those living here illegally?"

"Even some who were born here. So no one's safe. But your chances of being deported are much less if you get your papers in order."

"I've never needed any, not even as a muchacho."

"But you're not a muchacho now, my son. You're a family man, with responsibilities. You have an American wife and child. What would they do if you were sent back?"

"They'd follow me."

"Knowing Chacha, I'm sure she would. But think of her. Maybe you cut your ties in Mexico, but her family's lived here for generations. And think of little Imelda and the others to come. If things are bad here, what can they expect in Mexico?"

"I'll think it over."

"Please do. Remember, you're worse off than the muchachos. They're under Zoila's wing. They have bribes and political muscle behind them. All you have is my blessing."

That evening he discussed his dilemma with Graciela. "It seems," she said after hearing his arguments, "that if they're getting rid of native-borns like me, they might not want new outsiders."

"That's the risk I'd have to take."

It took her but a moment to decide. "Then we'll take that risk."

"And if they send me back?"

She showed her courage with a firm smile. "I've always wondered what the world was like beyond this valley. This could be one way to find out."

Chapter 17

In some ways Heraclio's marriage helped his legal efforts, but for the most part it only complicated matters. As a family man his hands were tied: unlike any muchacho, he could not erase his tracks in the U.S. and begin anew. "Putting your affairs in order is touchy," said the attorney handling his case. "Especially since you entered this country on the wrong foot."

"I didn't exactly walk across," he said.

His lawyer smiled wanly. "Well, now your first step is to return to your home town and gather documents: baptismal record, et cetera."

When Samuel heard Heraclio's plans, he insisted on coming along. His compadre's life in Mexico had rarely been discussed, but he suspected enough to fear trouble.

"I appreciate your help," said Heraclio, "but I have to arrive as unnoticed as possible. Besides, who'll watch over the family, in case . . . ?" He left the thought unfinished.

He returned to his birthplace and spent the night in a field he had often harvested as a boy. The next morning a young priest who tracked down his baptismal entry and inked out a certificate almost misspelled his surname. Asked if he planned to visit any kin, Heraclio shook his head. "The ones worth seeing are exiled or in the grave. To the rest I was the black sheep."

The priest stifled a yawn. "Once you leave you're as good as dead."

Nonetheless he looked back on his notoriety with a certain nostalgia, and when he stepped over a napping mutt without stirring it, he told a beggar, "Now even the village dogs ignore me."

Armed with a snarl of affadavits and a temporary visa he met Graciela at the border. They hand-delivered the papers to an Anglo bureaucrat who began stamping the batch like a bored baker with a cookie cutter. He was almost through when Graciela asked in a droll tone that matched his grimness: "In case he's defective, can I exchange him?"

The man excused himself and returned with two others who took Heraclio to a private room. For almost a full hour Graciela waited and cursed herself for the offhand remark. After his release Heraclio said nothing until they were safely outside. "All I can say," he told her, "is that after all those probings, your mail-order Mexican is guaranteed for life."

Two years later Heraclio, Jr.—Lalito—was born. By then little Imelda, under her aunt Fela's guidance, was reading fortunes from a Mexican deck. Doña Lola, in her near-sighted innocence, assumed they were educational animal cards until she overheard Imelda tell a lurid fortune. "Fela! What in God's name are you teaching this child?"

"The ABC's of life. Why, just last week she read Rita Molina's cards. When the six of clubs turned up in the Devil's trident, she insisted with her babe's mouth that the poor girl had a stomach ache that wouldn't go away. Rita finally admitted she was four months along."

Doña Lola turned to Graciela for support, but she seemed more amused than upset. "She's really quite good, mamá. None of this mumbo-jumbo about how you may or may not meet a handsome man who'll make you eternally happy unless a certain light-skinned woman comes along."

"One witch in the family is enough! I won't let you ruin her childhood."

Fela flung the cards in mock surrender. "I'll buy her some dolls then."

"Fine, only don't teach her to stick pins in them."

"She's already promised one last reading. Then it's over. I swear."

That evening Imelda had her godfather cut the deck, then studied the constellation. "There's something under your bed, Uncle Elephant. In a box."

"You mean in my suitcase?"

She nodded. "It's hidden and it's shiny."

He and Samuel returned later that night with a bracelet, an heirloom of antique gold. "This was in my treasure chest, waiting for a little girl to find it."

Graciela was awed like everyone else, but said, "I'm sorry, compadre, we can't accept it. It's much too expensive. I'd even be afraid to have it in the house."

"That's why I came along," said Samuel. "The muchachos' eyes almost popped out when they saw it."

"It must have a lot of sentimental value for you," said Heraclio.

"Besides," said Belia, "it's made for a young girl."

"Then I'll leave it in her care. If I never have a daughter, it's hers to pass along."

After Graciela reluctantly agreed, Heraclio pretended to examine it with a jeweler's eye and greed. "It's a perfect down payment for a house."

"You're looking for a house?!" said Samuel. "Why didn't you say so?"

"Don't tell me doña Zoila's leaving you the casa in her will."

"No, but last week she and her son were outside, talking like adults in front of infants. They plan to make a killing on the Suárez home. The family's staying up North for good, so they're selling it for a song."

When he heard the price, Heraclio said, "We planned to wait another year. But this sounds too good to pass up."

Graciela, though, had her reservations. "I don't feel right outbidding doña Zoila. If you hadn't heard it from her . . ."

"Suit yourself," said Samuel. "But she'll turn around and sell it to you for twice the amount. And she won't even lose sleep over it."

"Even at that price we'd buy it," said Heraclio.

"So then offer the Suárez family a little more. They'd stand a better chance if don Luis could compete against the Peñas. But his money's tied up."

"How do you know all this?"

"From doña Zoila. Don Luis' maid is her spy. The backstabbing between those families would fill a novel."

That clinched it for Graciela. "When can we look at the place?"

Samuel took them on an outside tour of the abandoned house. Weeds and burs had reclaimed the yard and reached their knees, so they watched their step for snakes. But Graciela was already planning ahead. "We can have two rows of flower beds leading up to the porch. Those pomegranate shrubs can still be saved. And with pruning, so can that orange tree by the bedroom window."

Within weeks they signed the necessary papers, but by then doña Lola was having second thoughts about their moving out. Cristina had already married, and Belia's talk hinted in the same direction. "Now that there's room," said doña Lola, "you're leaving me with this witch for a daughter."

"Mama's my guinea pig," said Fela, "for a potion against mothers-in-law. But so far she's only turned uglier."

Still, the Cavazos family lived close enough that one day Lalito showed up at his grandmother's house. Doña Lola was grinding spices when a small hand tugged her apron and made her scream. "I thought he was Fela's elf," she later told his parents, "the one who's always hiding things." She had with her a stack of steaming corn tortillas. "He says he only gets flour ones here."

Graciela was still upset at his having left without permission. "He eats what everyone else eats, mamá. What if he wanted cow-pie tortillas?"

"Then that's what he'd get."

Imelda teased him. "Why so picky? I used to feed you mud tortillitas when you were a baby. You'd gobble them up and ask for more."

"Well, he's not a baby now," said his grandmother. "He's a growing boy, and all Mexican. No pocho food for him."

"Mamá's suddenly a patriot in her old age."

That evening Heraclio had trouble sleeping, as if the spring evenings were already too warm. Finally he tossed out the idea he had been mulling over all night. "I wonder what it's like to work up North in the summer."

Graciela tickled his rib cage. "My cousins warned me against marrying a Mexican. 'The moment he gets his papers he'll go look for a gringa up North.' "

He rested his head on her arm. "It's in our blood. You've heard of Huero Nylon marrying a rich divorcee? Meet Prieto Khaki." He let a few minutes pass, then added: "The wages are a lot better. Besides, we've always wanted to see other places."

"From the back of a truck wasn't part of the fantasy. Every time I board don Marcelo's truck I feel like a steer in a cattle car. Imagine going all that distance. We'd get there with horns and tails!" He said nothing more, but she knew his heart was set on it. "Let's wait a couple of years, once Imelda's old enough to keep an eye on Lalito. Otherwise he'll bring back every disease up North."

"In two years time," he agreed, but in his excitement it seemed the moment would never arrive. A slight breeze stirred the orange blossoms by the window, and their fragrance filled the room.

Chapter 18

When don Marcelo stopped at the casa that Saturday, Samuel waved out the window to signal he was staying home. "El Elefante took my lunch!"

The Elephant told Heraclio as he climbed on board, "He bet his groceries in last night's card game and lost. Samuel may be the best bone healer around, but those poker hands left him crippled."

"But how can he buy food if he can't work?" asked Graciela.

"He should have thought of that before betting. I'll return his food tonight. Right now he needs to learn his lesson."

Just inside the town limits the truck pulled over, and Heraclio wondered aloud, "What's there to pick in a parking lot?"

"I'm helping papá drive again," said don Marcelo's adolescent son.

"He should take over for good," said Graciela. "I feel safer in his hands."

Heraclio agreed. "At least he doesn't hallucinate at the wheel."

The sun, barely risen, was slowly tearing through sheets of fog that made the hour seem ungodly early. The children usually helped on Saturdays, but at the last minute Graciela had left them with Fela and her mother. "The first hibiscus bloomed this morning. That means a scorching afternoon."

"Up North we'd be cool as cucumbers," he had said.

The field was far enough for a snooze, so he snuggled up beside his wife. He was glad the children were not around, since he always said napping on the road only made them sleepier. He was dozing off when the truck lurched to another halt, and a girl asked drowsily, "We're there already?"

Don Marcelo's son ground the starter several times. "Papá! I can't get this thing started."

A woman next to Graciela mumbled, "Now what?"

As if on cue they heard a faint noise, like a remote mooing, and Graciela smiled at the thought: "Good Lord. He ran over a cow."

Even the half-awake muchachos laughed when Heraclio hopped down and the Elephant yelled after him: "Get some hamburger for Samuel, compadre!"

As soon as Heraclio landed he noticed something odd. They were not near a pasture, as he had thought, but stalled on a steep railroad crossing. There was that lowing noise again, closer this time, and someone yelled, "Heraclio, please! Kill it before you grind it!" Then the realization hit him as if he had plunged into an icy current. It was not a cow at all, but the blare of a locomotive.

Several muchachos began to chant: "Sat-ur-day! Let's-go-home!"

He turned and almost collided with the Tomcat. "They're ready to call it a day, Heraclio." Then he followed Heraclio's gaze to the tracks beneath the truck bed. "Holy mother of . . . shit!" He pounced on the running board, climbed in and pushed aside the boy, already close to tears.

"Can you start this thing?!" yelled Heraclio.

The Tomcat crossed himself with a trembling hand. "I hope so." Heraclio scrambled back on board and sought out Graciela's faded green shirt in the chaos of colors. A woman squatting by the exit battled her rowdy brood. He started to alert her then hesitated, knowing that the warning might keep him from reaching his wife in time. He desperately scanned the crew and found her huddled in a far corner. But when he waved her to his side, her only response was a confused look.

"Let the man through!" said the woman, spanking two children underfoot and forcing them to sit screaming. "Whatever's out there is none of your business!"

Then came the most agonizing decision of his life: shouting over the rabble, he told them to evacuate the truck as quickly as possible.

A few hooters accused him of getting even for the teasing, but those who glanced over the topmost sideboard either spread the alarm or began shoving their own way to safety. Bodies suddenly began milling about, colliding as aimlessly as their incoherent questions. Several still sitting asked in all innocence what the commotion was about, while others hunkered in one spot like stunned livestock.

He cut a path to Graciela through the press of humanity, weaving around until push came to shove. Then he fell to the mob's level, kneeing an anonymous groin, elbowing a twisted face, cursing the stampeding herd whose lives he had elevated over his own wife's; above all yelling for his Chacha, shouting over the hoarse locomotive until he caught a faded green blur. But the moment he grabbed her, a canvas sack draped them like a huge party streamer. People shrieked on all sides, and for a furious instant he imagined them making fun of him. He struggled to break free but only tangled himself tighter, so he dragged away the struggling outline like a bungling kidnapper.

Brakes shrieked a short distance away, but the train's momentum kept it on a path as fixed as destiny, its horrible screech a mimicry of the screams it drowned out.

Somehow he managed to leap from the truck without dropping her, yelling as much at himself as at her, "Hold on! Don't let go!" The thought of being crushed in the collision lost its terror to that of crushing her in the vice of his arms. The rail's friction pierced his teeth, his skull and finally blotted out his words, but his thoughts screamed with an urgency he was certain she could intuit. His skin seemed covered with sun blisters. Then an eerie whine enveloped him and took on a force of its own, until its volume alone could annihilate.

He heard no impact; his senses seemed incapable of registering something so awesome. Instead, every whispered plea he had ever heard imploded inside of him. He found himself lifted off his feet with ethereal ease, and he recalled a fragile, childhood vision of a stained-glass Ascension. Then he forgot where he was or who he held, in a realm so alien yet everpresent that he was amazed he had never been there before. He managed one rejoicing thought: I'm alive! Then nothing.

But when he came to beside a man staggering among the carnage and praying to hold back the pain, what seemed even more unnatural than the corpses strewn about was his not being one of them. The drowsy girl who had asked whether they had reached the fields lay close by with her face mangled. She murmured only occasionally, and very faintly, as though her voice were too precious to waste, as if it were life itself. He thought it strange that someone so terribly injured should protest so little, until he realized she was almost dead.

For a long time he studied the bodies around him for a clue to his own identity. But their faces had the blankness of fetuses, and he recognized no one.

He arose and walked away. Several workers from the packing sheds that flanked the railroad were running to and from the bodies, which followed the tracks as far as the eye could see. A man with a sun-burned face that made him seem furious carried a large roll of wrapping paper used to pack produce. He began shearing life-size sheets to cover the odd-shaped corpses, ignoring the living until he mistook Heraclio for a gawker. "For the love of God, man, don't just stand there!" Then he caught the opaque, unfocused gaze of a survivor searching for his soul among the dead, and he stepped aside to let him pass.

The fierce sunlight scorched away the fog and made everything stark, and suddenly he remembered Graciela. He retraced his steps until he found her, his grip still marked on her arms. Very carefully he peeled away the canvas from her face and shirt. The ripping sound tore at his own insides and forced a protest from her lips.

It was not until he forced himself to stare at the blood-soaked face that his heart and abdomen caved into a single agitation: she was not Graciela! He wavered on the edge of an emotion that was both hope and horror and began the mad search for his wife.

He found her surrounded by splintered side boards, next to a cluster of mutilated bodies that made her apparent intactness all the more miraculous. Even though he only found a small cut on her neck, she was motionless. Desperate to hold her, but more terrified to move her, he lay alongside, oblivious to the stabbing in his own ribs, and delicately brushed the dirt from her face.

The distant sirens were barely audible until their piercing wail made them seem everywhere at once. The yells that finally brought an Anglo nurse were from the pain in his chest, and he kept waving wildly until she lowered his arms. "A woman here needs help!" she called out. "At once!"

"Hurry!" he urged in Spanish. "Please hurry!"

A doctor rushed to their side and searched for vital signs. His examination was brief, but for Heraclio it seemed an eternity. Finally the man faced him and shook his head.

Heraclio too shook his head and pointed at two attendants treating the woman he had accidentally saved. He asked in Spanish how it was possible for the other woman to be bathed in blood but still alive while his wife only had a superficial wound. Why, this was absurd, he babbled, she had cut herself much worse and her sister had dressed the wound with cobwebs. No, he insisted, this was a terrible mistake, and he began yelling for Fela.

He had no idea when the doctor left. The nurse tried to lead him toward the living, but he dismissed her with the growl of an animal guarding a corpse.

Later the justice of the peace who had once pronounced them man and wife arrived to pronounce her dead. Yet he too kept his distance. Unable to reason with him, he hurried on, for the dead were his priority.

The only other time Heraclio acknowledged a soul was when El Bruto staggered out of nowhere, carrying an old woman who everyone said had been around since the discovery of cotton. But that was all he remembered; the rest of her humanity seemed as insignificant as the blood on El Bruto's chest. She moved her lips, and El Bruto said, "She wants a little shade to die under." Then she whimpered and pressed closer to his chest, as if hoping to find a spot there.

Heraclio said nothing, because he no longer knew whether he was awake, or even alive.

He noticed then how utterly exhausted he felt, and wanted nothing more than to lay beside his wife. He needed to catch that interrupted nap before they reached the field, needed to bury the terrible dream under other dreams, needed to forget everything until Graciela nudged his ribs. Then and only then would he awake.

Chapter 19

Graciela's wake was held at home. On the morning of the funeral Heraclio paced the yard in an anguish no one dared trespass except to murmur a condolence. He finally crouched underneath the orange tree by the bedroom window, an ancient phantom who had long since forgotten the reason for his haunting. When Samuel grasped his shoulder Heraclio looked up but remained lost in his labyrinth.

"Father Coronado says it's time."

He acknowledged Samuel with eyes as reddened as Padre Adán's, and they walked to the front porch. All at once he remembered that last morning on the same spot: they were leaving the house when Graciela stopped and gave that little gasp that always made him imagine the worst. She pointed to the first hibiscus flower by the front porch, and her long-ago promise to wear one crossed his mind. Just then don Marcelo called out, "Enjoy the flowers some other time, lovers. We don't have all day."

He wanted to share the resurrected moment with Samuel, but an overpowering inertia drained his vigor until he no longer cared to talk. Instead, while the grinding gravel underfoot slowed his steps and seemed to drag his spirit as well, he paused by the hibiscus plant and picked the yellow bloom.

The living room was crammed with a mismatched collection of chairs that made walking difficult. He weaved past the mourners while the swaying hibiscus flecked an imperceptible trail. He meant to place it in her hands, then realized she already clasped a rosary that detracted from his everyday memories of her. So very gently, on that abundant hair whose touch of gray had once prompted her to ask whether he would still love her thirty years from now, he placed it and held his breath, hoping against all hope that his love held life enough for two.

She was buried in the stifling noon hour, on a day, as she herself would have said, when only mad dogs and lizards were out. He broke off from the procession before reaching her plot and stood his ground beneath some branches that offered a skeleton of shade. No one dared urge him on, not even when Father Coronado began the rites. Throughout the ceremony a pack of unsupervised children, innocent of his grief, circled him and chased the striped lizards that zig-zagged from one tombstone to the next.

From a distance, obscured in the weak umbra of the mesquite and far enough that his lined face softened in the blur, doña Lola imagined once more the young man leaning against the neighbor's tree in his untiring vigil.

The burial of the other twenty-six victims was staggered over several days to allow time to grieve each one. At times an entire cortege moved from one burial site to another, so that even the deceased muchachos without families received processions.

The Elephant, who had left no clue as to his next of kin, received a larger-than-life homage. At his burial an abandoned wife with a feverish, tubercular look repeated what everyone already knew: how in the last bewildering seconds, when the strength had left her legs, he had yanked her up like a rag doll and hurled her over the side boards. The trauma of that brusque act was apparent to all: a sprained arm treated by Samuel, and scratches from the dense brush that had cushioned her fall. But she was alive and among them, and nothing else mattered except her confused gratitude for a man she had scarcely known.

In fact, while the entire barrio had known him by sight, they knew little else about him. Father Coronado, baffled over what to call him in his service, had even asked Father Adán, whose memory went almost as far back as Creation. But even he was stumped. The only one who knew was the Tomcat, still in a coma. So in the end Father Coronado eulogized him with the nickname everyone had known him by and which now made him both intimate and unknown.

The county planned to bury him in a pauper's grave when Heraclio rose from his own spiritual death to donate part of Graciela's own funeral funds. "He was godfather to Imelda," he told those who pointed out that his wife's burial expenses were already meager.

Samuel suggested they pawn his bracelet, but Heraclio refused to let anyone touch Graciela's belongings. So the muchachos took up a collection and sent Juanito, who hemmed and hawed like a man unaccustomed to formalities. "We were saving up for a little fun. But nobody feels like celebrating."

The following week Father Coronado, aware that in the aftermath of disaster survivors often became converts, called on Heraclio to corral him into the fold. It was a hard way to do business, but with some it was the only way.

He started the homily he had rehearsed on the other bereaved families. Indeed, he had saved his toughest customer for last. But between parables Heraclio stopped him cold. "So every time that shepherd of yours gets crazy from loneliness, he takes it out on his flock. It's his herd, so I guess he can do whatever he wants." He escorted his guest out the door. "Only don't tell the sheep it's for their own good."

He took to disappearing at night, leaving little Imelda to watch over Lalito. When doña Lola found out, he overcame his apathy long enough to beg her to look after them, then returned to his wanderings. For three nights, at the request of the López family, Samuel trailed him until dawn, only to report that his haunts were always the same ordinary spots.

Soon he was so beyond the realm of even the walking wounded that one of his neighbors out watering her garden one morning failed to recognize the bearded, unkempt tramp who passed her without a word. "Good Lord!" she said to doña Lola across the fence. "Some man just walked into your daughter's house. Who in heaven's name is he?!"

"A corpse they forgot to bury," she answered, then left to look after him.

Sometimes those around him caught the trace of a smile, but without intimacy and with an abstraction that only made him more distant. Other times he stared long and silently at his children, who watched with confused, filial caring. But the moment he tried to share his grief, he fell into a mute indifference.

One morning he returned with his knuckles raw and bloodied and a deep gash in his ribs. He barely let doña Lola nurse his wounds, much less ask questions. At that point Fela stepped in, even though her mother warned, "He won't stand for help. Those demons inside won't let him."

Fela knew otherwise: what possessed him was a nothingness that could scare away the Devil himself. She also knew that to help him they must keep him home at night. Outright force was useless, so she simply hid his hat, knowing that the rituals that ruled his life would not let him leave without it.

That night he all but turned the house upside down in his stubborn search. He never once asked for help, and Fela held the others back until he collapsed exhausted on the couch. His lackluster eyes and the lack of tonicity in his wrists told the story. "Part of it is susto," she said, "from the shock."

"And the rest?" asked doña Lola.

"The rest is in his hands." He regarded her with a listlessness that sapped the energy of whoever looked into his eyes, and even Fela felt her powers wane. "Keep him away from the children these next few days."

"Dear God!" said doña Lola. "I'll hide every knife in the house."

"That's not necessary. He won't lift a finger against them. But he could injure their spirit without meaning to."

He listened with the furious impotence of a comatose man hearing his loved ones plan his funeral. She braced herself then entered the oblivion of his eyes. "We'll bring you back." She smiled and added. "We're not through with you yet."

He tried to show his gratitude, but only managed an absolute apathy.

Chapter 20

One evening he found himself in an alley that seemed strangely familiar. He looked back and realized he had just passed the casa. Suddenly he was a muchacho again, filled with dreams and optimism. He hurried up the stairs with the exuberance of a man cured of his crippleness, determined to begin where he had left off. But when he reached the landing, he imagined Samuel waiting as he did each weekday morning, walking down as though work were preferable to the casa, bracing his heart to soften the stone that was Fela's soul.

By the time he knocked on Samuel's door he knew that if someone had granted him peace in place of his past decade, he would have refused. And when he saw his friend's tender stoicism, he understood how no one who risked intimacy was immune from mourning.

"I thought we'd gotten rid of you," said Samuel.

"Just haunting old friends." His own voice spooked him momentarily.

Samuel invited him in. "How are the children?"

"They're fine," he said, ashamed that his neglect kept him from saying more. He had forgotten how spartan the quarters were. The room had only two beds. He sat on the larger one. "My compadre's?"

Samuel smiled weakly. "He needed space, so I was his only roommate. Besides, he talked in his sleep, and soon everyone else left. Even the Tomcat . . ." He knew from Heraclio's expression that the news had not reached him. "He died this morning. During the end he suddenly started yelling out a name."

Heraclio seemed elsewhere. "He could have been the first one to save himself. No family to worry about."

"Same with your compadre. He could have plowed through everyone else."

"He walked so slow, though. Graciela said he moved like an elephant with corns."

"That woman he saved . . . he had mentioned her before. He went into one of his rages once, wanting to know why mothers like her slaved in the fields while the grower's wife spent her days picking out hair-dos. Then he caught his reflection in the mirror. 'But who said life is fair? Right, you ugly elephant?' " He remembered something and reached under the bed. "I told him that kind of talk wouldn't get him into heaven."

"Heaven. Hm. The rich probably own it too."

Samuel pulled out a scuffed suitcase, its imitation leather peeled down to the cardboard. Heraclio suddenly remembered the time the Elephant had first yanked it from under the bus seat; it seemed like only days ago. Samuel jiggled open its one good clasp. "Everything he owned is here."

"Give El Bruto whatever he can use." He was already at the door when Samuel dug into the clothes and fished something out.

"And what do I do with this?" It was the smoking gun they had never hoped to find: the Love Bandit's shaving mirror.

Heraclio's chest swelled with grief and compassion, as if he had uncovered evidence of Graciela's infidelity. "Break it into a thousand pieces. Then grind it into dust." He walked out the door. "Let the dead bury their dead."

He spent that night with a field knife in hand, watching the faint, flourescent dawn that made him seem the lone survivor of a great dying. A canvas of old newspapers beside his bed soaked up, drop by drop, the spattered self-portrait done by his own hand, in his own blood.

He came to his senses, not by degrees but as abruptly as an infant taking its first breath. His first terrifying thought was how close he had come to the end. He sprang from bed, bandaged his wounds and crumpled the bloody newspapers, afraid that his new-found faith would evaporate like an alcoholic euphoria.

When he asked for Fela that morning doña Lola reacted as if he had summoned a priest. She was even more aghast at Fela's appearance, and expressed concern about her health.

"I had a hellish night." Fela exchanged a harrowing glance with him. "I had to push someone over the edge. That's how Chacha always brought me to my senses." She heard his first sign of emotion in weeks.

"Don't take my grief. It's all I have left of her."

She guided his gaze to the open bedroom door where Imelda was untangling her brother's hair. He was struck by her intense concentration, so like her mother's.

Fela articulated his thoughts: "She looks more like Chacha every day," then added, "God and the Devil help us both if she has her stubbornness too."

She brushed him with sagebrush for almost an hour, repeating phrases he found indecipherable but intriguing. Satisfied he was recovering, she said, "Have Samuel check your ribs."

"You're like those compadre doctors who refer their patients to each other. You two have a racket going?"

"You're getting your old spirit again. Remind me to hold some back, to keep you in line." She reached the front door then returned. "Samuel and the others stayed home today. They're burying your friend at two. I thought you should know."

At noon he finished grooming himself with the awkwardness of his son, leaving a mustache he would keep to his dying day. Then he visited Graciela's grave before going to his friend's burial.

During the funeral Father Coronado referred to him by the name he had repeated in his delirium. But when the muchachos buried a wooden marker with the name, the thought crossed Heraclio's mind that perhaps the Tomcat had been shouting the Elephant's name. But when the lopsided cross ended up between both plots, he kept it to himself.

That night Samuel patiently felt Heraclio's rib cage and sternum, then pronounced him healed. He scribbled some nonsense on a brown bag. "Your medical discharge. Tell your new crew leader you're as good as new." He noticed Heraclio's uncertainty and added, "Why don't you sign on with my boss?"

He nodded, less as a man eager to return to his purpose in life than as one too beaten to argue back.

His first day harvesting tomatoes was slow but supremely steady, his spirit so detached it could have stepped back and let his body continue through its paces. He moved through a monochromatic day where passion played no part, but neither did pain.

Suddenly the warm rush of a nosebleed flooded his face. He barely had time to pinch his nostrils and look straight up at the sky, but in that instant he glimpsed something that left him rooted to the spot: Graciela's profile, wearing one of her green work shirts; and close to her, the Elephant's broad back, stretching his favorite yellow shirt to its limits. He managed his first spontaneous thought the day: Impossible! I've gone mad! Unless . . . Fela brought them back!

His next thought was that she had bewitched him. He lowered his eyes for another look, but the throbbing nosebleed forced it straight up again. He had to stand there, staring upward, while just out of eyesight stood the two people he would have given the world to see again.

He tried to shout their names through his plugged nostrils, but the pressure was excruciating. It was just as well; if he were hallucinating, the last thing he needed was to publicize his raving. Yet they had seemed too ordinary to be anything but real, and he struggled to retrieve their everyday look.

He forced his attention on the sky while the pressure in his head eased. Storm clouds had collected overhead like tremendous, fossilized explosions that had burst only an eyeblink ago and whose detonations just now reached him. Then he felt more than heard a rumble that seemed to come from both heaven and earth.

Someone yelled, "Here it comes!", and dust began hissing round like matches extinguished in water. Fat raindrops pelted his face and sent the other workers running to the truck. Soon he stood alone except for the two figures at the far end of the field. An uneven gust brought their broken voices, and his heart started pounding, certain he had heard Graciela's unique timbre. He tried to lower his head but almost passed out, so he listened with all his will. Finally he heard: "Heraclio . . . idiot! . . . out of the rain!"

El Bruto's harsh words instantly broke the spell. Then he heard the first voice: "Hurry, papá! . . . catch . . . death of cold!"

He unclasped his nostrils and remembered Lalito's blue-faced tantrums. Smiling foolishly, he checked his moist hand: rain water, nothing more. All at once he caught the deep, organic scent of damp earth, so sharp and clean he could taste it. He stared hard at El Bruto, afraid that reality might plunge him back into his grim, ashen world. But his friend's movements stood out sharp and animated, his yellow, hand-me-down shirt welcoming him back into the vital present.

Imelda began running toward him, and suddenly sporadic patches of the world caught color all around. A pair of dungy objects in a nearby field combusted into twin calico cows with huge, rust freckles, grazing without a care on the good, green earth. Even the fire ants under his feet seemed to ignite in redness.

El Bruto gestured at the sky as though seeing the world afresh and roared above the thunder: "Move it, Heraclio!" Wasting no more words, he made a bovine noise and dug his feet in the furrows, pressing for a response.

Imelda fell into her father's arms and sought shelter from the rain. "El Bruto looks like a bull about to charge . . ."

"Yes! With steaming nostrils!" He made a strange noise of his own, then remembered it was laughter. He waved back and saw a man content to live and die in the same breath. "We're coming, buey!"

Imelda helped him pick enough tomatoes to fill his pail, then they hurried to the truck. For now only one thing mattered: bringing in the fruits of his labor.

Chapter 21

From his front porch, don Heraclio Cavazos continued to keep a careful eye on his grandson playing in the flooded street. By now the hurricane rains were a light drizzle, but before Imelda went inside she said, "If it starts pouring again, papá, bring Armandito in at once."

She was in the kitchen when her older son returned from the tool shed, a field hoe in one hand and rolled up.

"Thanks a million," she said. "Now there's man-sized tracks to go with Armandito's in the living room. I can understand him making a mess, but you, Esteban . . ."

" 'Buelito wanted a long-handled hoe."

"Don't tell me he's taking up field work again. We just went through that last year. Has he had any more crazy ideas about organizing farmworkers?"

"No, he . . ."

"Don Quixote had his lance, papá's got his hoe."

"He wants to clean up 'buelita's grave this weekend."

"For heaven's sake. He doesn't even believe in an afterlife."

"He goes to remember. If you ever came along . . ."

"Poor papá, still living in the past."

"Their anniversary's coming up," said her daughter.

She gasped and turned to Marina. "Good grief! Remind me to buy a wreath. Otherwise we'll never hear the end of it from Lalo.

Bad enough he buys those huge bouquets that make ours look like sick poinsettias."

"He has more money," said Marina.

"Don't remind me. As if life weren't already unfair."

Marina showed her the mementoes spread on the kitchen table. "I was going through grandmother Graciela's things for my history paper, and I found some love letters. And some photos aunt Fela took. Look. Grandma was so pretty."

"So was your aunt Fela," she answered without glancing. "But look at her now." She turned silent, then sighed. "Hard to imagine papá in love. . . . These days it's hard to imagine anyone in love."

"Oh, mom, people have always fallen in love."

"Maybe back then they did. But that's all dying, like your aunt Fela's devils and love potions. People don't believe in that anymore."

"Sure they do. You still love grandma, don't you? Just like you love dad."

"Why this talk of love all of a sudden? Are you getting ideas?"

Marina leafed through her grandmother's album with a self-conscious smile, as if seeing herself. "If you ever have another girl . . ."

"Please! I can barely handle you."

"Well, then, if I ever have one . . ."

"I knew it. You're hiding something."

" 'Please. I can barely handle you.' But if I ever have a daughter I'll name her Graciela."

Imelda let the name drift through her thoughts. "Gracie. Sounds nice."

"No. Graciela. Like my grandmother."

From the remoteness of her childhood, Imelda tried to rescue a single, intimate memory anchored to that name, listened for a maternal echo to guide her through the void of her adolescence. But nothing came to mind, except the overwhelming ache of abandonment.

Chapter 22

Imelda Cavazos, almost eighteen and still not the least curious about love, was brushing her hair for bedtime when she heard the first wave returning from the dance. She told herself it was too early for the crowd to let out, then concluded that for her the matter was moot.

"Next Friday I'm going," she insisted, loud enough for her grandmother to hear, as if needing a witness to hold her to her word.

"Nobody's locking you in your room," said doña Lola. "We even wonder who you're saving your dances for. You're going to wear out the poor boy."

Minutes later two of Imelda's friends, more animated than usual, stormed up the porch steps squealing from both fright and laughter. Doña Lola quickly unlatched the screen door. "Are the Garza twins after you again?"

"Oh, no!" said the older sister, as breathless from running as from the evening's events. "Did you hear what happened at the dance?!"

Imelda kept brushing her hair. "I couldn't care less."

Her father, though, put aside a Mexican newspaper and took a weary guess. "One of the Portales brothers threatened to stab someone looking at his girlfriend again."

"Oh, no, don Heraclio, nothing like that!"

The other one interrupted: "The Devil appeared at the dance!"

"Lalito's friend, El Diablo?" he asked. "Isn't he hibernating in juvenile hall?"

"Oh, no, not him!" She gasped and made the sign of the cross. "The real Devil!"

"It's true," said her sister, almost whispering. "Lupita Rivas was dancing with this handsome pachuco when she looked down and saw he had a hoof!"

"And a rooster's foot! Uuy!" She shivered and showed her goose flesh.

Don Heraclio suppressed a cutting remark about Lupita. For all her shortcomings she was an honest girl; her inability to say no had left her three children from different lovers and the nickname Lupita La Putita. But if he held back, his outspoken daughter did not. "She must have been high on something."

"But there were other witnesses!"

"And he's returning next week!"

Doña Lola touched the crucifix on the wall. "Thank God Imelda stayed home."

But her granddaughter, in a low voice that magnified her determination, only said, "Then maybe I'll run into him next Friday night."

By sunrise the barrio was rife with rumors, by noon divided into sheep and goats. The believers saw the incident at last night's wedding dance as punishment for the groom, a migrant worker who had reneged on a promise to tithe his earnings to Saint Joseph the Worker. But the skeptics smelled human sweat rather than Satan's sulfuric presence. The Devil's appearance they said, was meant to keep youth on the straight and narrow: some parents had probably paid a stranger to drug Lupita and stage the incident. They added that visitations by the Devil at local dances came in cycles, whenever adolescence reared its acned head too boldly.

Imelda had her own impudent theory: "Maybe he returns to keep up with the latest dance steps."

Dance steps aside, this Devil was no antiquated relic. Reports had him fluent in the latest totacha or pachuco slang. Dapper and elegant, he cut quite a fashionable profile: suspenders adorned with an elephant caravan hooked trunk-to-tail,—"elefantes en tirantes" was the quote one dance partner remembered; a shimmering nylon shirt with puffed sleeves; pleated seersucker slacks pegged at the ankles and ballooned at the thighs; a long watch fob that looped inches from the floor and that might have been his disguised tail all along; and topping it off, a stingy-brimmed hat at a rakish angle—to hide his horns, obviously. Of his dark face women only remembered the smoldering Pedro Armendáriz eyes and a gleaming gold incisor that gathered the dim light in a hypnotic pulse.

That was the composite sketch doña Lola brought back to the family. "And Lupita?" asked don Heraclio.

"They say she's turned a new leaf and become a devoted mother."

Imelda sneered. "The only leaf she'll turn is a marihuana leaf."

"Let's give the Devil his due," said don Heraclio. "He did in a bolero what Father Coronado's saints couldn't do in years of Masses."

In fact, Lupita was relishing her role as the woman who not only had danced rouged-cheek-to-red-cheek with the Devil but had unmasked his masquerade. Granting her eighth interview that day, she repeated, "So I ask him his name and right away he gets mysterious. 'El Diablo,' he whispers in my ear. So I say, 'Look, I couldn't care less if you're married and have thirty kids, just don't play games.' So he looks me in the eye and it's like I already know what he'll say: 'The party's over. I'm taking you home.' I mean, wouldn't that put out your fire right away? Then he mumbles something about needing a woman strong enough for his passion. I feel faint and look down, and that's when I see this horrible, hairy hoof!" She ended her performance with a nervous attack as spine tingling as the original.

She was not the only girl basking in his afterglow. Every one of his dance partners added a demonic theme to the encounter. "His hat was always about to slip off," said one. "It must have been hanging on one of his horns."

Another confessed with a blush, "When I admired his chain, he invited me to feel the arrowhead tip."

A third observed that when the band broke into a sweaty Caribbean cumbia, his tempo took on a feverish abandon, as if infected with a subtropical delirium. "Down there that must be the only dance there is."

Even a wallflower who missed her chance got into the act. "He must have sensed I'm a good Catholic girl, and that he wouldn't get anywhere. I knew wearing my crucifix would pay off some day."

Finally, a boy who had been closely watching the crowd's shuffling to unscramble the steps said there was something slippery about the stranger's footwork. But his crossed eyes seemed so eager to please that by the time Father Coronado was through with him, his objectivity was utterly compromised.

At the parish hall bingo that Saturday, Father Coronado was so pleasantly surprised by the overflow crowd that he told himself, Nothing like a good scare from the other side to bring them out of the woodwork. To meet the demand he cracked open three new bingo cartons whose illustrated Mexican boards included Satan's square on some. He considered removing the Devil card from the master deck but decided instead to pass it over if it ever turned up.

The Devil showed his face without fail in the first six games, always after the catrín card—the dandy in top hat and tails. The priest blamed the sinister coincidence on his sweaty palms adhering the cards. But even after he inserted each at opposite ends and shuffled, they still came up companions. A woman with an expression like an interrupted orgasm finally protested. "Father, that's the third time I've come this close. This close! And lost it because you're afraid to mention our friend's name. Last time that you passed him over, someone else won with 'the drunkard.' Now, I don't think it's fair for you to yell out 'el borracho!' like some hallelujah, then turn tail against the poor Devil."

His decision to ban the Devil from the deck altogether only penalized those with boards bearing his square. In the pandemonium he had to close down the hall and refund part of their fee. When he overheard a rumor that some timid souls were defecting to Fela for protection come Friday night, he let it be known that Fela and the Devil went back a long way. "That's like climbing aboard his crew leader's truck, my children." He added that he planned to hand out front-door posters that Sunday, warning the Devil, "Esta casa es católica," with a graphic background of Christ's last Passion. In truth they had been gathering dust for years; nowadays people only advertised their Catholicism to keep away Protestants peddling their religion door-to-door.

The following morning more people showed up for Mass than for Bernal's weekend raffles. By ten o'clock Father Coronado's stockpile was exhausted. He offered to get a fresh supply of placards, less bloody and in English, from an Anglo parish. But the phrase "This is a Catholic home" simply did not carry the same punch, they said. Besides, what if the Devil could not read a comma of English? Why, he would stroll right in as if he'd read, "Buenos días, Satanás."

And since he was obviously Tex-Mex, they needed potent stuff to keep that species of wolf at the door. There was no room for a wimpy gringo Christ with a blond perm and immaculate, three-piece robe. Only a half-naked, hard-core Christ would do, a Jesus oozing blood from every pore. They needed a champion, a Chicano Christ, the macho Christ tattooed on ex-cons who sweated blood for his image and identified with his masochistic machismo.

Leonel Madres, on parole from prison, was one such penitent, and he took advantage of the hysteria to announce a public viewing of the life-sized Christ's face on his back. Even those who had seen him on past shirtless strolls were urged to attend, for while paying his latest debt to society, Madres had freshened up the original tattoo. "Even our eternal father gets a few wrinkles," he explained.

The audience that gathered around his porch would usually have avoided him on the street, but that evening they fluttered around his evil aura hoping to innoculate themselves. "Look," he told them in that low, authoritarian tone drilled into him through prison etiquette. When he unbuckled his belt to pull out his shirt tail, several horrified onlookers covered their eyes, but he simply gave them his back and flexed the muscles bisecting the tattoo's mouth and thorned brow. The intended effect was a grimace, but the extra pounds Madres had put on led someone to whisper behind his back that Christ appeared to be pouting.

Don Heraclio thought he looked constipated. But while he kept his bad taste to himself, Father Coronado added to the display of Christian kitsch, solemnly blessing Madres' back with holy water. And the ex-con, who could play to a crowd's emotions as if before a parole board, vowed not to wash his back until Easter.

On the eve of the dance, Imelda's friends tried everything to discourage her from making her debut. "Sure we're going," admitted one. "But we're not stepping out on that dance floor. Only a fool would walk into his trap." But they only forced her pride into a corner, and their efforts were as futile as her grandmother's plea: "At least let Fela give you something to defend yourself."

"If I were my niece I'd worry more about street-corner Romeos," said Fela. "Besides, you can't stop the Devil any more than you can stop love."

Something told Imelda that her aunt knew why tonight of all nights was so important that it seemed predestined. But when she looked for understanding, she only found that enigmatic gaze that made her feel a closer kinship with strangers on the street.

A friend who intuited her fears said, "Maybe your aunt's making you do this against your will."

"What do you mean?"

"People in the occult make deals with the Devil. Maybe you're part of the deal. After all, you're blood."

She shook her head, more to convince herself than her friend. "Tía Fela would never do that."

The sheer size of the crowd outside the reception hall gave the night a carnival air. One enterprising cynic did a brisk business selling cardboard masks of the guest of honor, and masked teenagers greeted their friends with fiendish laughs. It took a careful eye to spot the crucifixes and holy medallions cushioned between damp breasts or hidden among hairy chests; and only an attentive ear could pierce through the superficial gaiety to the undercurrent of anxiety.

"Don't forget," said one parent, "this reception hall is Church property. He wouldn't dare enter sacred ground."

"What do you mean, 'wouldn't dare?' He's already been inside, slow-dancing with our daughters."

Another woman agreed. "I always said this den for dances and gambling would only bring more vice. Now look who we finally attracted."

Someone even called the police, saying that the Devil had sworn to show up at the dance that night, and that he was sure to bring trouble. "That's impossible," said the dispatcher. "He's in juvenile hall."

"No, not the kid with the alias. The real Devil!"

"Well, call us if he pulls out a pitchfork."

But for all the talk of confrontation, nobody wanted to end up in the middle once the sparks flew. And if the handful of men inside the hall entertained illusions about their courage, they were swept away in a rush of adrenaline when a boy tossed a lit firecracker into that powder keg of emotions.

The screaming reached the crowd outside. "What in God's name happened in there?!"

"They say a Roman Catholic exploded!"

"No!" said another. "A Roman candle!"

The first macho who turned tail, Ralph Ruiz, was well outside when he realized what had happened. He froze in his tracks but could not stop the hysterical trembling that prompted a lady to yell, "Somebody get Fela! We have a susto emergency!"

"It's not fright!" he yelled. "I'm shaking from rage!" No sooner did he publicly vow to give the little bastard a spanking he would never forget when a whiny retort came from the pitch-black alley. Afraid to go in, but more terrified of losing face, he groped his way in the dark, guided only by the giggles that kept shifting and that led the crowd to whisper, "Over there," or "To your left."

Then, during a space of utter quiet, his best friend called out softly, "Be careful. Sometimes he impersonates children."

His breathing tightened as though the hairs on his chest were retreating into their roots, while his mouth and anus went into an automatic lockjaw. An ancient instinct more primitive than pride pulled him back into the mob, where he managed to save face. "I saw his eyes!" he said through clenched teeth. "They were like huge, red reflectors."

That was enough to scatter most of the crowd and empty out the hall of all but the most dedicated dancers. Imelda felt even more lost among the diehards who sat in an isolated aggregate, like addicts waiting for a fix. The band, which had no choice but to honor its contract, started playing without tuning instruments or testing microphones. But in the end not one male walked over to name a partner, nor did the women encourage them, since no one knew what sex the Devil would assume that night.

Imelda felt herself sitting in quicksand. Suddenly the music turned louder, and the skittish girls huddled tighter and jarred her back to reality. She soon saw their cause for alarm: a dapper stranger was already half-way across the dance floor, hatless and with a cowlick that would not stay put. He never once looked her way, yet everyone sensed he had singled her out from the herd.

He began sneaking up on her on the oblique, with the studied nonchalance of a pickpocket, until she almost pounced in front of him to force an end to his cat-and-mouse game. A faint smoldering preceded him. She swore it was sulfur, and by the time she traced it to the lingering burnt gunpowder she was on her way to a full-blown scream. But in the end she surrendered with the bleat of a sacrificial lamb. Standing before her, silent and smiling, he politely extended his hand, but he might as well have put a pitchfork to her throat.

In the more idle and morbid moments of her adolescence, she had often choreographed her swan song, wondering whether she would stand up to death or simply cower under it. Now she knew: she ended up doing both, just as if death had asked her to dance.

She was still sitting when she noticed his legs trembling beneath his gabardine slacks. Then she heard his voice, as wavery as his knees: "May I have this dance?" A bold impulse made her reach down and raise his trouser cuffs. She gave an immense, audible sigh, then stood and patted his pomaded hair for unnatural bumps.

Only then did she gaze into the flabbergasted eyes of Gilberto Menchaca, who in spite of his shaking legs stood rooted to the spot. She had the simultaneous sense of being lost yet of having arrived at a predestined moment. Holding back an insane urge to wonder aloud whether this was love, she asked instead, "What took you so long?"

Chapter 23

Once he set his mind on something, Gilberto Menchaca prided himself on seeing it through as soon as possible. A month after meeting Imelda he decided he wanted to marry her; a month after that he was ready to meet her family and make his feelings known.

During Gilberto's first call, don Heraclio tried to put him at ease with small talk. But when the suitor kept drifting to more serious matters, he put him to the test. "Supposing you settled down . . . . could you support a family?"

Imelda looked away in shame, but Gilberto nodded then added, "I'm a crew leader, señor. I share a truck with my older carnal"— he backtracked over the pachuco slang that had slipped out—"I mean my older brother. He just got out of the Army." Before he could add that they had to work alongside the crew to make ends meet, Lalito asked: "Where are you parked?"

He felt both dread and relief, for sooner or later they had to see his ancient truck. "Out in the alley, away from street traffic."

"Oh, boy! Let's go see it!"

Crossing the backyard, Gilberto cursed himself for not taking the time to wash its two weeks of field mud. "That Carlos. I've wanted to wash it, but he says it's going to rain any day now."

But don Heraclio's attention was already on the cat's-eye reflectors on the mud flaps. "Were you driving this the night you met

Imelda?" Gilberto gave a puzzled nod. "And you parked in the alley that time, too?"

"The Devil's eyes!" said Lalito. "That's what scared Ralph!"

When it came time for Gilberto to leave, Lalito had to round up his teen-age friends to help push-start the truck. After the exertion don Heraclio paused to catch his breath on the porch steps. Surrounded by hibiscus flowers, he told Imelda, "He seems nice enough. But don't tell him. No sense spoiling him."

Naturally she told him the very next day. Gilberto responded with a marriage proposal that took her by surprise. "But I'm not even eighteen yet."

"I'm twenty-one. That's enough maturity for both."

Saturday morning she brought her father's response. "He says it's way too soon. We should give it at least a year."

Disappointed, he nonetheless honored the decision. That evening, after another crew boss invited him for a beer, Gilberto mentioned his predicament. His friend studied him with amused pity. "Imelda Cavazos, you say? López on her mother's side, right? Uuy, 'mano, good luck. Excuse the expression, but the women in that family will just jack you around till you're impotent."

Gilberto let the comment pass until well into their fifth round. "What did you mean, about the women in Imelda's family?"

"Ask the old man. He almost had to lay siege to her house before they'd let him in. And she has this weird aunt who's kept some fool waiting since before we were born. If I were you I'd give your girlfriend the usual good-for-ninety-days offer. This business of waiting around for ages is for the gringos. By then all you're good for is barbecuing hot dogs while your neighbor's inside with your wife. No wonder gringos wear those corny chef's hats. They must have twelve-point antlers. By the way, I'm going deer hunting next Sunday. How about you and I? . . ."

Gilberto went on his first binge, then showed up at Imelda's house with no idea how he had arrived but convinced that he was under the warm wing of a guardian angel. He felt inspired enough to serenade her and sway her father to his side, all in the same breath; why, he might even marry off her spinster aunt! The seconds stretched endless as stars, but he knew that his gift of gab would not wait forever, so he lumbered up the porch steps.

He tried muffling his knocks, but a light went on next door. Wondering if his impish angel had switched houses on him, he looked about and suddenly faced don Heraclio on the other side of the screen door. He started the speech he had committed to memory but found that the constant rehearsals had worn holes in it. "My honorable Señor Cavazos . . . forgive my showing up . . . unannounced. But my heart breaks when . . ."

After a long pause that was going nowhere, don Heraclio yawned. "I'll tell you what breaks my heart . . . being dragged out of bed at two in the morning on the one day I can sleep late." He knew it was useless to talk sense to a drunk, a love-sick one at that. "Son, go sleep it off in the truck."

Gilberto saw the tender concern in his eyes. "Sí, señor."

He woke up thinking he was in jail, then recognized the slat sidings of his truck. A neighbor's rooster was crowing atop the water barrel. Last night's fiasco came back like a bad dream. He thought of driving away forever, then remembered he had left his keys with don Heraclio. Besides, the whispering neighbors watering their backyard that Sunday morning made him realize he owed the Cavazos family an apology and a farewell.

Don Heraclio met him on the porch in an undershirt that reminded him of the time his father had disciplined him with a razor strop. "Señor Cavazos, I'm sorry about last night. I apologize for the shame I caused your family."

"If you mean the scene you staged for the neighbors, I couldn't care less. You're the one who came out looking like a fool."

He nodded, his face burning from humiliation and a hangover.

"Anyway," don Heraclio added, "I put on a circus or two in front of my wife's family." He looked the young man in the eye. "But don't you ever drive drunk again, or I'll put you out of your grief before you bring it on someone else."

Gilberto, in the vise of an inhuman headache, had already vowed as much, but it took a moment for everything to sink in. "You mean I can still see Imelda?" Don Heraclio nodded. "So we can still get married?"

"Unless last night's spectacle was so I could call it off."

Gilberto stammered through a tangle of apologies, then left before he could mess things up again. Afterwards Imelda hugged her father to get a hold on her own happiness. "So it's agreed. We'll marry as soon as possible."

"Why, no." He tried to retrieve his exact words. "What I said was . . ." Her sparkling eyes suddenly turned moist, and he was left standing as she rushed away to hide her tears.

For hours he agonized over what to tell her, a decision made more difficult by his empathy with the impatient fiance. That evening he sought his mother-in-law's advice. "When it comes to your children you're another Lupita," said doña Lola. "You can't say no. Why just yesterday Imelda was the envy of her friends for having a father who encouraged her to go to dances. That's how this whole thing started, remember."

"Maybe I wanted to make up for the times I didn't care if they existed."

He looked around the living room that was a museum of memories: the López family portrait, the first thing he had noticed that evening he came in from the cold; the sofa leg their puppy was gnawing when he had asked for Graciela's hand—the same one the pup abandoned to turn on his trembling ankle.

Three months later Imelda, like her mother before her, was married in a simple civil ceremony with Samuel Ochoa as witness. At the dinner that followed, Fela told her brother-in-law, "They say children are like an ear of corn, Heraclio. Once that first kernel drops, the rest follow right after."

But after Imelda's departure the bond between father and son took on the intimacy of old friends. Aside from an occasional helping hand from the ailing doña Lola, the two kept house and shared nearly everything—even, to Imelda's disgust, their undershirts. "Not even the muchachos in doña Zoila's pigsty go that far."

"That's because they're not blood," said Lalito.

But when Gilberto's bachelor brother offered to take Lalito to the red light district, don Heraclio opened his eyes to the inexorable changes in his son. Carlos Menchaca mentioned that Lalito had been asking about his Army adventures overseas. "I went through the same thing, Señor Cavazos. And pardon my French, but what I needed all along was a good lay. A trip to a whorehouse would work wonders for the boy. It's the perfect graduation gift."

Don Heraclio turned down the idea. "What he needs is a good job."

Four weeks later Lalito brought home a girlfriend whose mousy demeanor had helped her family camouflage its drug running. "We're getting married right after graduation," he announced, knowing that his father would never confront him in front of her.

Don Heraclio looked around at the everyday objects that faded before his eyes. "I . . . I had no idea."

"I know," said Lalito. "We wanted it to be a surprise."

That night don Heraclio asked point-blank whether he was being forced into marriage. "Don't be pushed into something you'll regret. You're both grown-ups, free to choose."

His argument only gave Lalito more ammunition. "Then this is what we two grown-ups want." But the whine in his tone betrayed his immaturity. "Besides, you gave Imelda permission."

Two weeks later don Heraclio gave in, and his first grandchild, compliments of his son, was born six months later. David, in fact, preceded Imelda's own first-born by almost a month.

At the first opportunity Imelda teased her brother. "Here we were, waiting to get on our feet before starting a family, and you couldn't wait to get off yours."

"I can't understand it," said Lalo. "David must have beat out your Esteban in those last three months."

Gilberto admired how well Lalo's mafioso in-laws had taught him the art of lying through his teeth. "And I thought we'd at least have a photo finish."

Lalo shrugged and smiled like a boy who could not help it. "Quick on the draw."

Gilberto finished the phrase for him: "And he never hurt the law."

Chapter 24

In time don Heraclio joined the Menchaca brother's crew. Aside from his contact with Imelda and her family, his life for the most part was uncluttered and private. The occasional barrio gossip about Lalo only added to the distance between father and son. But he was forced to face the issue one hot afternoon, when Imelda took him on a holiday picnic teeming with gnats and drunks. He was tending the campfire when he asked if Lalo had been invited. Gilberto, more out of wounded pride than malice, said, "Why bother? Our tripas and ground beef can't compete with his in-laws' steaks. Like everyone says, they're one big, mafioso family."

Gilberto quickly excused himself to gather more firewood, but don Heraclio followed him to the clearing. He snapped off a twig, sat on a stump and began scratching eccentric designs in the dirt. "Maybe Carlos was right. About six years ago he offered to take Lalo to a brothel to cool him down, but I said no."

Gilberto shook his head in mock shame. "That's my brother's home away from home. But don't blame yourself for how Lalo turned out, suegro. Going to a brothel wouldn't have changed a thing."

"I wanted him to realize the exploitation behind that sort of pleasure. I guess it's easy for an old man to preach."

Gilberto almost said he saw little difference between spending the night in a whorehouse and spending time with mafioso in-laws.

Instead he replied, more out of confusion than conviction, "Exploitation, uh, right." Actually he cared little for the political and moral dilemmas the older man was forever debating; he put up with it the way other men suffered fathers-in-law who went on binges. But the topic fit his own plans. "Exploitation . . . of course. And you won't find a bunch of more exploited people than down here. Things only change when they get worse. The only difference between hell and our summers is that the other place is a hell of a lot more crowded. Here anyone with an ounce of brains leaves before it gets fried. That's why people who stay turn to drugs and whores." He placed his hand on don Heraclio's shoulder. "And that's where my plan saves the day, suegro. We're taking Lalo and Carlos away from all this, long enough to put them on the right road."

Don Heraclio said nothing: he was all ears.

Gilberto had been incubating his plan for months, and he helped don Heraclio to his feet to get a grip on his own excitement. "Suegro, we're migrating North this summer! The family and whoever else wants to come along. Carlos and I have enough for a down payment on a decent truck. With this heap we wouldn't even cross the county line. We'll get a crew, find a grower up North, and say goodbye to this Texas hell!"

Don Heraclio seemed lost in a thousand thoughts.

"We'll need someone to help my brother translate when he gets stuck. That's where your son comes in. Anyway, he's not holding down a steady job."

"Lalo has a good head for figures."

"Perfect. He can take care of the books and order supplies without having to work much in the fields. He still knows which end of a cotton sack is up, right? Fine. His in-laws haven't ruined him yet." He plucked don Heraclio's hat. "And of course we'll need a cranky old man to keep everyone in line. Seriously, I'll need your help recruiting workers from your barrio. Most of my crew's already heading North by the end of the month."

Don Heraclio barely felt his feet touching the ground. Imelda had hinted at such plans before, but they had seemed vague and far into the future. "I don't know what to say."

"Just say yes." Gilberto replaced his hat, and only then did he discover that his head was uncovered. "Look, suegro, you once said this had been your dream long ago. Now it's here. A little late, maybe, but it's here. So what do you say?''

He did not have to utter a single word. His faraway look said it all.

Chapter 25

Gilberto and Carlos Menchaca discovered the truck of their dreams in the rear of Picudo's Used Car Lot. With extra rear tires which don Heraclio insisted served no purpose other than to waste rubber, and with an olive tone that stirred Carlos' nostalgia for his Army years, it resembled more a military vehicle than a field truck. "No one will climb inside," said don Heraclio. "They'll think the Border Patrol's rounding up people." But when the Menchaca brothers stood firm, he decided there was no explaining personal tastes.

Despite its military pretense, the truck had a dishonorable past. "It's left the county only once," said Picudo Flores. "On its maiden voyage it made it to a checkpoint an hour north of here. There the Border Patrol found contraband."

Carlos' eyes widened like a boy hearing pirate tales. "Smugglers! What? . . ."

Picudo shrugged. "I could make up a story, but why lie? All I know is they impounded the truck and placed it on the auction block."

After a morning of test drives and haggling, the Menchaca brothers left a deposit and a promise to find financing in three days. That evening, Picudo spread the news along cantina row that the Menchacas had paid cash for a new truck with a wad the size of a small cotton bale.

In fact they had not yet secured a loan, but the truck was, by barrio standards, new. As Picudo put it, "She's barely broken in. Just like Señorita Gertrudis . . . used only once on a church picnic."

They began gathering a crew that evening. Gilberto sounded out potential families while his older brother screened the more serious bachelors. Gilberto gave him the task with some reservation, for Carlos had the same soft spot for riff-raff that Samuel Ochoa had for homeless puppies. But since most workers had either gone North or were already committed to other crews, Gilberto had little choice.

His fears were well-founded. When Carlos recruited his best friend Rosendo, he never bothered to ask why his idol was so anxious to disappear up North for the season. On the contrary, Carlos seemed quite pleased, for Rosendo was a tireless worker when the inspiration struck him. Unfortunately, it only struck him for as long as he stayed stoned. "This weed gives me the stamina of two men," he never tired of saying. He failed to add that afterwards it left him with an ego allergic to work, so that when all was said and done, his prowess as a packing shed worker was mediocore.

The instant Gilberto heard that Rosendo was coming along, he said, "Not no, but hell no! That pachuco will bring nothing but trouble."

"You were once a pachuco too, carnal."

"Wearing a zoot suit on weekends is one thing. Living in pool halls is another. We'd have to bring a pool table for him to sleep on."

"He hasn't picked up a cue stick in almost a month."

"He's probably too stoned to remember which end to hold. Look, Carlos, it's very important to weed out characters like him. This time we won't be taking the crew home at the end of the day. We'll be with them round the clock, all summer. A whole new barrio, with countless problems and emergencies. We can't lose sleep babysitting some pelado whose own mother won't trust him with the rent."

"He only borrows when he's broke."

"Which is most of the time! How much does he still owe you?" Carlos did not answer, and Gilberto did not press the matter, since

Carlos had the same luck picking friends that he had picking women.

In the end, though, Gilberto's fraternal pity spoke over his better judgment. "Well . . . he can come along under two conditions . . ."

But when Carlos had to spell these out to his friend, he skirted the drug issue the same way he solicited sex from prostitutes. "Gilberto doesn't want you to, ah, bring anything to, you know, get us into trouble . . . ."

"Why, carnal, carnal, carnal!" said Rosendo, as though the mere thought injured his integrity. Ordinarily that plea which promised nothing and delivered as much would have sufficed, but now Carlos insisted on something more binding. So Rosendo gave his word, but with an amoral indifference which would have convinced no one except Carlos. The second condition, though—how good a picker he was—no amount of sweet nothings could fulfill. Packing shed workers often threw in the sack after a day of stoop labor, and when Carlos escorted Rosendo to the fields the next morning, the crew flocked around the greenhorn wearing zoot suit slacks and a peacock's plume on his hat. He placed his sack between his legs, its mouth gaping under his crotch, and they grinned as if a dude had mounted his horse backwards. Lupita even whispered to her cousin, "From that angle it looks like a giant condom." But the instant he straddled his row and began furiously scooping cotton, he left any doubters in his trail. Father Adán compared him to a kleptomaniac kangaroo, and the technique triggered several imitations.

By the end of the week the truck loan was secured, along with the remainder of the new crew. "Let's do this right," said Gilberto. "I don't like to throw a dart at a map and go where it lands." He and Imelda consulted several crew leaders, asking what crops were grown where, who was going to which state, then reported their findings to the family. "Indiana's our best bet," he said. "Few crews are headed there, so there's less competition."

"And there's cotton," said Imelda, "so we'll take to it like ducks to water."

That evening they contacted La Gorilita, a squat, heavy-set crew boss who moved as though he might suddenly break into a knuckle-walk. He gave them the phone number of a Mr. Hutchinson in Indiana who needed a crew in two weeks. After Carlos and Lalo reached a long-distance agreement with the grower, the entire family cheered—even the cautious don Heraclio, who warned the Menchaca brothers, "Just don't turn into tyrants once we're up there."

"This isn't tío Porfirio's Mexico, suegro. Here people respect each other."

"You're the one we have to watch out for, Señor Cavazos. My brother said you organized strikes in Mexico."

Gilberto laughed. "Some men sow their oats in Mexico. My suegro sowed revolution."

On the day before the annual blessing of the migrant fleet, Father Adán baptized the truck La Golondrina. "The Swallow," said Gilberto. "Let's put that on her mud flaps."

Imelda agreed. "Each summer she'll take us north then bring us back."

Carlos spent his last Saturday night at home waxing La Golondrina's cab under an outside lamp whose moths kept him startled but alert. He barely had time to test a new array of roof lights before the first rays of dawn.

That warm and breezy morning Father Coronado held the mass blessing in the church parking lot. The tradition went back to don Heraclio's bachelor days, and crew bosses in starched khakis parked their field trucks in a neat row as if awaiting automotive Communion. But the center of attention was La Golondrina, gleaming beneath a cloudless sky and sporting immaculate, stenciled mud flaps. Carlos had expected to score points with Dina Zuñiga but ended up so exhausted he sat out the service unshaved and asleep behind the wheel.

"He must have spent the night in Mexico," Dina whispered to a sister under an Our Father. Suddenly Father Coronado's flock bleated a collective "Amen!", and Carlos startled awake, blasting the "Aoogah!" horn with his elbow.

That afternoon Gilberto caught his six year-old son trying to smuggle his puppy in the truck's tool box. "What did we agree on, son?"

Esteban's fright squeezed a yelp from the pup. "That Lobo's staying with 'buelita Lola. But he won't listen."

Gilberto took the stowaway, a gift from Samuel Ochoa, and handed it to don Heraclio. But its whimpering made him feel he was separating two close friends, so in the end he decided to bolt a sturdy crate behind a running board. "You can't carry him with you because he'll bother the workers. So I'm making him a little dog-house on wheels."

But the childish requests were not over. Carlos arrived at the eleventh hour with a local musician who waited in the yard like a reluctant petitioner. "One-eyed Lara wants to bring his conjunto along."

Gilberto shook his head. "This is a work crew, not a touring band. Besides, there's no more room."

"No sweat. They'll take their own van to play at other camps on weekends."

"That's all I need! A marihuano musician with a burnt-out head-light!"

Don Heraclio shushed him. "He's not deaf, Gilberto."

"But we need people to pick cotton."

Carlos had a ready answer. "How do you think he makes money between dances? In the fields, like everyone else."

"What's he do, take his harp along?"

"He plays the accordion, carnal. Damn good, too."

"Great. He'll get the men in a drinking mood every night."

Don Heraclio took Carlos' side. "They'll help keep our spirits up. We'll be out in a strange land. Homesick. Anyway, there'll be no one here to play for." He picked up Lobo, who began sniffing out his new home. "Even the dogs are leaving."

"Bad enough we're taking Padre Adán's ark," said Gilberto. "A crew of odds and ends, headed for who-knows-where. Maybe we should name our truck the Santa María." He searched the ground for an answer, then finally signaled One-eyed Lara a thumb's-up approval. "Tell that pirate we sail at dawn."

Chapter 26

La Golondrina had barely pulled into the grower's driveway when Esteban sprang from a pile of picking sacks and peeked through the sideboards. "Toys!" he yelled. "Look at all . . ." Suddenly he remembered there was no one else in back and held in his excitement until his father put the parking brake on. He jumped down for a closer look and noticed there were no other children around; the toys lay discarded like abandoned treasure. He ran to the truck cab to tell his father and his uncle Carlos, but they were already approaching Mr. Hutchinson, who flashed a nervous smile. "Why, it's the Menchaca boys!"

Gilberto wasted no time instructing his brother: "Tell him we came to Indiana as farm workers, not tourists. Today makes thirty working days he owes us. We have a crew to pay and payments to make on a truck." He stared at the grower through the translation, nodding at the little English he understood.

The grower claimed he had difficulty with Carlos' accent, then reneged outright on an earlier agreement. But Carlos had sharpened his English and mechanical skills around redneck sergeants, so Anglos did not intimidate him.

"Tell him the crew would love nothing better than his freckled butt," said Gilberto. "Either he pays on the spot or they collect their slice."

Suddenly Esteban ran from the truck and buried himself in the group. The grower gave a high-pitched yell, as if a wild animal had brushed him, and Carlos had to fight back a grin to keep their business serious.

Later, driving to a Terre Haute bank, he mussed his nephew's hair. "You almost gave Hutchinson a heart attack."

"Then we'd really be out in the cold," said Gilberto, patting his shirt pocket as if the check might have gone up in smoke. "I still don't trust him."

"Maybe he doesn't have money in the bank," said Carlos.

"Ha! He probably owns it."

Esteban, sitting between them, was certain of one thing: "He had so many toys!"

His eyes widened when his uncle said, "Before he coughed up the check I was ready to load them on the truck."

It took a bank teller's critical eye to catch the discrepancy between the name on the driver's license and that on the check, made out to one GILBERTO MENCACA. His refusal to cash it hinged on the missing letter.

"Carlos, is this man saying I'm not me?"

The teller did not wait for a translation. "Mister Men-ca-ca?"

"No!" Gilberto said in Spanish. "Your father!" He glowered at the startled customers and grabbed his son's hand. "Let's go. These goddamn gringos all sleep under the same blanket."

Carlos drove in silence until they reached the creek that separated their camp from the woods. "So now? Do we stop working?"

Gilberto rubbed his knuckles on his incisors. "No. But he'll sure have a hard time getting his cotton once it's picked."

The strategy sounded dangerous, even for the impulsive Carlos. "He's going to shit in his bib overalls."

"He can ask Mister Mencaca for some cotton to wipe his ass."

"What about our payments on La Golondrina?"

Gilberto lied. "There's enough money left."

"Enough for a few more lights on the truck?"

He almost smiled. "It's a long way to Christmas, carnal. Besides, my suegro's still crabbing about the extra rear tires."

"That don Heraclio," sighed Carlos. "Duller than a communist."

During the family discussion that evening, Imelda voiced her doubts. "Keeping his cotton can get the whole camp into trouble. And let's face it, people here only let us stay because we pick their crops."

Don Heraclio agreed. "Ask him once more, without threats. We need time to rally the crew."

They consented, for in times of trouble the camp turned to him. He had calmed them when the Menchacas took the wrong turn and overshot their northern destination. "We almost made history as the first migrants in Canada," he had said, then helped them backtrack and bivouack in family tents outside an unknown town. The residents, never having seen migrants before, had mistaken them for a band of gypsies, and several people had shown up to have their fortunes told.

"Then it's settled," said Gilberto. "Carlos drops us off and pays him another visit. Esteban, tomorrow you ride shotgun with your uncle."

By dawn Carlos was up before the other bachelors. Walking by the Zúñigas' tent and wearing his favorite guayabera, he shivered as much from the morning chill as from the thought of running into Dina Zúñiga. The crisp air sharpened his senses, and he swore he felt a feminine warmth from her tent.

He finally admitted his blunder during last week's dance. Dina, complaining of a headache, had decided to leave early with a male cousin. Although disappointed, Carlos should have left it at that. Instead, under the influence of several beers and Rosendo's advice, he had hinted at incestual goings-on. She had slapped him in the middle of the dance floor and had stormed out arm in arm with her chaperone, leaving Carlos smarting from her swift hand and from the wagging tongues all round. But her anger had only fueled his jealousy, and the following evening he had put Esteban on her trail. His nephew, of course, had bungled the assignment, infuriating her further.

Esteban was still lying bundled on the floor, listening to the secure activity of his parents getting ready for work. The thought of spending the day with his uncle cut both ways: it offered a chance to see the toys again, but also the risk that his uncle might want another spying mission. He heard his mother at the far end of the tent. "I don't feel right leaving him with Carlos." He hid his head under the blanket just before his father looked his way. "He's in good hands. Carlos drives carefully."

"That's not it. Last week he got Esteban into a fight with David."

"A playful round between cousins never hurt anyone. Besides, Lalo didn't mind."

He felt her come quite close, pulling a silent tension while she gathered blankets from the floor and swallowed hard to keep her words down. Then, before he could pretend to wake up, she asked, "And that time at the Zúñiga's?"

He slipped deeper into the cocoon of his blanket and stoppered his ears until his skull buzzed, but the memory had already spilled through: he was peeping through a slit in the Zúñiga tent, carrying out his uncle's orders to the letter—keeping an eye on Dina. The Zúñiga sisters were retiring early when suddenly an enormous hand gripped his neck and smothered him against the canvas. Don Edelmiro Zúñiga dragged him back to his parents, yoking him under a hand that stank of pesticide. One eye, the one Esteban had kept shut while spying, was covered by a paralyzed eyelid; the other was pie-eyed with fright. "Just look!" said don Edelmiro, pointing to the petrified wink. "I caught him getting an eyeful, and now God's punishment fits the crime." His uncle Carlos, going over the books with his uncle Lalo in a corner of the tent, became more absorbed in his work.

As soon as they were alone his mother had cornered him. "Qué chulo!"—how lovely! "I'm dying to hear what you were up to."

He stood her stare with as much dignity as possible with his one good eye. "Playing hide-and-seek. I was looking for David."

"Playing hide-and-seek," she mimicked in a likely-story tone. She wanted to let him suffer a bit longer but instead knelt to nurse his eye. "I think you're the one who's playing hide-and-seek with us."

His father turned up the kerosene light to give her a better look. "The old man's insanely jealous of his daughters. No wonder Carlos suspects the family's too close for comfort."

Except for his uncle's questions over what he had seen—a probing he had evaded twice—that had been the end of it, until now. When he unplugged his ears and the buzzing faded, his mother's voice was the first thing he heard. "Our poor, sick son."

"Why sick? He didn't get a sty."

"Go ahead, laugh!"

"If you have to worry, then worry about your nephew David caught wearing his sister's panties. Anyway, what's Carlos got to do with this?"

"When I brought up the incident, he and Esteban glanced at each other and turned dumb. Then . . ."

At that instant his uncle entered the tent and lifted the mosquito net above Esteban. "Open your eyes, sleepy head!" He tickled and tousled him until he was left tangled in the blanket.

Nothing more was discussed, and Esteban gathered his things while his mother put out cornflakes and evaporated milk. "Don't forget to add water," she said, "or you'll get a tummy ache again." She handed him a bundle in butcher's wrap that had the texture and color of paper on a doctor's examination table. "These tacos are for the road. Share them with your uncle."

His father unlocked the small tool box they used as a safe and counted each bill, hoping he had missed one. Then he handed them the empty box. "This time screw the courtesies, Carlos. And no more checks. We want legal tender."

Chapter 27

While his nephew christened passing animals with first names, Carlos drove in silence, insulated in a cozy daydream about Dina. He had settled into a slack-mouthed reverie when he realized Esteban was watching him. All at once he felt caught with his pants down, like the time he had gone to the field's farthest corner with a handful of cotton only to find a cow in an adjoining pasture placidly contemplating him. He had blushed fiercely, like now, although there had not been the slightest judgment in those large bovine eyes.

He stared into the rearview mirror to distract Esteban. "Say, what's that truck following us?" It was their favorite pastime on long drives, and his nephew's knowledge had become his source of pride among other crew leaders.

Esteban stuck his head out for a better view. "International, fifty-five!"

After they parked in the grower's driveway Esteban opened his door to get out without asking; with his father he could only tag along when invited. They were shown inside by a lady in a stiff, coiled hairdo. Carlos removed his hat—a soft crease rimmed his hair from always wearing it in public—then put it back on after catching his reflection in the hall mirror and deciding he looked subservient. His dark, angled eyebrows turned stern as he told himself to keep his concentration and control.

Mr. Hutchinson was buffing his shoes in the living room. "Why, howdy, amigo! We were just going to Tear-ass-hood for a little shopping."

He placed the check on the coffee table. "So were we, until this came up."

The grower slapped his forehead without even reading the check. "Don't tell me I got the name wrong! I'm terrible at spelling Mexican."

"Don't bother writing checks anymore." He opened the ledger to show him the new totals.

Esteban felt restless; not understanding a word made the minutes itch like his uncle's Army blankets. Then his gaze wandered to an adjoining room and settled on a chest crammed with toys. A small truck caught his attention: a miniature Golondrina, down to the extra rear tires! He almost interrupted his uncle, who closed his ledger and handed Mr. Hutchinson the tool box. No sooner did the grower leave the room than Esteban said, "Look, tío, a baby Golondrina!"

His uncle's eyebrows arched from anger to surprise. "You're right! She must have come up North to have it on the sly!"

Esteban moved in for a closer look when suddenly another boy blocked the play room. He had very pale skin and red hair, a crayon red that with a few freckled exceptions seemed to have drained the blush from his face. He uttered some noise and nonsense, and when his mother answered from the hall in the same gibberish, Esteban understood: he was facing a flesh-and-blood Anglo boy.

The boy began showing off his toys from a distance. Esteban smiled to show he was an available playmate, but the boy only sneaked him sidelong glances. Then during one hard turn a small airplane slipped his grip and taxied to Esteban's feet. Esteban stooped to return it, but the boy yelled, "No!" and pounced on it. After that Esteban ignored him until the boy grew tired of playing.

Carlos followed their rivalry with a quiet fascination. "Ask him this, Esteban," then carefully enunciated in English: "What's your name?"

Esteban said nothing. The last time he had repeated one of his uncle's English phrases, his mother had scolded him. "It's only to find out his name," his uncle added in Spanish, then repeated the words like an hypnotic suggestion. Esteban tested it under his breath, then blurted out what was less a question than a command: "Juas jur neym!"

"Jimmy."

He beamed as if he had taught Lobo a new trick. But when the boy asked, "Do you work for my daddy?", he reacted as if a lit firecracker had been tossed back. Sensing a reply was needed, he turned to his uncle.

"Tell him to screw his own mother."

Esteban's ears burned. "Why?!" he asked hoarsely.

"That's what he told you."

He had never understood exactly what the phrase meant, except that he had to fight. His breath came and went in desperate pants, until Carlos realized the prank had gone too far. "It's not fair, though. He's smaller than you." Either he did not hear or the dilemma only made it worse, and he lunged at the boy the moment Carlos corralled him. "Whoa!"

Esteban struggled against the bear hug, knocking off his uncle's hat and yelling at the stupefied boy in Spanish, "Screw yours, and your grandmother too!" Carlos muzzled him and drew him closer until the grower came back, then cautiously turned him loose like a half-tamed cub.

The tool box was returned half-filled with small bills. "I'll have the rest five days from now," said the grower and offered his hand to honor his word. Carlos took a deep breath, emptied part of the payroll over the outstretched hand, then littered the rest all the way to the door.

Suddenly the world reached Esteban in disconnected episodes: his uncle striding away, so determined he did not even stop to retrieve his hat; the grower shouting after him with jerky gestures, the way barking dogs chased La Golondrina; the frightened boy trotting after his father. He heard his name in the commotion outside and began making his way around the scattered toys. Then, without understanding why, he paused by the small, green truck. Perhaps he only meant to touch it farewell; but seeing it at his feet, he realized that at times things were placed in one's path by magic.

He tried tucking it under his flannel shirt, but when the bulge turned out too obvious, he smuggled it out under his uncle's hat.

While the men argued in the yard, he unwrapped his mother's tacos and put each in a shirt pocket. Then he covered the toy with butcher's wrap and stuffed it under the truck seat.

On the way back he broke the long silence. "The boy was a gringo, right?"

Carlos nodded. "What did you make of him?"

He remembered his first glimpse of newborn puppies, how they had seemed more like mice than dogs. "They look different in the movies."

His uncle sighed. "Everything's different in the movies. Say, since we're all going to hell anyway, let's treat the crew to a drive-in movie tomorrow night."

"A monster movie?"

"No, about two lovers . . ."

He ignored the rest. But even after a boring movie he looked forward to the discussions in his uncle's tent. Since few of the bachelors knew English, several versions were invented, and by the time he went to bed he had enough plots to keep him in dreams all night long. The best ones came from Rosendo, who included himself in the cast of characters.

"Tío," said Esteban, "your friend says movies stay in the air, and if you look hard you can still see them. Even enter them."

Carlos wondered whether Rosendo had kept his promise to stay clean, then decided it was the least of their worries. "Well, don't look too hard or you'll see flying saucers land in the fields like him."

Esteban brushed off flannel lint from his tacos and shared one. Carlos returned the favor: feeling under the seat while Esteban's stomach tightened, he pulled out a warm soft drink. "Don't let it pop in your face. It's been under the seat all morning."

After reviewing his plan, Carlos decided that a drive-in movie was the perfect cover for getting back on Dina's good side. But the moment he imagined himself inviting her face to face, his Adam's apple corked the courage in his throat. A note would be better, and better still if his nephew delivered it. He looked about and spotted the butcher's wrap. "Hand me that paper." Esteban sputtered carbonated water through his nose and fell into a coughing fit. "Easy, muchacho, I need you in one piece." Finally he settled on a more

personal touch for stationery—a blank page from the ledger. Ma-
nuevering his penmanship around pot holes, he creased the note
and tossed it into Esteban's lap. "This goes out air mail to you-
know-who, Cupid." He winked. "Top secret."

Esteban stared at the note without touching it. "What's it say?"

"Don't worry, it won't get you in trouble."

He held it upside down by a corner, as when he picked up
horned toads by the tail. "Why write a letter, tío? Why not just tell
her?"

"This is more romantic. Take charros in the movies. Say Jorge
Negrete, rest his soul, likes a woman. He doesn't just blurt it out.
No, he serenades her, or shoots someone who insults her."

When his nephew failed to see the connection between serenades
and shootings, Carlos wondered whether he was being put on the
spot on purpose. But searching the child's eyes he found the same
solemn innocence as on that windy day when he had taught him to
send kite telegrams: after tearing a page from the ledger and scrib-
bling a message, they had cheered its spastic climb skyward. Then
Esteban had asked, "But who's going to read it, tío?"

That time he had a ready answer: "The little birds flying by take
the message to heaven. That's how prayers are answered." Esteban
had thought a moment, then had smiled, satisfied.

After they returned the crew back to camp, his uncle signaled
him on Dina's trail. He clenched the note and went through the
motions of dashing after her, but once out of sight he backtracked
and retrieved his truck. Then he sneaked off to a secluded bend in
the creek and played until Rosendo and Dina Zúñiga stumbled onto
his hide-out. "We . . . we were looking for a robin's nest," she
said. "I mean . . . a bunny that ran into the woods." She stared for
an instant at Rosendo, then hurried back to camp.

Esteban returned to his parents' tent to find the crew gathered
around La Golondrina. His father hoisted himself on the running
board and displayed the tool box. "He offered us a half-filled box
and his word . . ."

"Meaning he offered us a half-filled box," said an elderly
woman.

Don Heraclio disguised his voice in the crowd, a tactic from his
organizing days. "Why, that's handmirrors and beads!"

Samuel Ochoa added, "It won't even cover the snake extermination we gave his fields."

"I say we finish picking his cotton," said Gilberto, "then keep it in a safe place until he pays up."

"And if that doesn't work?" someone asked.

"Then we take him to court."

"And if he takes us first?"

When don Edelmiro Zúñiga backed the Menchacas, Carlos sought Dina's attention, but her eyes never left the ground.

Imelda promised to pay the two families who refused to join them. "Lalo and Carlos will tally up your earnings tonight. You'll have your wages first thing in the morning."

That evening Esteban molded a play mountain from a pile of blankets and began punching in some caves for his new truck. His mother was replacing the warped carboard slats in her sunbonnet when the toy caught her attention; his attempt to hide it only fueled her suspicions. "Gilberto, when was the last time we bought Esteban a toy?"

"About a year ago. And at this rate he'll be lucky to get the next one when he's thirty."

She fished out the truck from under the blankets. "So then, what's this?"

He showed the same childlike joy as his son on seeing a replica of La Golondrina; then her point sank in. "Where did you get this, Esteban?"

His stomach jammed his chest as if he had been hurled from a tremendous height. He struggled to say something—anything—but his will melted like a puddle at his feet. "Well?" she asked. "We're waiting."

From across the tent, with his back to them and without looking up from the ledger, his uncle Carlos spoke for him: "You mean a little truck like ours?"

Esteban managed to think, He remembered!, and then even his inner voice turned dumb.

"How did you guess, Carlos?"

He continued adding figures. "No guess. I bought it for him last week. It was rolling under the seat till today. I figure if we end up losing the truck we'll at least have a toy to console us."

128

She rapped her knuckles on a box that served as their table. "Don't even joke about it. Esteban, did you thank your uncle?"

He answered with a saucer-eyed stare, wondering why he should be grateful. Then he remembered the gift of the lie. "Thank you, tío."

On the surface things returned to normal, but when he tried to incline a plank for his toy, nothing obeyed his rubbery grip, and the board whacked to the floor. The moment his mother stepped outside the tent, his uncle said, "Your boy saw his first little gringo, carnal. Gave him a chinga tu madre, and threw in the grandmother for good measure."

Esteban braced himself for a lecture, but his father simply gave a sigh that seemed to come from long ago, then brought himself back with a shake of his head. "He had to open his eyes sometime. Try to keep them blind and you only hurt them more."

That night the world lost its sleep to chirping insects and Lobo's sudden barking at the darkness surrounding them. But the shared insomnia also added to the camp's solidarity, and a melancholy accordion over a card game serenaded Esteban with a security that felt like an extra blanket at night. Even his father's murmurs, muffled by a canvas partition and soothed away each time by his mother's voice, took on a rhythmic serenity.

By sunrise the entire crew was on its feet. Imelda checked the canvas sack she had washed the day before and found it dry and gleaming. The families who were leaving came in together and avoided her eyes, staring with exaggerated interest while Esteban played with his truck. They made him uncomfortable, but he held his ground until they were paid with a minimum of words. Then he tossed his toy into the pillowcase that was his cotton sack and checked his pocket for the note. By now the paper had worn soft as tissue.

The radio was forecasting a splendid Saturday morning when several Anglo teenagers cruising the countryside in a late-model convertible were drawn to the neat rectangle of tents. Carlos stopped chatting with Rosendo and hurried to intercept them. "This is no circus," he said. "There may be trouble, so please leave." He went ahead to escort them out, but Rosendo crossed the car's path and forced it to brake. An acned couple in the rear, jeans damp from beer quarts wedged in their crotches, smiled nervously.

"You want big fun, eh?" he asked in English. The girl in back took a drink to appear courageous, but Rosendo mocked her by sucking his thumb. "That for little babies," he whispered in a hiss that mesmerized their fear into curiosity. "This for big boys." He reached into his chest pocket and was about to let them in on his secret when Carlos whistled sharply, and they zoomed off in a dust storm.

"What was that all about?" asked Carlos.

"Spoiled brats with nothing to do." He nudged him. "But the two blonde bimbos gave me the eye. Maybe we can squeeze their pimples at the drive-in tonight."

The workers entered the field with a vigor that belied last night's insomnia. Everyone seemed aware of each other, and they cheered when don Heraclio went to weigh his sack and said, "I'll finally sleep on a mattress tonight."

"As long as it's not the county's," said Father Adán.

Noon came, but no one thought of stopping for lunch. Their only rest came from the close watch for dust clouds over the country road, which they checked every so often, as if a tornado funnel were slowly sending its root to earth.

Esteban was emptying his pillowcase into his mother's sack when a pickup truck parked behind La Golondrina. He recognized the grower and the men who had been paid that morning. Two policemen in a patrol car joined them, and his heart turned into a trapped rabbit.

The workers stood and turned to his parents. Don Edelmiro loped across several rows, herded his daughters, then left them standing in midfield while he followed the group, which grew as it neared.

A few feet from Esteban, Rosendo ducked between rows and stashed something in his sack. Esteban followed his lead: in one quick move he hid his toy inside his mother's sack and wadded it down with cotton. When don Edelmiro shouted something at his uncle, he buried the note, too.

His mother gripped her chest strap. "I'll weigh this and bring back Lalo's books. Don't worry, Gilberto, they won't stop me." She tugged her canvas sack, immaculate under the blazing sun and trailing a shearing sound as though rending the earth. The men closed ranks but at the last moment let her through.

In the distance El Bruto cinched her sack to the scale's cradle, steadied its arc and barked a figure to Lalo, who entered it in the ledger. When El Bruto hoisted the sack up the trailer ladder, Esteban imagined him carrying an unconscious angel back home. Reaching the top, he untied the tail drawstring and shook with bonecrushing strength until cotton vomited from both ends.

Esteban strained for a sign of his truck or his uncle's note, but they ended up buried in the silent avalanche. Then the empty sack fell to earth like the carcass of a cloud.

Chapter 28

Gilberto and Carlos Menchaca were escorted to the back seat of the patrol car. A second policeman followed behind and kept the crew at bay, which managed to distract him long enough for Imelda to push the ledger through the car's half-opened window. The policeman at the wheel gunned the engine to disperse those in front, and Gilberto acknowledged his wife with a terse smile. "We'll be back when we get back."

The sun had already set when they finally returned. The crew tried to read their faces in the fading light for clues of the outcome, but no one could tell whether their fixed gaze spelled victory or failure. Then Gilberto repeated the grower's ultimatum, but so softly that the crew in turn had to pass it along by word of mouth:

"He wants us out by noon on Monday. We'll get half our wages that morning."

"And the rest?"

"The rest we write off to experience."

"That's it?"

"That's it. That's the best I could do. I'm a crew leader, not a crooked lawyer." He said nothing about the lawsuits and civil charges he and his brother still faced.

Even Carlos had a silence which gave him an enigmatic maturity. Later, when he left for Gilberto's tent to begin working out the details of their departure, one of the bachelors wondered aloud if the brothers had struck a deal to save their own skin. "A man can get mightly cold feet after a few hours in a cell."

Rosendo, who considered himself an expert in illegal matters, thought otherwise. "Ever try getting a J.P. to set bail on a weekend? The Menchacas could've squealed on both grandmothers and they'd still be there. Even if they were out on bond they couldn't cross the creek to take a shit, much less the state line."

"Speaking of crossing state lines," said One-Eyed Lara, "I heard there's some wild nightclubs in Illinois. By the time we finally get a little money we won't have time to celebrate."

"Celebrate what?" said someone else. "That it's all over except for the crying?"

Rosendo sat on the edge of Lara's cot and closed one eye himself. "I don't have money, but that doesn't mean I'm broke. I can always trade."

One-Eyed Lara suddenly remembered the trunk Rosendo had stored in his van the minute they had returned to camp. He stretched his neck, slowly scanned the tent perimeter like a periscope, then teased out a riff on his accordion so that only Rosendo could hear his words: "Once these guys jerk off and say their prayers, let's take a midnight ride . . . maybe even have a going-out-of-business sale."

"If we do, it won't hurt to take along a little protection. Just look at how these gringos double-crossed the Menchacas."

"And those are the law-abiding ones. Imagine what the others are like." He lifted a corner of his blanket to show the revolver that the band took on their tours.

Rosendo knew he had found a kindred soul. Before coming to Indiana he had packed most of his mother's trunk with enough marihuana to last him the harvest, even hibernate through the winter if need be, and now he faced the closest thing to a moral dilemma in his life: to return with a season's stash that would soon grow stale in a land of plenty or risk unloading it up North on unknown clients.

On the morning the camp was supposed to pack up, the police arrived with Mr. Hutchinson and searched each tent without explanations or apologies. When the dragnet reached the stag quarters, the bachelors began clearing a week's worth of recycled underwear and abused girly magazines. Rosendo rested on his upended suit-case with a forced nonchalance, and it suddenly dawned on Gilberto why the pachuco had worked steadily up to then. "Shit!" he hissed under his breath.

He was not alone in his dread. Even the grannies who waited outside, and whose toothless smiles made them appear as innocent as the toddlers they babysat during the day, even they would not have backed Rosendo any more than they would have bet their meager life's savings on a drugged nag.

What the police did find in his flimsy suitcase was money, lots of it, stuffed inside rumpled zoot suit slacks. "Goddamn!" said Mr. Hutchinson. "These people sack away more money than Jews! So why the hell are they whining?"

"I save for rainy day."

"These aren't just pennies from heaven, boy! I should be so rich!"

"And I not steal one nickel."

While the police put out an all-points inquiry on recent holdups, Rosendo protested his innocence in Spanish. "Why won't they be-lieve I had a good season? Don't they say God helps those who grow their own?"

He was even first in line when Mr. Hutchinson finally paid the workers a part of their summer wages, and he offered to trade what he called his "filthy lucre" for the grower's crisp, new bills.

Don Edelmiro had half a mind to back him up. "This money looks a little strange to me, Heraclio. Is it real?"

"Must be. Looks like he just made it."

La Golondrina had barely returned to Texas when the rumors began flying that the one worker who had made a killing was Ro-sendo. It was being circulated by One-Eyed Lara, who had brought back a small nest egg himself. When Gilberto crossed paths with him in cantina row, Lara was buying everyone drinks and bragging that he was going to Mexico to have an alabaster eye fitted. Gilber-to's own friends hoped to baptize him into the rites of macho mourning, but he insisted on nursing the same bottle throughout, saying he had already made an ass of himself once. Lara, though, was beyond discretion and already well into an account of that Indiana night when he had been unanchored from his migrant moorings and resettled in an Illinois nightclub. His recollection had the unreal air of a movie set, "like Cantinflas versus the midwest mafia. There you had us, gangsters on all sides and Rosendo's trying to charm the pants off a cocktail waitress."

But if Lara admitted to having felt ill at ease, Rosendo had felt right at home. After a few trick shots on the pool table and some practice licks in English, the pachuco had plunged into a monologue that would have put even the incessant Cantinflas to shame. His clients, already under the influence of his samples, had sat speechless under a rambling tribute to those universal vices which made Mexicans and mafiosos alike, all brothers in sin. In the end Rosendo had exchanged the contents of his mother's trunk for a grocery bag of assorted bills, even finagling an expensive fedora he later found too large.

One-Eyed Lara tried to salvage a moral from his tale. "At least someone took those gringos to the cleaners."

Only sheer cynicism gave Gilberto, sitting within earshot, the strength to keep his temper. "So that Robin Hood walks out with new zoot suits, and the rest of us lose our shirts."

The following morning, as he drove La Golondrina through the barrio one last time, he had no choice but to acknowledge the bizarre tale as fact. To add insult to injury, Carlos, who rode shotgun, was wearing a new, cream fedora, compliments of Rosendo. Simply thinking about the camp's near-brush with drug charges soured Gilberto's stomach, and he tried to neutralize his bitterness with a strong dose of sarcasm. "At least we ended up with a pimp's hat for a souvenir."

"Don't forget, Rosendo also gave us money on the way down."

"That's the least he could do, after putting everyone's ass on the slave block. Even the Pope couldn't have pardoned us."

"We risked sending the camp to jail, too. What's the difference?"

"The difference . . ." Gilberto rolled the reply on his tongue as though it were a bitter pill to swallow. "The difference is we consulted them first, told them the dangers. We were in it together, win or lose." But the words sounded as superficial as the mutilated rote of his son's Pledge of Allegiance. For even as they worked against the clock to sell La Golondrina and stay out of jail, many insisted they had struck a deal with the grower to divide the crew's earnings. "In the end," Gilberto admitted, "Rosendo and I were both out to make a buck. The only difference is I failed. Now he's a hero and I'm a heel."

They were barely home and already Gilberto was a changed man. His pessimism had infected Imelda, who had started out agreeing with him to humor his dark spells, but she too was fast becoming a convert. Everyone noticed his embittered about-face, but only don Heraclio understood how the world could warp a trusting young man into a premature cynic. So while the circle of friends and family mouthed the obvious—that Gilberto had ended up bankrupt—don Heraclio knew that the bankruptcy was less monetary than moral.

Even before leaving Indiana the Menchaca brothers had decided to sell La Golondrina for a loss and let the buyer assume the lien. They had no choice, since their liberty from the snarl of lawsuits, fines and verbal agreements hinged on the condition that they scrape up money, and quickly.

The greetings of compadres and friends in Chale's garage that morning were subdued, and the only remark on the new pin-up in the corner was that it be taken down in case doña Zoila showed up for the bidding. She did not, but several barrio merchants poked their heads inside, saw the group and walked on by. "They don't want an audience seeing how dirty they can get," said don Heraclio.

Finally Carlos' godfather, don Ramón, walked in, burdened with his eternal economic concerns and a remorseful aura that followed him like an unforgiven crime. He wore his perennial khaki shirt like a sackcloth. His gloom prompted Chale to ask if he was facing major surgery. Because he lacked the arrogance that typified self-made men, he was pitied by laborers and servant girls alike, who drew the moral that the well-to-do were, after all, worse off with their cursed wealth.

His offer was fair for a businessman who had his sellers over a barrel. The Menchacas in turn saved face by saying that the truck had stayed in the family, although Carlos had seen his godfather only twice in the last twelve years.

After closing the deal don Ramón paused at the door and said to no one in particular, "I'll need new mudflaps for the truck."

Carlos was standing with the blank look of the newly dispossessed, and the idle aside galvanized him back into action. "You've got it, padrino! I'll have a pair in seven days!"

He went straight to the truck and yanked off the mudflaps he had stenciled just weeks before with his surname and a swallow's silhouette. A horrified friend looked on as if he were removing the shoes from a still-warm corpse. "At least old don Ramón will remember you in his will. You could choke half the elephants in India with the pesos he's squirreled away in Mexican banks."

While Carlos was naive about many matters, he had no illusions about an inheritance; his godfather's last gift had been a snowcone during a record heat wave some fifteen summers ago. But for the moment, Carlos had nothing but time on his hands, which he felt were better suited now for painting canvases than for picking cotton. He saw too how time was already corroding Gilberto's soul.

He threw himself into his art work with a discipline nobody thought him capable of. "He's working like a man possessed," they said. That in itself said a lot, coming from field workers who picked and pulled hundreds of pounds of cotton over suffocating fields, and for whom artists were bohemians who lifted nothing heavier than a brush or a bottle.

He unveiled his twin masterpieces in Chale's garage on the seventh day, as promised. The identical mudflaps each had a voluptuous harem girl reclining in utter abandon. Their veils were precisely that: a lace veil someone had torn and thrown away, and which he then cut and pasted over the nude figures. For jewels he had riveted chrome studs and a fanciful assortment of truck reflectors. Beside each girl lay a bowl of exotic fruit, also invented from colored reflectors; each held in her fingertips and above her mouth a jewel-like purple sphere. "I got the idea from a María Félix movie," he said. "She makes eating grapes a sin."

Gilberto crouched for a better view. "What's a sin is getting them muddy." It was his first lively remark in weeks, but seeing him on his haunches, Carlos could only think back to his boyhood, to the time they had bet all their marbles on one shot against the

Maldonado brothers and had lost. He remembered Gilberto rooted to the spot, his arm still outstretched from the losing shot.

Don Ramón's pragmatic eye, though, overlooked esthetics. "Cover up those shameless strippers, unless you want Father Coronado to roast us in his next sermon." He said nothing about the faces on the two figures, but their resemblance to Dina Zúñiga's twin sisters was not lost on the other onlookers. By dinnertime the garage became a crowded, one-portrait gallery. Carlos was guarding the garage door, keeping a cautious eye out for don Edelmiro Zúñiga, when he heard an urgent echo from inside: "Menchaca, come look!"

Pushing his way through, he overheard fragments of the tragedy: someone had used the distraction from a backfire to spill battery acid on both mudflaps, dissolving the faces. At first he stood in mute shock, as though the disfigurement had trespassed vandalism and had entered the realm of flesh. But the edgy crowd, pressing in on all sides, chafed the layers of his dulled senses until he reached a raw outrage. With a low voice which made his threat more menacing, he vowed revenge. When someone asked what that vengeance might be, he answered, "An eye for an eye."

"A real eye?"

"As real as One-Eyed Lara's only good one." He scanned their faces for the culprit's flinching betrayal. Then, blinking back his tears, he hurled the ultimate insult: "Whoever it was, he can screw his mother through the same place he came out of." Even the innocent stiffened as he turned more explicit. "Up her . . ."

"We get the picture," said don Heraclio. "But what's done is done."

"Right," said an anonymous wag. "No use crying over spilled acid."

Carlos glowered again at the crowd, but don Heraclio's whisper sent a shiver down his spine that paralyzed his bravado: "Be grateful it wasn't your face."

After the others had left, he added, "Besides, who in his right mind would paint a pin-up of Edelmiro's girls, knowing it would be paraded through every street in town?"

But he doubted the point sank in after Carlos answered, "Why couldn't he just smear the faces? I could have repainted them. I'm an artist, not a surgeon . . ."

But don Heraclio had other hearts to mend, and he hurried after Gilberto, who was returning home through back alleys with the slow, painful gait of a convalescent. Don Heraclio caught up with him, then caught his own breath. "I guess that Hutchinson out-son-of-a-bitched us."

"I guess so." Gilberto's gaze never left the ground, as though an inner fog made it difficult to see more than a few feet ahead.

"We should have known, though. Anytime it's us against the gringos, you know who gets the breaks."

He stopped in his tracks. "So let's stop being us and start being them."

Don Heraclio smiled, uncertain whether his son-in-law was serious. "And lose our pride?"

"Pride? What's that? Can you eat it?" He dug his heels in the dirt. "Can you at least grow crops on it? No, suegro, you can keep your pride. What we need is to become as low-down as them. Don Luis or doña Zoila can tell you that. Like the gringos say," and he tossed out the English he had started fracturing recently, "it's a doggy-dog world. You mount the other mutt from behind before he sticks it to you first."

The following week Lalo called Mr. Hutchinson from the pay phone outside Bernal's grocery store and emerged with the smug smile of success. "We're almost out of the woods. One of us has to appear in court, pay a few fines and settle up with the man."

At the family meeting, he volunteered as their go-between, arguing that he had been their bookkeeper and that only he could do business without anger. "Besides, my brother-in-law's going to the Illinois border this weekend. From there I can catch a bus to Terre Haute."

Gilberto and don Heraclio exchanged uneasy glances. They had heard of Tonio's mafioso dealings too often to dismiss them. Imelda also worried that Lalo might end up an unwitting accomplice. "Be careful. Tonio would hide stuff under his mother's skirts if . . ."

But Lalo laughed away their concern. "I've been around him long enough to know the score. If it'll make you feel any better, I'll have Father Coronado bless his Ford."

"I'd feel better if Fela did the blessing," said don Heraclio. "But

I guess if you're traveling with so much money, Tonio's the one to take along."

Gilberto agreed. "He looks like a mouse but fights like an upside-down cat."

A week later Lalo sent a telegram so long that don Heraclio feared it could only mean bad news. Carlos translated the first sentences and set the family at ease. "Hutchinson dropping other charges, stop. Settling out of court, stop."

"Lalo was right, suegro. We needed a level head doing the dealing. Me, I'd have ended up with murder charges as well."

"They'd hang you in Indiana," agreed don Heraclio, "then fry your corpse in Texas."

Carlos mumbled through the details then added, "Gilberto can keep his underwear, stop. Lost La Golondrina but driving back in new car, stop."

"Good Lord," said Imelda, "don't tell me he stole the grower's car."

Carlos too was baffled, but also more optimistic. "Maybe Hutchinson let him keep most of the money." He read the cryptic ending: "A big hug for Rosendo."

"Rosendo?!" they asked in unison.

When Rosendo dropped by asking about Lalo, Carlos read him the wire. "Why, that sly devil!" said Rosendo in that narcotic candor which assumed everyone else was either stoned or trying to get there. "No wonder he wanted those names in Illinois. When he returns, remind him to do unto those who did unto him."

In the vacuum that followed, the pieces slowly floated into place. "We can't say he didn't warn us, suegro. He said he'd been around Tonio long enough to know the score."

Carlos figured out every angle but one: "But where did the money to buy the stuff come from?"

Rosendo thought no one else was smiling because he alone had an answer. "Tonio, of course. Always use other people's . . ."

"Not Tonio," said Gilberto. "Us. Every penny we gave him."

Only Rosendo saw the bright side. "So? He got it back, and then some!"

Don Heraclio retrieved his hat from atop the ice box. He stepped outside without being followed because no one had the strength to console him. He sat on the porch steps and listened to Gilberto's histrionics, and wondered why the memory of his wife kept coming to him. Then he felt the answer in his eyes: her death had been the last time he had wept.

Chapter 29

The drizzle from the hurricane rains had stopped, but the humidity had taken over. Imelda returned to the front porch to check up on Armandito, who was still splashing in the street. She stared at the flooded lawn in a tired stupor while her words dragged out. "One-Eyed Lara was so sure the hurricane would hit here that he'd already composed a corrido."

"He can still record it," said don Heraclio. "Anyway, you only get a ballad after you're dead."

"Not always." She perked up for the first time that day. "I know—or rather we know—someone who got one in his lifetime." It was a tidbit she had meant to mention but had forgotten in the hurricane scare, and now she savored the suspense.

"Well, who the devil is it?"

"Lalo, who else? Actually the song's about Tonio, but Lalo's mentioned once. Nowadays they only sing about love, drugs and disasters."

Don Heraclio managed an indifferent tone. "Dealers are the only ones rich enough to call the tune."

"Mm-hmm." She hummed and waited for his curiosity to get the better of him.

"When did you hear it?" he finally asked.

"Last week. But I didn't want to upset you."

"Why would it upset me?"

She failed to catch his sarcasm. "You're right. Anyway, rarely he mostly deals in drugs anymore."

He answered with the same irony as before: "Now it's only human flesh."

"Exactly. He's even helping the community, smuggling wetbacks up North. At least he takes them far from the border."

"So what's the ballad say?" She tried to carry an off-key tune until he interrupted, "How about an accordion, too? Just give me the lyrics."

"Oh, it's the usual rags-to-riches stuff, with mafiosos called modern-day Robin Hoods. They used Lalo's alias, but everyone knows it's him."

"He's asking for it."

"The law can't touch him now. His mules do all the dirty work. The song's about the first time he and Tonio disguised themselves as farmworkers and ran dope up North in a beat-up car. The moral of the song . . ."

"The moral?!"

"The whatever . . . tells migrants to take their own crop upstate. It's called 'Los migrants del carro roto,' by that bilingual band. Our people eat it up."

He wondered whether she had brought up Lalo to make herself look good by comparison, until she added, "Funny how a person can be so nice and yet . . . Why, before the storm he offered Gilberto one of his apartments across town. Said we'd be safer there."

"Gilberto said no, of course."

"Of course." After a while she added, "I still think his in-laws led him down the wrong road."

"They showed him the way, but he took the first steps. And he can stop whenever he wants."

"I still say he never got over his fall from La Golondrina. Head-first, papá!" She warned Armandito of approaching traffic, then added, "That reminds me, I was talking to Carlos' ex-wife the other day. She saw his old truck across the border . . ."

"Which one?"

"Which truck?"

"Which ex-wife?"

"Dina, his first. She was partying across the border . . . you know how wild she got after the divorce. Anyway, she noticed this truck with her first name on the mudflaps. She was probably on the point of passing out . . ."

"Mexico makes trucks and parts by that name."

"So she wasn't that far gone, then. Anyway, there was La Golondrina, hauling blocks of ice! It had a paint job like an ambulance and enough lights for a bordello, but she swore it was the same truck. She even shed a tear or two, like in the movies, when some-one sees an old nag from his childhood."

"I wouldn't doubt it. Ramón sold her down the line to some Mexicans. Down there they squeeze every last fart from a truck, and then some. It'll probably outlast us."

Chapter 30

With Gilberto paying rent while struggling to recoup his losses, it was only a matter of time before don Heraclio convinced his son-in-law and his family to move in with him. "If not for my sake, then for the mice in the house. They're fed up with my face."

By then Esteban and his cousin David were in grade school. Every afternoon that they stopped by doña Lola's house, Esteban was lured by the candies his aunt Fela brought back from Mexico on her forages for herbs. After Miss McAndrews read them the story of Hansel and Gretel, David began spitting his aunt's candies out. "Pendejo," he told his more trusting cousin. "Aunt Fela's a witch, too. She'll fatten you up for dessert."

Esteban tapped the baby bottle that was always at David's side. "She won't have to worry about you." That was how doña Lola, blind from diabetes, told them apart—by feeling for David's bottle. His parents tried every trick to break his bottle habit, even taking Fela's advice of smearing chile picante on the nipple. But he overheard the conspiracy and the following morning, after his mother eagerly prepared his bottle, replaced the nipple on reaching school. When he returned that afternoon and asked for a refill, they decided to let him quit when he was good and ready.

His size had insulated him from schoolboy taunts, until one day a sixth-grader asked, "How's mama's milk?" David forced him to find out for himself. Afterwards the boy scrambled to his feet, spat wildly into the crowd, and threw up all over David. The insult had succeeded where everything else had failed: after that even the sight of milk repulsed him. However, he developed a substitute craving, guzzling several soft drinks at one sitting. His parents found the new addiction the lesser evil, and he started treating his poorer cousin Esteban to root beers at Bernal's store.

After doña Lola passed away, their after-school get-togethers in front of Bernal's grocery became a ritual. Occasionally doña Zoila's muchachos brought over adult magazines and asked them to translate the captions. Both boys tried to outdo each other in crudeness, but they were no match for the muchachos. Other times, from sheer boredom, Esteban would tell David, "There's that penny-pinching Bernal at the window again. Let's pretend to leave with the bottles." And the ancient don Luis, the animation on half of his face erased by a stroke, would holler out after them as though they had held him up.

That era came to an end when after numerous false starts Luisito Bernal inaugurated their supermarket. Opening night featured automatic glass doors, air conditioning and local conjunto bands in the parking lot. Father Coronado was on hand to bless their business, and everyone flocked to its carnival atmosphere, including the muchachos.

At first doña Zoila dismissed their patronizing the enemy as the fleeting curiosity of children. "The same thing happens whenever there's fresh meat at the whorehouse. They go crazy for a few days, then settle down."

But judging from her general store's monthly receipts, the muchachos were either defecting in droves or else on a mass hunger strike. Something had to be done, but with betrayals on all sides, she trusted only three boarders: two cousins in their teens and an older man, all illegals and so daring that after running errands in her pickup they would stop at El Camello Lounge, a watering hole for off-duty cops.

When Bernal's supermarket ended up vandalized by the trio, everyone assumed she had hired them as saboteurs. Why else had they had ransacked the aisles but left the cash registers intact? By the time the police arrived after midnight the fracas reached the end of the block. The older man, living up to his nickname, was drunk as a skunk, as were the other two. The older cousin pushed a shopping cart, weaving through aisles and picking cans at random while plowing into the few pyramids still standing. He had pried open several bottles of warm pop with his buck teeth to wash down a rainbow of powdered drinks on his tongue. The other boy was in the midst of a feeding frenzy, surrounded by cookies and sweet bread, and scraping the sugar coatings with incisors as impressive as his cousin's.

The neighbors had turned them in when the noise made it impossible for the early risers to get any sleep.

With that the sun began setting on doña Zoila's little empire. Soon afterwards several muchachos rented a house of their own, calling it la casa chica. Veterans like Samuel and Father Adán stayed on from force of habit, but with doña Zoila's political patrons either dead or retired, no one stood in the way of the threat of a mass deportation. There were even rumors that the Border Patrol was cruising the area.

Dona Zoila tried in vain to turn back the clock. She started amassing her son's laundry again and having his shirts hung out all at once, like the rows of colorful pennants around Bernal's new store.

One night the damp laundry was left on the line. For two down-and-out muchachos from Michoacán whose rent was three months in arrears and who planned to skip town after the full moon, the clothes were manna from heaven. Moving up their departure, they ran off with a small fortune in dress shirts. By the time the other muchachos left for work, the ex-boarders were in another county. Doña Zoila had her maid empty out every suitcase and chiffonier into a pile on the patio. She turned up nothing and nearly incited a riot among the muchachos who returned to find a stray mutt mauling their guayaberas.

Later a crew boss said he saw the pair in the back of an immigration car. "They were down on their luck again, and by then the shirts were filthy. But quality shows. They must have gone back to Mexico with some real stories. I told myself, 'Here I'm wearing patches on my ass while these two mariachis are picking tomatoes in monogrammed dress shirts.' I ask you, where's the justice in this world?"

Chapter 31

With three alleged killings to his name, Border Patrolman Eligio
Canchola squinted into the summer evening sun, rechecked the
casa's address and hobbled up the side stairs in full uniform before
anyone could sound the alarm. There was a tense standoff in the
hall when he interrupted the banter of several muchachos. Yet no
one bolted, and Eligio Canchola, whose trained eye and hunting
instinct told him he had stumbled across the largest nest of illegals
of his career, held back the way a crippled predator swallows his
pride before quicker prey. He banged hard on Samuel Ochoa's door
and immediately doubled over in pain, shooting a defiant glance at
the wide-eyed wetbacks in a vain attempt to outstare them. The
stabs along his back humbled the knocks that followed, until Samuel peeked out from a blocked opening the width of his face.

Canchola asked, "Are you Samuel, the healer?"

He neither nodded nor shook his head, but simply addressed
Canchola by Father Adán's nickname for him. "Are you the Blood-
hound?"

Canchola ignored the comment. "I've had this pain for months."
He mapped an area from his right shoulder to his hip. "Doctors
can't do a thing except knock me out with painkillers. In this job
that can cost you your life." Samuel heard out his complaint but
refused to open the door an inch more until Canchola added,
"Someone sent me to Fela la curandera. She told me where to find

you." He smiled through his grimace. "She didn't say you . . ."

Samuel gestured him into a room filled with the healing spirits of volcanic liniment and rubbing alcohol with camphor. Canchola sighed nostalgically, as if he had returned to a recondite corner of his childhood. He unbuckled his gun belt, less out of good faith than from the weight's sheer torture. The old man placed it atop a rickety chiffonier that was crammed with votive candles and pictures of saints. Canchola cautiously bounced his behind on the bed springs. "I haven't slept on one of these in ages." He glanced out the door. "This stag tenement's all illegal?"

"You're the only real man here." Samuel sprinkled liniment into the creases of his hands, then rubbed them as though warming himself by a fire.

"How old are you, señor?"

"A hundred."

"Really?"

"People think that's a milestone in life. You tell them anything less and they say, 'Well, here's hoping you hit a hundred.' "

Canchola sized him up. "I can't see you swimming the Rio Grande, much less working in the fields."

"I've worked here since before your father was a gleam in his father's eye."

"And never been deported?"

"These wrinkles are my passport." He grinned, and the wrinkles multiplied. "They get me through spot checks that trap the younger ones." He smeared salve on his fingertips. "Now pull up your shirt, lower your pants and lie face down. Don't worry, I'm too old for perversions."

Samuel left the door ajar so the rest could hear the patrolman's groans. Canchola smothered his cries under a pillow as a small gallery glued itself to the crack in order to enjoy more intimately his suffering. They wondered aloud whether someone who hunted his own kind looked any different. "He loses his shadow when he's after you," whispered one muchacho. "That's why he's so dangerous."

"I don't know about his shadow," said another, "but from this angle his ass looks as dark as ours."

Afterwards Canchola zipped up his pants with ease, strapped on his weapon and offered Samuel a handful of dollars. "Take it," he insisted. "I earn more in a day than you make each week."

"I don't take money for people's misery."

Canchola pretended to shield his eyes from a brilliance. "Christ on a crutch! You'll have your picture beside those saints the minute you're dead." He tucked the bills into an empty votive vase. "Then buy some candles for your miracle workers." He paced the room with the joy of a man cured of a congenital crippling. When he calmed down somewhat, Samuel dispensed a simple prescription: "Don't bathe for a week."

"What?!"

"The salve has to do its job."

"How about a sponge bath?"

"Not even a tongue bath. That's seven days, like in siete machos."

Canchola sniffed the ointment smeared on his back. " 'Seven he-goats' is right! I can't go like this around the Anglos at work. Anyway, I'm a new man already." As proof he drew his gun in one fluid motion.

"Then bathe. They'll bring you back more crooked than the Rio Grande." He turned a deaf ear to the protests and searched through Father Adán's chiffonier. "You need to relax," he said, "make your peace with the world," and handed him a shriveled stem with dried leaves.

Canchola first mistook it for a charm, then had a delayed startle. What the hell is this?!"

"Don't act innocent. You boys confiscate tons of the stuff."

"Don't press your luck, señor! I'm a federal officer."

"Why the fuss? I'll bet your grandmother took it for labor pains." He wedged it into the tooled gun belt.

Canchola stared at him but left the stem in the empty cartridge clasp. "Anything else?"

Samuel stepped back and gestured with his eyebrows at the gun. "If you could live without that dead weight for a few days . . ."

He tugged his belt a notch tighter. "You must be mad, old man! With every wetback and his brother dying to ambush me?" He cocked his hat and swaggered out the door with his spine erect.

Months later another patient arrived unannounced at the casa. The muchachos were playing poker in the patio when a mongrel pup with a fresh scrape among other battle scars limped up the casa stairs. Father Adán glanced up and said, "That crazy mutt lost another fight," but the rest, suspecting a trick to reveal their hands, ignored him. When the puppy dragged itself to the edge of the second story landing, he put aside his hand. "That little animal's going to jump."

El Bruto, married but still a regular at their poker games, peeked over his shoulder and remarked, "No dog's that dumb," when they heard a fragile crack, like a sack of eggs dropped on concrete, and a screeching yelp that put their hairs on end. Even neighbors from the end of the block rushed over to investigate.

The puppy was still writhing on the bricks, its forelegs mangled like flippers, and howling—pure, ignorant pain indistinguishable from man or beast. Several onlookers from across the street, a moment earlier secure in their Sunday repose, now stood dazed and vulnerable, aware of how suffering turned things so hideously alive.

El Bruto returned with an old revolver and drew a bead on the animal when Samuel stepped in between. He cradled the raw mass of nerves in his arms and took it to his room, where Father Adán began blowing marihuana smoke in its muzzle. By nightfall Samuel's eyes were as bloodshot as his roommate's, and his head swam with the indifference of a drowning man, but the puppy had fallen into a fitful sleep.

From ice cream sticks Samuel improvised slats and patiently bound the forelegs. A roller skate donated by a little girl became a scoot-about. Secured to the toy, the puppy learned to maneuver by oaring on the floor. The girl named it Superpup, after its leap from the second story, and clapped her hands on seeing it scuttling. "He looks like a turtle from outer space."

One afternoon she brought canned food which Samuel identified at once. He showed her his own provisions. "We eat this when we're too tired to cook."

She screwed up her face. "It's dog food!"

He imitated her gesture. "You mean it's made from dogs?"

"No. But it's for dogs, not people."

He jerked his face away as if from a blast of heat. That night he confessed his embarrassment to the others.

"Ridiculous," said the Armadillo. "Pets eat table scraps. That's why God put them on this earth. Right, Padre Adán?"

"Anything's possible. I once bought a package at Bernal's that looked like a banquet on the carton. But inside it was frozen solid! Maybe you're supposed to eat it like a snowcone, but I lost my appetite."

"Ever since I saw a grower feed his dog that crap, I've laid off it," said Reynaldo.

"So?" asked the Armadillo, who had acquired a taste for the stuff. "If he fed him rice and beans would you stop eating that too?"

El Bruto argued that in all his years as a slaughterhouse stunner in Mexico he had never seen good meat set aside for dogs; in fact, any canine who came sniffing around ended up on the butcher's block. "It's just a label," he said, "like bears on molasses bottles."

Samuel emptied a can on the puppy's dish. "Why would she lie?"

"Maybe lying's not the word," said the Armadillo. "More like a runaway imagination. I mean, 'A turtle from Mars?!' "

"There's your proof, though. He's like a gringo wolfing down hot dogs."

"What a waste," said the Armadillo. "Next you'll be saying those cans with kittens are cat food. Where will it end? Tacos for coyotes?"

"What I can't get over," said Reynaldo, "is how tame he's become. Look, I can even pet him while he's eating. That fall must have knocked some sense into him."

Samuel finally admitted, "I've talked to him."

The Armadillo stared at him. " 'Talked to him?!' How can you talk to animals?"

"Just like I'm talking to you. Actually I was only trying to help him sleep. Maybe my advice took."

"Now I've heard everything! This world is going to the dogs."

Father Adán chuckled. "I heard you and thought you were talking in your sleep." He picked up the pup by the scruff to confirm the change. "You have a way with animals, Samuel, like Saint Francis. Damn it, quit toiling in the fields like some beast of burden and put that talent to use." His eyes glowed. "Hell, I'll be your partner. I medicate them, you put them on the couch."

Reynaldo agreed. "There are plenty of rich gringos with crazy pets. Why, that grower I told you about . . ."

Samuel stood and waved the thought away. "The only thing I meant to straighten out was its legs. After Canchola I gave up trying to reform animals."

Chapter 32

Fela la curandera already had an idea of her country's conflict in Viet Nam, but the events of that remote battlefield first touched her by way of an urgent and unusual request. One April afternoon doña María Valenzuela asked her for a spell to keep her son from passing his Army medical exam. Only doña María's desperation kept Fela from smiling. "You want me to make him sick?"

"Anything to keep him home."

"Lots of people have asked me to hex their enemies. This is the first time I've been asked to curse a loved one."

María pressed her hand as though she were her last hope. "I don't see any difference."

"Neither do I," said Fela, already intuiting that the well-intended request might turn out as complicated as the war itself. "That's why I'll tell you what I've told them. No." But the maternal pleas awoke an anguish she thought had long since atrophied. "I guess there's no harm in trying," she said against her better judgment.

Three weeks later a somewhat disappointed but infinitely relieved Chato Valenzuela was back from San Antonio after failing his physical. Whenever he tried to explain the snarled but benign symptoms responsible for his deferment, he ended up tracing them to a different organ. By the time he recovered his health, he felt comfortable enough with his 4-F stigma that the only person he told about his recuperation was his mother. She in turn told her comadre, which amounted to a barrio press release.

When word of her alleged miracle got back to Fela, she shrugged it off, as well as any accusations of abetting the enemy. "As far as I'm concerned, I agree with Heraclio. Our real enemy's across the tracks, not across the ocean. Anyway, what can the government do? Send me to that Viet Nam?"

Yet several mothers with sons already overseas insisted that if their boys were facing death, so should everyone else's. That selfish logic lasted until doña Panchita, whose own son had recently received a military burial, publicly shamed their patriotism. "If by some sorcery I could spare a single mother half of what I've gone through," she said, "I'd sell my soul this instant."

Finally, a mother who had refused to seek Fela's help now came to her for guidance. "My boy was inducted last week," she told Fela. "His father warned me not to come to you. Now I have these nightmares . . ."

Fela vowed then and there to stop playing God. "I stepped into my own no-win war," she said. "Now I have to step out."

But it took a visit by Luisito Bernal to show her how the best of intentions might backfire. She already knew that Luisito's son had exhausted every draft dodge short of leaving the country, that his college deferment had been revoked after trying to bribe a professor, and that his family had lost a petition with the local draft board. Now, Luis Bernal II was an infantryman running the same dangers as the rest.

"It's just not fair," said Luisito, "with so much waiting for him here. I want you to bring him back. I heard you can do such things."

She was about to say she had closed shop when he added, "And I'll pay you well to see Nava's boy take his place."

She thought back to the time Luisito had set in motion the falling dominoes that had toppled her own happiness. "Amazing how little we've changed," she finally said. "I'm still as heartless as in my youth, and you're still the same son-of-a-bitch." Then she offered a ruthless but sure-fire solution. "You want your son back? Fine. I can put a bullet through his heart this very instant, if you'd like."

He held back his rage for the same reason his own father had cowered before her many years ago: she would have made good on her threat.

The following month her nephews David and Esteban graduated from high school in a ceremony steeped in patriotism and the separation of future soldiers from scholars. David's future was already secure: his father had promised tuition and a new car, so he did not have to worry about loans and part-time jobs like Esteban. But the thought of spending four more years in school paled alongside the glory of fighting for his country. His middle-class friends, though, made no bones about their motives for going to college: to avoid the draft.

At the graduation dance David mingled with the well-heeled boys who already bragging about their future alma maters and were making plans for a holiday reunion. He noticed Esteban standing in another crowd and glancing his way, so he crossed the floor before his own friends could notice.

The conversation was oddly similar to the one before, but when Esteban's friends spoke of leaving home, they were not talking about going to college.

"Marines, eh? Well, I'll keep your girl's parts oiled till you return."

"Hah! With your own ass in the Army?"

A third boy who was already tipsy said, "I got me a full scholarship to Saigon City College. Pays room and board."

"Bullets, too," said Esteban.

"Screw you, Menchaca. I'm saving you a seat on the plane, just in case."

David smiled uncomfortably with the rest, knowing that Esteban's loan was still in limbo. After a long silence he added, "Jeff Atlas was saying a minute ago that some of us fight with our pens, others with bayonets."

"Ha!" said the future Marine. "Easy for that son-of-a-doctor to say." He grabbed his crotch. "Here's his bayonet! One thing for sure, you'll never see one hair of his ass where we're headed." He turned and playfully punched both cousins. "Yours either, not if your tía Fela can help it."

Esteban took the teasing in stride. "Maybe I can sell my soul for a scholarship."

David, though, was utterly in the dark. "What's she have to do with this?"

The drunken kid hugged him, "Come on, Cavazos. Don't act innocent."

Early next morning David marched straight to the local Army recruiter, armed with a story as incredible as it was incoherent. "Let's make sure I follow you," said the red-neck sergeant. "You're saying she gave this guy a drug to flunk his medical exam?"

"No, not a drug! The Army would have found out in a minute."

The sergeant, who at first thought he had reasoned his way out of a labyrinth, now found himself back at step one. "So if she didn't drug him . . ."

"She's a sorceress."

"You're saying she put a spell on him?"

"Long enough to fail the physical. I know it sounds . . ."

"Listen . . ." interrupted the recruiter, then floundered for a response. "I've worked with your people for years. I know their superstitions. But you expect me to believe this Mexican mumbo jumbo?"

Something told David then and there that as much as he wanted to live alongside this man and share the same patch of geography, at that instant they were planets apart. He should have walked away while they were still strangers. Instead he stayed rooted to the spot, waiting for a revelation to open the other's eyes. But the only sound that filled the room was the scraping of the sergeant's chair. "Well, now, 'less you're interested in signing up . . ." The accent was at once exotic and nostalgic, and he found himself in his first day of grammar school, blushing at the sound of sweet Miss McAndrew's drawl: "So what should we call you, dear?" she was asking, all creamy skin and the faint smell of strawberries. "DAY-vid, or Dah-VEED?"

He was still under the influence of that heavenly encounter when he asked starry-eyed, "So how's a red-blooded American boy enlist in this war?"

Chapter 33

David's first letters from Nam were stamped with one obsession: staying out of harm's way. Even after he resigned himself to the danger, he wrote to his uncle Tonio that he would rather be dodging bullets from narcotics officers than from the v.c. "If I'm going to get shot at," he wrote, "at least let me get some money out of it."

Later he came to love the things for which he suffered, and his self-pitying prose gave way to a self-righteous patriotism. Told that his grandfather Heraclio had publicly denounced "the gringo war," he wrote back, "Tell him to go all the way—wear black pajamas, find an AK-47 and come grease us on the side of the gooks."

In the last weeks of his tour, when every short-timer kept his moves to a minimum, his letters took on a terse, telegraphic style. There were no more tears, no gung-ho harangues, only a naked witnessing. What the pages lacked in detail they made up for with a bare-bones realism, so that on July of that year he wrote home, "Today we found a corpse on the perimeter wire," and left the observation at that, knowing that no degree of artifice could resurrect the dead.

He returned home not so much a changed man as a distilled one, as if his spirit had filtered through the charcoal countryside and out the other end of the world, leaving him much more of the same. His aunt Fela assessed him in a single glance. "Uy, this one came back even more enchilado." Later she told his mother, "You prayed for him to come back in one piece but forgot about his soul."

Yet he adapted well to civilian life. His sexual appetites were stronger, but with an aggressive edge, and his highest compliment to women was, "For her I'd go one round with every guy in Viet Nam."

Still, it took him two weeks to finally approach Angelita, the girlfriend who had suddenly stopped writing just weeks before his return. He found her more reticent than ever, and every question got the same response: Was it something he had written? No. Something she had heard? No. At first, compared to civilian conversation, her direct answers were a welcome change. But after racking his brains, already riddled by combat, he tired of the game. He took her in the litany of those no's mistook her protests for the weakness of willing flesh, convinced that her denials were face-saving formalities. He could not see beyond his own macho myopia, could never put her carnal wants on a par with his. And Angelita, unable to tell him outright, finally gave in, explaining in body language—the only one he understood—what she had never dared write.

Three mornings later he shuffled to the bathroom and felt his penis turn into a flame thrower. His eyes seared shut, his tears burned like tequila on an open wound, and in the agonizing seconds it took to spew his firewater, he was back spraying jungles, but now he was on the receiving end, too.

One tour in Nam! he cursed in silence. Four long seasons in that very small hell, gassing out v.c. from jungle tunnels one day, checking love tunnels for v.d. the next. All for what? To come home to the clap from the woman who had been his reason for staying safe and sane.

"There's a lot of this going around," Dr. Peña consoled him that afternoon. He sterilized a thin strand over an open flame and nonchalantly fished for a specimen from his patient's urethra. "I just hope hope you boys don't bring back a strain that eats the barrio for breakfast."

"I got it here," said David, in a voice thickened as much from insult as from injury.

"You don't say," said the doctor, for once showing more than professional interest. "Well, then, our home-grown variety shouldn't be too hard to stop."

Doctor Peña, like his patient, had underestimated both the appetite of sexually active women and their capacity for incubating virulent strains. David had contracted a dose so resistant that after several office visits the irritation still flared up occasionally. "If I pump any more antibiotics into your butt," warned Dr. Peña, "you'll start molding." His years in the profession had changed him from a make-believe miracle worker into an amused realist. "It's something you'll have to live with. A war wound from the sexual revolution. You won't appreciate the itch till you can't get it up, though."

But when his frequent office visits started tongues to wagging, David decided that the only face-saving alternative was to re-enlist. His announcement triggered the traditional nervous crisis in his mother, who cried that he might as well put her in the front lines. "You're too old to pull a tour," he said. "Besides, they don't take women grunts."

When she failed to talk him out of it, his grandfather tried the opposite tack. "Why not join the Foreign Legion?" said don Heraclio. "I hear there's a special platoon for men with the clap."

"That's a low blow, grandpa. Let's not get personal."

"You're the one who's taking it personal. Look, son, I'm against this war, but I respected your decision."

"I only want to fight for my country's honor . . ."

"You mean your prick's honor. It's the injured party in this mess. But why take it out on innocent people?"

Their talk made him think twice, long enough for his wounded pride to heal and to seek his aunt Fela's help. From his vague gestures and English she suggested he see a plumber instead. If she understood more, she was not saying. Finally she added in Spanish, "Come on now, talk to me in that same tongue you used to cuss me out."

He stammered through his story in Spanish as if his throat were a rusty pipe coughing up stagnant water. Fela spared him nothing, then put some herbs to boil. "If it works, I'll name the cure in your honor." She added after he downed the bitter brew, "That's for the one you owed me."

He had the chilling certainty that she knew of his attempt to turn her in years ago, and he would have confessed had not the aftertaste left him speechless. Finally she explained: "For the time you out-foxed me with the chile pepper on your bottle."

That night, after a sudden urge to urinate, he locked the bath-room door and passed a stream of liquid lava worse than the origi-nal. He hissed his first spontaneous Spanish since his combat prayers: "¡Pinche vieja bruja!" Then he stumbled backed to bed and fell into a profound, healing sleep.

The following day he arranged to run into his uncle Tonio. The word was out that Tonio planned to pass along part of his drug operations to his own son. "My Mario's willing to start from the bottom up," he said, putting his arm around David, "and he needs a partner. It's time for new blood, but the transfusion has to come from the family." He added in that slightly strangled voice in vogue with local padrinos or godfathers, "It's a job, like any other. We hire workers, worry about deadlines and the competition. About the only thing we don't do is advertise on the tube." Except for his affected voice, he resembled more Bernal's fresh-produce manager than a drug-pushing padrino.

Before his nephew had left, Tonio made his pitch, and his voice took an added strain, like an overworked engine in low gear. "When you wrote saying you wanted to make money, you reminded me of your dad. He started out the same way."

David promised to think it over, and Tonio nodded with a needles-and-pins uncertainty, not knowing that his nephew had al-ready made his decision. After keeping his uncle on tenterhooks, David relayed his acceptance through his cousin Mario. That done, he went straight to Angelita and proposed. She not only accepted but agreed to see both his doctor and aunt.

That weekend Fela ran into Dr. Peña at the supermarket and said, "I hope to see you at my nephew's wedding. After all, you helped make it possible."

For all of his candor in the privacy of the clinic, his face flushed as they stood in the middle of a crowded aisle. "I'm not sure I catch your meaning."

Fela, unfettered by licenses or lawsuit threats, asked, "Aren't you his penicillin godfather?''

 But the most cynical assessment came from the groom himself, after his best man asked in drunken candor why he was marrying the same woman who gave him a dose to end all doses. David thought it over, then gave a motive as pragmatic as his decision to work for his uncle: "This way I know exactly who I'm dealing with."

Chapter 34

"Papá's old friend, El Bruto, was naturalized last week," Imelda told her husband over breakfast. "He's a U.S. citizen now, eligible for old age assistance. That's the third one this month."

Gilberto scooped up a tortilla from the griddle the moment it puffed up. "I've told you. Almost everyone past sixty in this barrio's made his peace. Your father's the only rebel left."

"Forget the rebel part. We sure could use that monthly government check. Prices these days are up in the clouds." She hushed on hearing don Heraclio in the hall telling his grandson a joke. Armandito entered the kitchen laughing, but his mother evaporated his humor with a stern look.

The old man followed, his thin legs swimming in the wool trousers that knew all seasons. What his erratic hearing sometimes missed, the soft, brown eyes rarely overlooked, and taking his place at the table he sensed a conspiracy in Imelda's smile. He turned more guarded than usual and began grooming his mustache with his fingertips. He had honed the white fringe to a minimal essence that seemed to have unhinged from under his nose and now hung above his upper lip. The hair along his temples had gone past gray, to the amber of aged tequila.

Imelda tried to soothe his suspicions with a forced cheerfulness. "And what'll it be this morning, papá?"

"You mean I have a choice? Like a condemned man?"

She overlooked the sarcasm. "Of course."

"In that case I'll have armadillo sausage with bull's testicles."

Gilberto gestured her to humor him. "What a pity, papá. Armadillo's out of season at Bernal's, and there's a shortage of bull's . . . uh . . . eggs. They're just not laying this year. How about huevos rancheros?"

"I hate huevos rancheros."

"But you have them every morning."

"There you have it, then. I'm fed up."

She watched him stir the steam from his coffee while he read a Mexican newspaper. She repeated the news to Gilberto: "El Bruto passed his citizenship test." She tried for spontaneity, but it was too early for a convincing performance.

"Hell, if he could do it, my father-in-law here should pass like a chili seed through an intestine." But either don Heraclio had lapsed into one of his deaf spells or was playing possum, so this time Gilberto told Imelda the news. Finally don Heraclio glanced up from his paper.

"What's this business of trading old gossip back and forth?"

"I was telling Imelda that your friend . . ."

"Yes, yes." He dismissed the news as ancient history. "They shot Kennedy."

At that moment Marina came in and tore whatever net her parents were trying to snare the old man in. "Not another one! Esteban, turn on the news!"

Esteban rushed into the crowded kitchen. "What's wrong?"

"Your parents." Don Heraclio showed him the newspaper. "The people are up in arms in Guerrero, and here your folks are honoring . . ."

"What 'people', suegro? What 'up in arms?' "

"Here, read! Open your eyes a bit."

"Working men don't have time for political crossword puzzles."

"But they do have time to sit and watch soap operas or gossip about an old-timer turning americano."

Imelda answered without thinking, "At least that old-timer's bringing in some money with his old age assistance." She immediately wanted to bite her tongue.

Don Heraclio carefully folded his paper. "No need to throw

stones. I'm sharpening my field hoe first thing tomorrow morning."

"Heavens, no, papá! Why, as soon as the carrot season starts I'll join Gilberto at the packing shed." She pressed her plump side with a grimace. "I'd sooner rupture my inflamed gall bladder than have you suffer a nosebleed in the sun."

Gilberto hid his admiration. Actually she had planned to join him next week but had postponed her decision, fearing it might ease their pressure on the citizenship question. This time Gilberto sided with her, but his objection was less sentimental: "All you do is get in the way of other workers." He reminded the old man of his last attempt as a field hand three years ago. Besides chopping more plants than weeds, he had tried to organize a strike for higher wages.

"I would have pulled it off, too," said don Heraclio, "but the muchachos without papers couldn't afford trouble."

"Naturally!" said Gilberto. "The grower was the mayor's brother! Is nothing sacred, señor? Don't you have an ounce of respect?

"Respect for my gray hairs is what I should have gotten from that crew boss. Instead he almost left me stranded."

Gilberto anchored his argument to mundane concerns. "See? There's no need to suffer heat or humiliations. Not at your age, not with a monthly check waiting for the picking."

"Now you're saying it's for my own good . . ."

"For the good of the family!" Gilberto said crossly. "My miserable wages barely keep our noses above water."

"I had no problem raising a family on a tenth of your salary."

"Stop living in the nineteenth century. Now that wouldn't even cover burial insurance." He lowered his voice before his children. "These days even beans cost you a nut."

Don Heraclio raised his. "I'd rather have a huevo hanging than end up castrated."

"Nobody's out to castrate you, señor. But face the facts. You've lived here over forty years. Your children and grandchildren were born here. Your wife was born and buried here. You're practically an americano already."

Don Heraclio buried himself behind his newspaper once more.

They thought he had conceded the argument when he added softly, "In some ways leaving Mexico was the best move I ever made. In others it was my biggest mistake. Now I'm stuck in a swamp, unable to turn back or move ahead."

Esteban censored a flippant remark on the tip of his tongue. Even Imelda, calloused by their daily skirmishes, had trouble swallowing her morsel of food. Don Heraclio stood, sopped up a coffee ring with his newspaper and said hoarsely, "If anyone needs me, I'll be at Bernal's."

A small, elderly flock had queued by the bus bench in front of Bernal's supermarket. Most were waiting for the shuttle to the free breakfast program at the Christian War Veterans Center. Others, like don Heraclio's neighbor, don Clemente, came to chat and hear Heraclio harangue the rest for accepting alms. Don Clemente's relatives had placed him in five different rest homes, and each time he had slipped back to the barrio in his bedroom slippers. "Like an old cat," he said. "If I don't come back one day, just go scrape me off the highway." His excuse for returning was the same one he gave for refusing to eat at the free meals program: the gringo diet gave him diarrhea.

Doña Gertrudis, a regular at the Veterans Center, caught sight of don Heraclio and passed the word. "Here comes that old Quixote. Too bad the bus is late."

Don Clemente offered him a cigarette, but he shook his head and pointed to his friend's khaki shirt, peppered with pinholes from live ashes. He scanned the faces around him. "Someone's missing."

"Josefina," said doña Nestora, then calmed their fears. "Sprained her leg shooing a dog from her garden." Doña Nestora was compact and intense, and a facial tic added to her energetic image. The tremors mimicked rapid head shakes, and people speaking to her had the uneasy impression she was not believing one word. Don Heraclio often wondered whether it persisted in her sleep, since she insisted she would stay active until her dying day. "The day I stop shaking, don't bother winding me up again."

He would have liked her except for one fault: her living room had turned into a small museum of Kennedy memorabilia. Between icons of obscure saints that even Father Coronado failed to recognize and religious calendars going back decades, she had crammed Kennedy plates and portrait plaques that switched faces at different angles. "She's not content with church fairy tales," he once said. "Now she worships millionaires."

The dislike was mutual. Whenever he said, "They shot Kennedy," she winced and crossed herself.

The group carried on several conversations at once until an ex-smuggler from the tequilero days caught their attention. "I'm thinking of turning gringo before the government changes its mind."

Someone chuckled. "Just don't give them your old alias."

"They're almost giving away the test answers to old mexicanos like us," said someone else.

Don Clemente frowned. "I heard you have to spit on the Mexican flag."

"I myself did no such thing!" said doña Nestora.

The argument splintered into several chatterings. From somewhere in the crowd, someone seeking a little excitement asked, "Heraclio, when are you turning yankee?"

Don Heraclio rested a hand over his groin. "On the day this gets stiff and swollen"—he continued down one leg—"from rigor mortis."

Señorita Gertrudis, the barrio's vintage virgin, looked away in case the other old men had ideas. Someone else said, "Quit being such a diehard, Heraclio. With a pension you could guzzle a few brews now and then."

He looked at them as if they were whores on promenade. "You're like those Anglo mummies in make-up and girdles . . ."

"It's not just women," said doña Nestora.

"Men too," he agreed. "One foot in the grave and they still pester bar maids for polkas. Remember Edelmiro Zúñiga? He barely broke in his new name—Eddy—when his warranty expired. A month after becoming a señor citizen. Didn't even cash his first check."

"All the more reason to enjoy life a little."

"That measly allowance just brings out the worst in you. Enough for your vices and maybe an aspirin afterwards."

"Maybe that's true for some," said the widow Clotilde. "But a lot of us live hand to mouth. That check is our only salvation. We don't have a family to care for us like you do."

Don Demetrio Chávez, the oldest, voiced their resentment. "You criticize everything, my friend. The americanos are only trying to help."

"Help screw us, you mean. Where were the decent wages when we were their farmworkers and maids? You, Clotilde, slaving for that politician's family for fifteen years. Did they lift a finger after you got t.b. and couldn't iron their shirts?"

She lowered her voice, but the memory had not lost its bitterness. "They almost threw me out in the street, as if I had the plague."

He nodded as if he had heard similar stories. "And now they throw us peanuts and expect us to kiss their hands."

"So what's your solution?" asked don Demetrio.

"It's too late for solutions. But we can take a stand, toss back their slop, like we organized our strikes in Mexico." For a moment the hoarse nostalgia in his voice made him imagine he was rousing the rabble. "We showed them in Nuevo León! Shut down their company stores . . ."

"Stop being an anachronist," don Demetrio said wearily.

"Anarchists? Never! We were organizers!"

"A-na-chro-nist, Heraclio. In your fantasies Jacinto Treviño still terrorizes Texas Rangers. Those times are dead."

"Not until we are."

Don Demetrio snorted and lifted his friend's arm. "And how much longer for that? Look at your own carcass."

"Then let's die with our dignity, as Mexicans."

"Mexico never gave me anything except plenty of reasons to leave."

A bowlegged woman bent by the years added, "Nowadays all you hear in this barrio is that rock-and-roll noise. It's even worse in Mexico."

"Face it, Heraclio, the whole world is turning gringo."

He had no time to reply; someone shouted, "The bus!," and the more nimble ones jammed in line first.

He waited until they started inching slowly in single file, then said, "There goes the hyena pack." From within the silent crowd an empty stomach growled its agreement. "Hear that, Clemente? That tit barely keeps them alive."

After the driver shut the door someone answered back: "I hope the Devil catches you confessed, Heraclio! You might be the first planted this season!"

He threw them a farewell taunt over the diesel's roar. "You're going to get freckles from all those hamburgers!"

Chapter 35

What had started out as a warm day was now being roiled by the beginnings of a freak norther, and high school students out for the afternoon were enjoying a respite from the heat. Marina was walking home with her friends when a patrol car cruised by. She heckled with the rest, then someone passed the word that her grandfather had been seen in the back seat. At first she dismissed it as the crude humor on the level of grandmothers being busted in cantina row for prostitution. But the witnesses were so insistent that she hastened her steps along with the others. "I know it's not 'buelito," she kept saying. "I just want to see his look-alike."

After five hours at the packing shed Imelda was resting at home when the commotion made her glance outside: a small crowd surrounded a patrol car parked out front. There had been no sirens nor flashing lights to announce its arrival, but from the spectators one would have thought otherwise. When a policeman escorted her father to the door, the rowdier youngsters gave the old man an ovation.

Her first thought was that he had suffered a stroke. But seeing him walk on his own, as alert as ever, she decided not to face the crowd. Soon the officer was explaining the string of incidents:

A Zapata poster on a community center window had caught the old man's attention. Inside, several workers and volunteers had greeted him with "¡Viva la revolución!" and assorted slogans of solidarity.

Beyond himself with excitement, he quickly left behind their half-baked rhetoric and concocted a series of strategies to rattle the barrio out of its apathy. From his experiences as an organizer he divulged the ingredients for a Molotov cocktail. "Personally I'd add detergent to the recipe," he told his flabbergasted audience, "so that the fire sticks to the walls." For starters he suggested the Veterans Center. "Just an outside scorching during one of their meetings, to loosen their bowels a bit. Most of those men saw more action in bars than at the front." At that point someone had called the police.

"Some thought he was on drugs," said the officer. "Others . . ." He tapped his temple, then sternly shook his head as if reproaching a mischievous child.

"He's on medication," Imelda lied.

Don Heraclio stared out the screen door the entire time.

When the officer left, Imelda's meek facade exploded. "How humiliating, papá! We should have sold tickets to the neighbors."

He waved out the window, and some boys cheered. "What's so humiliating? I wasn't out begging."

"Putting up with you like some common delinquent. I swear, you'll end up in court one day."

"Listen, Imeldita, I'm not Armandito afraid of the boogieman." He indicated his immunity in the mirror. "At my age who'll throw me in jail?"

That evening she related every detail to Gilberto, and then some. Rather than correct her exaggerations, don Heraclio expanded them. "Don't forget the tear gas," he said. "And the puppy I took hostage."

She retired early with a pain in her side. At two in the morning don Heraclio got up to urinate and found his son-in-law alone in the kitchen. His first impression was that he had never suspected Gilberto was an insomniac. "It's her gall bladder," said Gilberto. "Happens when she's upset."

"Call Dr. Peña." His voice sounded ragged and uncertain, as though his conscience had torn through.

"We already know the prescription," Gilberto snapped, his anger sharpened by the insomnia. "The scalpel, sooner or later." He raked back a stray lock, and for the first time don Heraclio noticed his son-in-law's eroded hairline, already quite gray. He felt at that moment a bond more intimate than any kinship.

"So? Does she lack the nerve?"

Gilberto faltered, incredulous that the old man was so removed from their household affairs. "What's lacking is money, señor."

"But you're holding down a job."

"And then what the Devil do we eat?! Unless they take out half her stomach and intestine while they're in there. At least we'd have menudo and tripas for a few days."

Don Heraclio ambled oddly around the room, his world turned upside down. He gently brushed his wife's faded needle point to verify its reality. But returning to the despondent man sitting in his boxer shorts and with a day's growth of stubble, he seemed to have stumbled into that alien realm Armandito witnessed on waking fresh from a nightmare and surprising the vampires and werewolves that roamed the house while everyone slept. This was the same place, only here his son-in-law stood guard against another beast at the door.

He left for the sanctum of his room but was up again before dawn, without a moment's sleep but with an anguished decision. Gilberto was still up, but his eyeballs, hardboiled from a night of worry, no longer registered recognition. Don Heraclio gulped down a mouthful of yesterday's cold coffee to brace his nerves. "I'm turning yankee," he said, and then his voice broke. "You two do whatever has to be done."

Gilberto surfaced from his stupor long enough to decipher the hieroglyphs streaming from the old man's mouth. He congratulated his father-in-law for coming to his senses, then drifted off into an incoherent litany on the cost of eggs, Armandito's broken crayons and his suspicion that Marina was no longer a señorita. Don Heraclio retreated to his room, wondering whether Gilberto would remember in the morning.

He assumed the matter had been forgotten when one day he found a review booklet for the citizenship exam on his pillow, along with a note from Imelda: "Homework for papá."

Again nothing more was said until one Sunday morning when Imelda cleared the kitchen table of Armandito's clay figures. She kneaded the little men into a single mass, set aside the lump of dough, then rolled the citizenship booklet into a makeshift megaphone. "Papá! Pop quiz!"

Don Heraclio fidgeted as if needing a tortilla to feel complete at the table. Imelda riffled the booklet. "Ah, let's start at the beginning: who discovered America?"

Armandito's hand jerked up, but Imelda raised a finger to her lips. "I knew it too," don Heraclio told his grandson, "when I was your age."

He rumaged through the attic of his memory, then answered, "Culón"—big-assed.

Armandito shrieked, but she hushed him with a special stare and turned her attention to the old man. "Colón, papá. Columbus in English."

Marina and two girlfriends came in from the backyard. "You should have known that one, grandad. You once told me Mexicans call it El día de la raza."

"I forgot. After all, I'm old enough to be his compadre."

Imelda eyed him to see if he were faking his lapses. "Here's another easy one. When was independence declared?"

"In Mexico?"

Imelda reached the end of her short fuse. "Quit clowning around, papá!" She mangled the booklet in frustration, then pressed her side with a grimace. "Why, you haven't glanced at a single page." She had hoped to shame him into submission but only pushed him into a mute stubbornness.

He tested his shoelaces without a word then retrieved his hat from atop the refrigerator. From the living room he murmured his usual, "I'll be at Bernal's," then remembered it was Sunday. He stared out the screen door and wondered if it was already dog days. The mere thought parched his throat, and he turned back for a drink of water, but a pair of adolescent laughs blocked the way. Suddenly it occurred to him to use the backyard faucet, although he had not done so in years.

Outside, a chorus of cicadas pressed their shrill siege on the barrio. The humid air grew hotter with insect friction until it

173

seemed to simmer in a stew of noise. Graciela's garden was long since overgrown with the weeds Armandito gathered for don Clemente's rabbit warren. Side-stepping a porridge of rotted mulberries, he touched off a mad buzzing of flies. For one frantic instant they swarmed around him, then in the startle of an eyeblink the cloud vanished without a stain.

The faucet spigot was lower than he remembered, and the tap coughed and gasped before spitting out a rust-colored trickle. He stooped for a drink, cupping his hands while the water leaked along his wrinkles. In the end he was forced to kneel among the weeds and suckle at the warm stream. Afterwards he felt too bloated to walk, so he numbed the colic with a fist to his stomach and returned to review for the test.

Although he was always the first one up and about, the morning of the exam he stayed in his room until sensing that his grandchildren had left for school. He had been wearing the heavy pepper-pattern suit since sunrise, and his cautious steps as he entered the kitchen gave his frame an added stiffness. His timing, though, was premature.

Marina, still having breakfast, gave a wolf whistle. "Who's the hunk?"

"Why, it's Beau 'Buelito."

Imelda, who had kept the event as guarded as possible, only added to the commotion. "Don't make him nervous! It's his day in court."

In a last-minute inspection Gilberto smoothed the old man's collar, bunched around his turkey throat. "Ignore them, suegro. After the swearing-in you'll never have to wear another suit."

Don Heraclio corrected him matter-of-factly: "You're forgetting the day the undertaker powders my nose."

"Then don't shrivel too much between now and then. No sense spending good money on a smaller suit."

Imelda glanced at the clock. "The courthouse is a good half-hour's drive. We should skip breakfast and get a head start, papá."

"What the hell is this . . . fasting for my first communion? At least let me have my last breakfast of huevos rancheros."

"Your last breakfast, 'buelito? Are you facing a firing squad?"

"No, I'm not moving to the other barrio yet. But once I'm a yankee I'll only get toast in the morning."

At the last moment Esteban had to loosen the old man's necktie after he broke out in a rash. "Why, 'buelo, you're changing color. Turning redneck already?"

They were barely out on the street when Imelda unveiled her remodeling plans. "I can see it already. First on our block with a bay window. And I can get it on monthly installments . . ."

"Hold on, honey. This car's a total moving violation. The tires are slicker than an Apache's ass. After all, safety first. Right, sue-gro?"

From the back seat came a confused question: "And Imelda's operation?"

Gilberto gave a knowing laugh. "Cancel that surgery, suegro. Nothing cures her quicker than money."

Betrayed, he edged toward the door for support. He considered jumping out at the next red light, but they were already on the freeway. Besides, he had given his word to go through with the test. He remembered the times Gilberto and Imelda had dressed Armandito with the promise of going shopping for toys. At a critical turn in the road the boy would realize they were taking him to the doctor, but by then it was too late.

His fatigued, solitary outline in the window brought back a rhyme popular with the barrio children: "Marta García was left all alone, wearing a bridal maternity gown."

He had always thought its sad humor a pacifier for those too innocent or too wise to believe in God, and thus more real than prayers. The refrain looped in his thoughts until he murmured it aloud: "Dejaron a Marta García panzona, vestida de velo y co-rona."

"What's with Marta García, papá?"

He retreated to his reflection. "Nothing."

She edged toward Gilberto. "She already had the baby."

"Who?"

"Marta, poor thing. The father was Mexican, and all of a sudden he got the urge to go back."

Gilberto shrugged. "So? There's always el huero feo."

"Who?"

"Welfare."

She took out the review booklet, already dog-eared and stained with table scraps, and twisted toward her father, who waved her away.

"I'm up to my mustache with your riddles."

"Let him be," whispered Gilberto. "He knows the book better than Father Coronado knows the Bible."

After a long silence, almost as an afterthought, don Heraclio added, "Leonel Madres was denied citizenship."

"No wonder," said Gilberto. "If serving time were a career, he'd have a gold watch by now. They put him in an old folks' home for the hardcore and he organized a Mexican Mafia."

"I wonder if the boys down at the courthouse know about my own past."

Gilberto's eyes darted to the rear-view mirror. "You mean that episode with the cop? Relax, you weren't even booked."

"I mean long before, when I'd spend weeks in the shade."

"You've never been inside a jail, papá. Tía Fela would have told us."

"This was during my bachelor days in Nuevo León. I owe my last jailbreak to a well-bribed guard."

The suspense stretched out when Gilberto eased on the accelerator. "Anyway, that's ancient history, back when snakes walked upright."

"If you say so. But you know how touchy these gringos are about the law."

"Gilberto's right. How could they possibly know?"

"Gringos keep files for God Himself. They'll tell you things about yourself you didn't even know."

"Be serious, papá!"

"I am. When Tomás Aguirre's son enlisted in the Army they told him he'd fathered a boy three years earlier. It was right there in the records. Took him totally by surprise, but he admitted he'd slept with the woman."

"So what are you telling us, suegro? You knocked up some old lady?"

Imelda said, "I think he's afraid they'll lock him up."

"I'm afraid you'll have a hard time explaining to the barrio why you came back empty-handed."

Gilberto glanced at his wife but found little support. Finally, more out of desperation than decisiveness, he floored the accelerator.

Mr. Olivares, the courthouse examiner, wore a pastel guayabera to hide his ample, civil servant's backside. He escorted them through a maze of corridors and elevators until they entered a large room with fluorescent lights and no windows. Its spartan furnishings caused echoes to collide. When he bent to check the bottom file of a cabinet, the target proved too tempting for don Heraclio's barbs: "That's how Japan lost the war."

"What about Japan's defeat, Señor Cavazos?" he asked with the monotone of a man with his mind on other matters. Without waiting for a reply, he added, "Some time back this old Japanese soldier surrendered almost forty years after the war ended. Imagine, everyone's made peace and he's still out in the jungle." He retrieved a folder and read it carefully. "You lived in Nuevo León before coming here?" Imelda and Gilberto held their breath until he added, "I have relatives in Nuevo León. Never bothered to meet them, though. I'm afraid they'll ask me to help them get citizenship here." He turned and smiled. "We have enough people here to take care of."

He opened another file cabinet. "The exam, then." He sat and sighed audibly the moment his contours assumed their former inertia. "Let's see . . . I think one question should be enough."

Imelda immediately saw the risk. "Just one?"

Mr. Olivares turned to the couple with a faint wink. Don Heralcio, who had not dropped his guard once, caught it too. Then, unable to look the old man in the eyes, Mr. Olivares glued his attention to the sheet in front of him. "Now tell me, señor . . . who discovered America?"

Don Heraclio looked at Imelda and Gilberto, who were grinning from ear to ear, then at his examiner. No one returned his gaze, and in the midst of the mockery he assessed everything: he had committed to memory states whose odd names mirrored their gerrymandered borders, had shuffled and reshuffled scores of dates, in the end had come prepared to answer trivia too obscure even for most gringos, and it had all come to this—the farce of answering something his grandson could have told them.

Imelda's rasp ricocheted off the walls. "His hearing goes at times."

Mr. Olivares, his hand still shielding his eyes, pencil suspended a fraction of an inch from the answer sheet, raised his voice: "Who discovered America, señor?"

Don Heraclio gave them a final, disappointed gaze, then answered truthfully: "Los indios."

In that moment of collective horror the answer flew wildly around the room like an exotic, expensive bird loose from its cage. Mr. Olivares dug the pencil point in his right ear and returned it to the same infinitesimal distance from the answer sheet. "Beg your pardon. I don't believe I heard you right."

"LOS INDIOS!" his echo thundered. "The Indians discovered America!"

Mr. Olivares hesitated a split second then slashed a bold check on the sheet. "Correct, señor!"

Gilberto and Imelda stood and hugged each other as Mr. Olivares navigated around the desk to shake hands. Congratulations were offered as enthusiastically as bureaucratic protocol allowed. No one paid much attention to don Heraclio, who was now only a warm technicality.

Alone within the celebration, he chastised himself for always falling for the same ruse. "Americanos and their rules," he told himself aloud. "They won't even give you the pleasure of losing."

Chapter 36

Marina's eyes darted from one boutique to the next as she led her grandfather through the shopping mall. "Just look, 'buelito. The minute I step inside I get a tingly feeling."

"Maybe the air conditioning's too high." When she pouted in mock anger, he added, "If you're happy, then so am I."

Imelda, walking behind with Gilberto, could not help but overhear. "I see something I like and papá says I'm greedy. My daughter does it and she's adorable."

"You both are," said Gilberto. "Greedy, I mean."

"I'm not denying it. I'm just saying it's not fair."

"But you're supposed to be mature."

"What's more mature than knowing the value of money?"

He was not about to argue with that. He remembered the reason for their trip to the mall. "Then let's hope we've taught her well."

"Marina may be sentimental, but she's not stupid."

Gilberto noticed his wife slowing down every few steps. "What's wrong? Getting cold feet?"

She shook her head. "It's just that papá looks like a wetback in that hat."

"Well, for now put your pride in your purse. Speaking of purse . . ."

"It's right here." She opened it so he could see for himself. Inside, wrapped in the same handkerchief Marina had found it in, was the heirloom bracelet that had been her godfather's gift. "I'm still afraid papá might mess things up."

"This is between you and Marina," he said, then made the sound of a miniature lightning bolt striking. "We'll kill two birds with one stone! I'll buy the old man a new hat while you head down to the jewelry store. That way we'll help keep America beautiful and take him off your scent at the same time."

He hurried on ahead and steered the old man away from Marina. "So, suegro, planning to see the end of the century in that hat?"

"I've grown attached to it."

"I'll say. Worn it all your life, eh?"

"Not yet."

Gilberto paused in front of The Tall Texan. "Look at those ten-gallon beauties. Don't they stir up every John Wayne fantasy you ever had?"

"I never found him that sexy. But if I ever go trick-or-treating as a Texas Ranger I'll buy my costume here."

Gilberto pointed to a far corner of the store. "Over there's your type."

"Over where?"

"Over there." He guided him through the entrance and waved the women away.

No sooner were they inside than he asked, "Who gave you this sombrero, señor? Zapata's grandfather?" He yanked it away, and don Heraclio suddenly felt as if his fly had been open in public. He went after Gilberto, but a salesman headed him off with a smile.

"May I help you, sir?"

Before he could answer, Gilberto was back with the hat they had seen from the window. "We already had our eye on this." He set it on don Heraclio's head, stepped back and framed him with his fingers. "Why, it's David Silva in 'Espaldas mojadas!' "

Don Heraclio could not resist checking for himself. "Where's my hat?" he asked, but his gaze stayed on the mirror.

"It's on your head, señor."

"I mean my old one."

"It passed away in my hands." Gilberto tossed it inside the empty hat box. "We'll bury it later, but since it's my fault, I'm buying."

Don Heraclio examined the new one from every angle. "I don't know. Looks sort of expensive."

"It's on sale," said the clerk. "Discontinued merchandise. Only $49.99."

"Hear that, señor? It's your lucky day. Maybe it'll even help you pick up some old lady cruising the mall."

The clerk made out the sales slip and entered the amount into the register. "That's $52.99, total."

Gilberto saw it coming a split second before the old man said it: "You just said it was $49.99."

"It's my treat, suegro."

"That's not it. He raised the price under our noses."

Gilberto took the clerk aside. "My father-in-law has this thing against paying taxes," he whispered.

"But it's the law, sir. Everyone pays taxes."

"Not him. Look, show him another hat, figure out the tax beforehand and quote him a final price."

"But that's the last we had of its kind."

"Then take it back to the stock room and put it in another box. Add an armadillo feather or something."

"An arm . . .?"

"Something! That way you'll have a satisfied customer, and I'll have a satisfied father-in-law."

But by then don Heraclio had resurrected his old hat and was already at the door. "Hold on, suegro! Where are you going?"

"To find the women while I still have my pants on. This place is a den of thieves."

At that moment, halfway across the mall, Imelda was making a beeline for the jewelry store. Marina, hurrying behind her, wondered aloud why her mother was ignoring the bargains on display. "Because I have to take the bracelet to The Treasure Chest," said her mother. "Maybe they can fix it."

"So can I have it after all? Please?"

"I thought you liked flashier things."

"I do. But this belonged to 'buelita."

"I've told you a thousand times . . . it was mine." She quickly corrected herself: "I mean, it's still mine. Anyway, that clasp is so hard to figure out I doubt anyone'll wear it."

"That's not true," said Marina. "That's why I found it."

Several days before, she had discovered the unclasped bracelet while rummaging through her grandmother's things. And although no one could figure out how to work the intricate lock, a dispute had broken out almost at once: Marina claimed it for herself. "After all, if I hadn't found it . . ."

"If it hadn't been given to me in the first place," said her mother, "there'd be nothing to find." Don Heraclio's reminder that the Elephant had wanted Imelda to bequeath the bracelet to her daughter fell far short of a Solomonic solution. "Fine," said Imelda. "She can have it when I'm good and dead."

But if don Heraclio's advice was too abstract, Gilberto's was practical and to the point: "Sell it," he told her in a private moment.

"But Marina will never forgive me."

"Sell it," he repeated, "or you'll never forgive yourself. Just give Marina half of what you get. What's the use of sitting on top of a small gold mine if you can't spend it? Unless you start digging with that pick it's just a pile of dirt."

Suddenly all that mattered was the thought of sitting on riches, like a queen on a throne. "But I wouldn't know where to start."

"I did some digging around for you. I went to The End of the Rainbow, A Girl's Best Friend . . ."

"What on earth for?"

"Pricing diamonds for my mistress, what else? Anyway, it turns out the owner of The Treasure Chest buys old coins and antique gold on the side. For guys like him even a hobby's tied to money."

Imelda's antennae were already up. "What did he say?"

"It's what he didn't say. He acted indifferent, but I know the type."

"Did he make an offer?"

"He has to see it first."

The moment she entered The Treasure Chest she had no trouble singling out the owner. Dressed impeccably in a dark double-breasted suit, he exuded a patina of tradition, as if his precious metals had passed along their timeless luster. His interest in old gold seemed only fitting.

She pretended to admire a pair of emerald earrings to get his attention, then carefully placed her heirloom on the glass counter. She checked his body language but found only silence. "This bracelet's been in the family for longer than I can remember," she said. "But we've never figured out how to close it." She tried jamming it shut. "See . . .?"

He snatched it as though she were juggling a priceless crystal, then took out from his coat a small tool that resembled a slender fountain pen. With a concentration she dared not disturb, he teased the bracelet's female end for what seemed an eternity. Finally she heard a delicate click. He exhaled a sigh of satisfaction and showed her the locking spring inside.

"That's what was driving me crazy?" she asked.

"This is a very special piece of jewelry. Once you shut the clasp, it's closed for good."

"You mean you can't reopen it?"

"Only if you remove the first link and use the next. One for each generation that wears it. That's why they're called life chains. What's so rare about this piece is its mint condition."

She seemed all thumbs as she set it on her wrist. "Now I'm even afraid to touch it." She paused until he took the bait.

"Perhaps you should sell it, then. In fact, didn't your hus . . ."

"Sell it? That's a thought."

"We're not here to sell it," said Marina.

"Marina, dear, don't interrupt." She turned to the owner. "So how much were you offering?"

He seemed confused, wondering whether she had read his thoughts or whether he had forgotten his own words. "Well, I couldn't give you top dollar. Its true worth is sentimental."

"What are you saying in dollars and cents?"

"I'm saying that people expect a small fortune for their grandfather's pocket watch. For me it's simply an old watch of historical value."

Her disillusioned voice lowered to a more pragmatic octave: "How much?" She studied his tight-lipped pensiveness and added with a lilt, "Gold's gone up, you know."

"It'll come down soon enough," he said, still eyeing the bracelet. "One thing's certain in the universe: the law of gravity." He sheared a slip from the register's receipt roll, scribbled his offer and examined her uncertainty. "Of course, it's only a working price."

She became aware of her expression. "Oh, it's not that. My daughter has to agree first. Half is hers."

He slipped the paper along the counter top so discreetly that Marina failed to notice it until she glanced down. She brought it closer to believe her eyes, then stared at her mother. "Half of this is mine?!"

"Like pennies from heaven."

Her high-pitched squeal sounded tiny. She spun, flinging her arms, and heard a voice that seemed at once distant and immediate: "Watch out!" The next thing she knew she was rubbing her forehead without any idea why. She recognized her grandfather's face inches from hers, but failed to realize he was not rubbing his own head to make fun of her.

Gilberto rushed into the store then suddenly slowed down as if he had entered a sacred place. "He walked out of the store. Just up and left. I tried to warn you . . ."

"Ay, papá. You know Marina's worse than a mountain mule."

The owner, on seeing the old man's nosebleed, started to improvise first aid with a silk handkerchief, but Imelda insisted on using the one in which the bracelet had been found. "He'll be all right," she said. "He just bleeds as easily as a señorita. We'll walk around the mall if you don't mind. Please excuse us."

Don Heraclio tried to protest and look after Marina at the same time but ended up more disoriented. He let himself be led by the hand to a concrete bench where the wobbly world slowly resettled in its axis. He forced himself to concentrate on an indoor fountain just in front of him. He still had trouble tracing its shape, but the uncluttered esthestic of its stream became a prism that cracked open the surrounding light.

Suddenly he found himself returning to a crossroads in his life, on a pilgrimage to a cathedral four days' walking distance from his village. His uncle had taken him, hoping to cure him of his strange affliction: although well into puberty, he hardly talked. Even for a family that bred men of few words, his silent spells were unusually long. And although he read whatever he could get his hands on— besides being taciturn, everyone else in his home was illiterate—he often went without uttering a word for weeks. Whenever his brittle, atrophied voice made itself heard, he would cough up perhaps a dozen words, then turn mute again. "This Heraclio's going to explode from keeping all those words he reads inside," said the uncle who finally took him on the pilgrimage.

At the cathedral his aunt and uncle approached the altar on their knees, but he entered with unbound wonder. He barely glanced at the ornate icons or the gold-leaf altar. Instead he went directly to the gallery of colored windows that appeared to hover in the afternoon air like another realm. He had never seen sunlight pass through stained glass, and the sight left him spellbound. Yet it was not the pantheon of saints that fascinated him but the animals in the ensemble: bronze lions with flaming manes; burros in assorted shades of chocolate; above all, a crowing rooster with chanticleer colors so translucent that he sensed its very spirit. His relatives, fearing that the revelation had left him stone-dumb, took him home without a word, debating what to tell his parents.

But when he finally talked at his journey's end, urgent to retrieve his lost autistic years, his rapture lacked a shred of Christian dogma. Instead he tried to show through the poverty of language how his vision had been as vibrant as any living thing.

The same village priest who had taught him to read knew that to polish a peasant youth into a folk saint one needed a saintly patience himself. He let the boy devour the philosophical tracts he had saved from his own youth in the seminary. But just where did one begin with a man-child pagan who placed Christianity on the same plane as raw pantheism, who preached that the first ray piercing that crystal mystery could engender every species anew?

The local cacique, who said that a little knowledge only drove campesinos crazy, had finally discredited his vision with a cynical and more secular explanation: "He must have nibbled Devil's mushrooms on the way. No wonder the Indians down there are always seeing God."

" 'Buelito! 'Buelito! Are you okay?"

Don Heraclio reentered reality by degrees. He recognized Marina's voice before he realized that her " 'buelito" was none other than he. Then he heard another voice with a deliberate echo.

"Suegro, are you still with us?" Gilberto applied a gentle pressure to his bump. "Good thing you didn't get that hat. Your head just grew two sizes."

"Papá, are you all right?" He gave her a cautious, confused nod. "Good," she added. "Your granddaughter has something to tell you."

Marina searched for the right words. "The owner of the jewelry store . . . wants to buy 'buelita's bracelet."

"It wasn't your grandmother's," Imelda repeated.

"He offered all this." Marina placed the slip so close that his eyes crossed. The blurred figures seemed superfluous, though. "Mamá says I can keep half. Is it all right, 'buelito?"

Imelda turned his own words against him. "He's happy if you're happy, dear."

"But is it right to sell a gift?"

At that moment he did something that had been done to him before, something he had sworn never to do: he avoided her gaze.

"Marina, mi vida," said her mother, "it'd be different if I at least remembered my godfather." She placed the open bracelet on her own wrist to force Marina's hand. "But if you'd rather not sell it, just say so. I could easily grow attached to it."

Marina seemed torn between rejoicing her good fortune and cursing it. She turned to touch the bracelet one last time, when the solution came to her, crystal-clear in its simplicity: she locked the clasp on her mother's wrist.

Immediately, almost instinctively, Imelda tugged at it, but she was too late. When Marina finally looked up at her parents, she seemed bewildered yet relieved. "I needed more time," she said.

Her father's voice had a shrill edge of disbelief. "You had plenty of time! That bracelet wasn't going anywhere."

"I mean time to . . . grow up."

For once her mother agreed. "Yes, you need a lot of growing up to do." She looked long and hard at her wrist, then managed the indifferent shrug of someone who had neither lost nor gained a thing. "Now you have a whole lifetime."

Marina buried her head on her grandfather's shoulder and confessed, "I came this close to selling it."

He began guiding her out the mall when the owner of the jewelry store called out: "Is something wrong?"

"She needs to think it over," said her mother. She waved good-by with one hand and measured a gap of time with the other. "Just give us this much."

Chapter 37

By day's end the hurricane clouds had started to scatter. Gilberto returned from work to find the street flooded all the way to the yard. He estimated where the curb was, parked, then came splashing up the walk.

Don Heraclio called out from the porch, where he had been all afternoon: "Running through puddles only makes it worse."

"I passed the fogging machine a few blocks back, and I want to have dinner before it gets here."

"They're spraying so soon?" asked Imelda. "The mosquitoes haven't even started breeding yet."

Gilberto shrugged. "Anything to send our tax money up in smoke." He tossed a newspaper on the old man's lap.

Don Heraclio thanked him, then noticed it was useless. "One of these days I'll learn English." Still, he was impressed his son-in-law had brought home something besides cheerleader posters for the den he was working on, until Gilberto added:

"I needed an umbrella this morning."

Don Heraclio studied a front-page photo of politicians sandbagging a levee, then asked Esteban to translate the caption underneath. He smiled at their rolled-up sleeves and their rubbing elbows with the common people. "I'll bet they stayed just long enough for the picture."

Esteban singled one out. "Where have I seen this Chicano?"

"He was at Bernal's before the elections," said don Heraclio. "Everyone was hoping I'd shock him with my Kennedy line." Esteban wondered aloud why he had not heard the phrase in a long time. "Because I was only playing into the hands of hypocrites. When I told them I stopped out of respect for their loved ones, someone suggested I wear a 'Viva Kennedy' button. They're no different from Luisito Bernal, who offers Mass for the brothers, then looks for ways to cheat his workers."

Esteban recognized the politician on the front page. "I remember now. He was on t.v., saying we Hispanics have a proud heritage. But he wasn't around two years ago when we were trying to get the barrio flooding fixed."

"These guys take the plunge when the water's safe. Nowadays it's acceptable to be ethnic, especially if there's a buck to be made or a vote to be won."

Imelda overheard enough to interfere. "There's no pleasing you, papá. If you're not cutting down americanos, you're after your own people for being proud of their culture."

"You mean an instant culture, like the frozen enchiladas at Bernal's. Every Cinco de Mayo our people pig out on mole poblano and get drunk."

She shook her head, convinced he would never make his peace with the world, then stooped to pick up Armandito's toys. "If you can't get along with the rest of the world, how about a little sympathy for this housewife? Everyone in the barrio has a maid except me. Just because I'm not at the shed anymore doesn't mean I don't work my fingers to the bone."

Gilberto made the sound of weeping violins through the screen door. "What do you need a maid for? So you can both watch soap operas?"

"No. To help look after papá, for one."

"Don't drag me into this. I can still wipe my own ass, thank you."

"Imagine some sweet young maid getting a hold of my suegro with his check hanging out. Burial time!" He plopped his middle finger into the trench of his other cupped palm. Imelda gave Marina a mortified glance, and Gilberto suddenly realized the double meaning behind his words and gestures. "I meant she'd marry and bury his bones that same week."

"Never mind what you meant. Forget I mentioned it."

Don Heraclio started to protest when Armandito came running up the porch. "Here it comes!"

The billows of pesticide were not yet visible, but the fogging machine's faint drone was already in the air. The southeast wind, reduced to a breeze once more, brought traces of the intoxicating vapors that made barrio boys trot after the truck to get high. Soon the generator's sputter descended on the house with a metallic whine that reminded Armandito of evil robots. He was the first to bolt inside, and the others followed, afraid he might lock them out in his panic. Only don Heralcio stood his ground. Imelda quickly shut the doors and windows, a ritual she followed without question ever since doña Zoila had stuck her head out the door during a spraying and had ended up with a monk's bald spot for her curiosity.

Don Heraclio ignored his daughter's pleas to come inside. It was his latest crusade, protesting the fact that the barrio was always fumigated around dinnertime while the affluent side of town had a more convenient hour.

"Papá, your hair's going to fall out!"

He pushed his hat over his ears. "Who'll know the difference?"

"You'll end up looking like a mangy street dog."

"Good. Then everybody will give me the right of way."

The house was padded in fog when Gilberto said, "Let him battle his windmills. Better here than out in the street."

Armandito tried to wipe the window panes clean from the inside as in cold weather, then peeked out and giggled. " 'Buelito's jumping up and down! Boy, is he mad!"

Imelda barely heard above the noise, and by the time she glimpsed outside, the house seemed to float in the clouds. She thanked her stars that his spectacle was eclipsed from the neighbors.

Outside, a pack of street kids followed the fogger in fighter formation with outstretched arms, echoing its hoarse sputtering. One, overcome by the fumes, pulled out to straighten the tailspin of his thoughts. Through a gap in the clouds he saw a man gesture wildly, then disappear, so he pushed through the fog and water to see what he wanted.

Although the mist had not fully settled, Imelda opened the door because the knocking was so persistent. "Why bother coming in now, papá?" she said, then came face to face with a stoned boy staring with huge eyes through the screen. Unable to get a coherent word out of him, she took the precaution of latching the screen door instead. "Esteban, there's a muchacho loco out here. I think he's high on something."

Esteban had to pacify him through the screen before he could step out into the porch. That was where he found his grandfather's body sprawled by the railing, clutching a hibiscus branch in his fist while a wisp of fog hovered over him, then disappeared.

Chapter 38

Although the water was nearly knee-high, several neighbors crossed the street to the Cavazos house after the ambulance arrived. The driver gave the family a hurried apology. "The water was so high coming in that we almost got stalled. They really should fix these streets . . ."

"I don't think it would have made a difference," said the other paramedic. He tried twice to get a pulse, then stood and muttered aside to his partner, "The old man was already dead in the water."

Unable to find the curb, they had parked next to Gilberto's pickup, and as they brought the body, Gilberto followed with a stunned look, carrying don Heraclio's hat. But after they cruised away like a patrol boat in unknown waters, Gilberto returned with the hat in his hand.

The neighbors who had gathered around continued to stare at the porch corner where don Heraclio had fallen, as though he might miraculously reappear. Marina reached for the hibiscus flower on the porch floor but could not bring herself to take it until her aunt Fela did it for her. She led her niece inside, then said through the screen door, "We need to be by ourselves."

For a while Imelda ignored everyone. When Gilberto handed her don Heraclio's hat, she placed it on top of the refrigerator as though her father might need it any minute. She drank some herb tea Fela had prepared, then asked Esteban to get his uncle Lalo on the phone, taking the handset herself. "Lalo?" She braced her voice by erasing all emotion. "Papá's gone." She said nothing for a moment, then repeated, "Papá's gone." She barely heard his reply, thinking only of the time when she had tried to explain their mother's death and his only concern was that she be back before dark.

She turned silent again, and Esteban realized she could neither listen any longer nor answer his uncle's inquiries. He took the phone without any protest on her part. "Mamá can't talk now, tío . . . What she wanted to say . . . is that 'buelito's dead . . . Yes . . . Right . . . I really don't know . . ." He tried to console his uncle and interpret his father's gestures at the same time. "Papá wants you to come over. He says we should start making funeral arrangements this evening . . . Well, he already had a plot next to 'buelita . . . Thanks all the same . . . Yes, we know the place gets flooded, but we have to respect his wishes . . . So you're coming right over, then?"

In what he called the last gesture of a son's love, Lalo insisted on assuming the cost of his father's funeral. While the expense left barrio mouths gaping, it was but average by mafioso standards. An earlier over-reaction to grief was still fresh in Lalo's mind: upon the death of his father-in-law, in a moment of sentimentality, he had publicly vowed to pay for the lavish services. His in-laws had sworn on their father's grave to share the burden but had later scattered to the four winds. Even Tonio had gone underground, then resurfaced with a tale of Houston businessmen reneging on a drug deal; he had extracted his pound of flesh, but claimed the setback had left him in the red.

"Papá's death took us by surprise," Lalo was telling a group of men, and several of the mourners nodded solemnly. "I was all set to go north for a week of hunting."

"Really?" asked Carlos Menchaca, whose two divorces had left him with little more than a wry sense of humor. "I thought you'd had enough of roughing it after that summer we lived in tents." They were drinking discreetly in the parking lot, just beyond the lights of the funeral home, and his loud voice made a few of the others uncomfortable. "Lalito was so squeamish while picking cotton," he told them. "If he accidentally squeezed green juice from a caterpillar, why he'd be gagging all day."

His irreverence made them wonder whether don Heraclio's spirit was floating about. Lalo ignored him and asked his son to bring his sport coat from the car. "Gentlemen," he explained, "I've decided to have the pallbearers wear matching coats. My tailor's working round the clock."

David returned with an iridescent coat that seemed a blend of silk and a space-age fiber. His father draped it over Gilberto's chest, adding, "Of course, there's no time for custom fitting, but . . ."

Gilberto, a pallbearer and never one to turn his back on a gift, expressed his gratitude. Esteban, though, voiced his doubts.

Lalo mistook his confusion: "Don't worry. I'm paying."

"That's not it." Esteban picked up a coat sleeve, then blurted out his misgivings before the group: " 'Buelo wasn't some gangster shot in the street."

Even Father Adán, not known for conservative tastes, agreed. "Heraclio always said he'd end up in hell, but who'd think they'd send him off in fireproof suits?"

Despite the humor, or because of it, the group turned uncomfortably quiet. Esteban, knowing he was the cause, excused himself. A moment later Samuel Ochoa, El Bruto and Father Adán joined him and began reminiscing about their days as muchachos. Samuel and Father Adán did most of the talking while El Bruto listened. Esteban assumed they were merely trying to cheer him up, until the memories began acquiring a life of their own, and he found himself drawn into their anecdotes, with his grandfather at the center of each. Their words were respectful yet intimate. Even hard times had a nostalgic edge, by virtue of being shared.

He had always seen his grandfather as just that—his grandfather—and it had seemed enough. Now, through their eyes, he was seeing him as a friend. His loss seemed all the greater, but so did his life.

El Bruto continued to say little, content to nod and smile with a soft tenderness every now and then. Then Samuel turned to him and said, "And remember the time he hooked a corn-silk tail on your pants?"

Father Adán, recalling the incident before El Bruto could,

slapped him on the back. "And when we got back to the casa he yanked it off, showed it to you and swore he'd find the joker!"

"It was him all this time?! Heraclio, you bastard!"

Minutes before the funeral home closed, his uncle and several other men came and asked him to reconsider. "What's to reconsider?" said Esteban. "Look, tío, I know you're trying to do what's right, but so am I. And for me these clown suits are an insult."

Samuel, the only pallbearer who was not family, took his side. "The muchacho's right." He added a comment whose meaning was lost on everyone there except Father Adán. "It's as if we buried him in peach guayaberas."

The awkward silence from his uncle's camp made their wish obvious, and when they looked away Esteban would have preferred they stare him down. Finally, when even his father sided with them, he settled the standoff. "I'll step down, then."

The words were barely out when his uncle said, "Find a replacement, David."

"Find two," said Samuel. "I'd end up deported if I wore that outfit." After the others had left he told Esteban, "Heraclio used to say that sometimes a boycott is the only way, even if you're left out in the cold." Then he went to pay his last respects to his old friend. "I wouldn't put it past him to walk out on his own wake."

Esteban was on his way to the parking lot when he crossed paths with a flock of elderly mourners. A couple of them cleared their throats while a third lowered his voice. He had already unlocked his car when the soft evening breeze carried a comment deliberately made audible: "And then psst!, they exterminated Heraclio."

He stood motionless, sensing the tension of those who felt they had trespassed their immunity. For a moment his chest tightened in a knot of anger and pity that seemed impossible to unravel. Then he closed the car door, certain his grandfather would have appreciated the epitaph.

Chapter 39

In the aftermath of the hurricane, beach fronts were left studded with starfish and dunes littered with driftwood. Even a few doubloons from sunken Spanish ships turned up to lure treasure hunters with fantasies of easy money. The wind and rain had also scooped up fauna from swamps around the Gulf and had resettled it elsewhere. That was how David Cavazos, waiting by a cotton field for his drug connection, found a baby alligator floating in an irrigation ditch. He thought of naming it Moses but decided on Heraclio in dubious honor of his grandfather who had died that same week. The choice was really his mother's: she saw a strong resemblance between her late father-in-law and the reptile's biting personality.

At first David kept the gator in his backyard. There, submerged in a miniature, man-made lagoon, Heraclio would lie in wait for curious alley cats that wandered inside. When David received a city summons ordering the pet destroyed, his wife Angelita felt a sweet vengeance. Besides becoming as much of a neighborhood nuisance as his namesake, he was her prime suspect in their poodle's disappearance.

"It was thieves who took him," said David. "You know you can't keep valuable dogs in this neighborhood for long."

"Since when do dognappers leave a chewed ear behind? Either you get rid of him, or he ends up as a purse."

"I can't just flush him down the toilet."

Her reply was an unconscious association: "Then take him to your uncle Tonio's farm."

The suggestion seemed logical to him, for what better place to keep an animal? His cousin Mario agreed. "Our pond's been taken over by shit ducks. He'll be in alligator heaven."

Tonio, though, had his doubts. "Talk about a useless beast. What a waste of jaws. At least our Doberman keeps the narcs away."

Teased by his uncle for keeping an animal unable to pull its own weight in work, David came up with a money-making scheme and offered Mario a partnership.

"It sounds crazy," said his cousin on hearing the plan. "Not only that, if they bust us they'll throw in cruelty to animals."

"If they bust us, that'll be the least of our problems. Look, our dads are always boasting about all the tricks they've used in the trade. It's time we invented one of our own."

Mario tapped the muzzled pet's snout and agreed. "I guess the worst that can happen is having your pet sent up the river."

A few weeks of training was all Heraclio needed. They selected a remote spot on the Rio Grande where a line of willows along both banks gave ideal cover.

The trick lay in crossing the exposed patch of river. "Perfect," said David. "This is the last place they'd expect us to cross." He was right: anyone trying to swim across would be spotted instantly, and at night a nearby power plant's floodlights made it off limits to smugglers and aliens alike.

For David and Mario, though, it fit their needs to the letter. They simply stashed their kilos in plastic trash bags on the Mexican river bank, and the reptile did the rest, hauling with the patience of a pack mule. Clamping a bundle in his snout, he crossed the river submerged, silent and unseen. On reaching the other side, he swam upstream along a ditch overgrown with river sedge then scuttled into the brush. There he left his load under a pile of logs and headed back for more. After crossing each bundle with the stealth of a submarine, he was rewarded with a shit duck, which he took back and buried next to the stash until it was putrid enough to eat.

Afterwards David and Mario loaded the stash on their jeep and tethered Heraclio with enough carrion to last through the next crossing.

While tedious, the strategy was as safe, as David put it, "as inhumanly possible." Best of all, Heraclio was a perfect partner in crime—clamp-mouthed, tireless, dirt-cheap and without a back-stabbing bone in his body. Plans were in the works to find him a bride and launch a flotilla at different points along the river.

The idea might have worked had not Joe Jara, who was digging up cottonwood saplings to sell as shade trees, crossed paths with the alligator, already full-grown. Joe's sighting lasted an instant, but it was fueled by flash-backs of a movie monster spawned in industrial waste. By the time he reached the power plant, the reptile had taken on prehistoric proportions. "He had a plastic trash bag in its mouth," he said breathlessly. "Looked like marihuana to me."

"Mm-hmm," said the plant foreman. "Maybe you smoked some with him, eh?"

The Border Patrol found the alligator next to a nest of kilos left to dry. A chewed brick told them he was skimming off the top. But no one thought he was more than a watch-animal until a rookie unleashed him. Like a reptilian robot, Heraclio scuttled away on his programmed route while the startled officers jumped back and drew their weapons. The rookie who had to pursue him into the river waded up to his crotch when the alligator dove back from the opposite bank and headed straight for him like a live torpedo. The young man scrambled ashore as terrified as the original Heraclio on the day he had first touched U.S. soil.

When the animal returned with an old burlap sack half-filled with culls, Patrolman Eligio Canchola put the pieces together. He staked out the lair, but by then David, with his customary caution, had scouted the area and had spotted trouble.

That same afternoon the cousins placed an anonymous call to the sheriff's office, asking how much bail was needed to spring Heraclio the Alligator. It told the authorities two things: their prisoner's underworld alias, and the fact that their trap had been sidestepped.

In a press release, one official cited the incident to show that the criminal mind would stop at nothing. But neither would the law, he added, and unveiled an apparatus tested in the jungles of Viet Nam and soon to see action along the Rio Grande. With it they could sense the body heat—human or otherwise—of smugglers and other undesirables. No one asked whether reptiles, being cold-blooded, could escape detection.

For his role in the stakeout, Eligio Canchola posed for the papers alongside the animal. "Alligator Express," read the byline. "Pet Fetches Kilos Across River." A grinning Heraclio, jaws pried open, had a county jail placard dangling from his upper snout; Canchola stared steely-eyed at the camera in the tradition of frontier lawmen. The caption informed readers that Heraclio the Alligator was on the left.

Chapter 40

The spring downpour had ended during the night, and with it Esteban's pretext for not seeing Consuelo. The past two mornings he had stood before the living room window, hiding behind a skirt of rain that blurred the world beyond, praying for a deluge to wash the world clean. But now, that time only added up to two more bouts of morning sickness, two days lost in pressing Consuelo for an abortion.

His cousin Licha, also expecting, was having breakfast with the family. She caught him staring at a naked patch of stomach, taut as a peeled grape, and covered up. "Any day now," she said.

He glanced up as if thinking back to a forgotten time. "Funny, you said that months ago." No one laughed, and the room suddenly seemed too warm.

"Any later and they wouldn't have let her into the country," said his father.

"That's right," said his mother. "Immigration's sending back any mexicana who looks the least bit pregnant."

These days Licha did not have to lift a finger in her defense, all the more incredible because that winter she had waddled into their lives out of nowhere, shopping bag crammed with underwear and magazines, her password some obscure relative's name and the Cavazos hooknose. He remembered her words: "I want my child to be an American." His parents had agreed, for who could wish on any child the life she described back home? From then on she had played on their patriotic vanity.

"You're lucky to be an American," she told Armandito at the table that morning. "Your cousins in Mexico only eat one meal a day. And nothing like this, mind you."

Esteban poked Marina's plumpness with his fork. "Let's send you in exchange."

"Kids today take everything so lightly," said Licha, even though she was his own age. The remark won his parents' approval. "By the way, Casanova, a certain Consuelo Mejía called." He had to make an effort to chew calmly.

"Who is she, Esteban?"

Licha added, "She said that if anything's going to be done it has to be today."

"Goodness," said his mother, "are you two robbing a bank?"

He excused himself. "Sure. On a Sunday?" He went to the living room phone, but Licha followed and began browsing through her stack of fotonovelas for unusual names.

"I like Yvette-Xochitl," she said on impulse, startling him.

"For what?" She patted her belly. "And if it's a boy?"

"Ricky-Cuauhtemoc."

"Why not Charly-Cantinflas?" he said on the way out.

He arranged the meeting from a public phone, then quickly hung up for a waiting woman. Flushed with guilt, he felt as if he were leaving a confessional booth after those in line had overheard his sins.

Soon he reached the Anglo suburb where Consuelo worked as a live-in maid. He waited at the same corner where he had first seen her chatting with other undocumented servant girls who had little to do with their free evenings but stroll the block and back. Only one muchacha could go farther without worrying about being caught, and Consuelo had explained: "She works for some judge."

At first he had been content to sit absorbed in her Spanish—so effortless and fluid, so unlike his tongue-tied Tex-Mex. And Consuelo, starved for conversation, was an all-too-willing talker. She had learned English fast, overhearing loose-tongued phone calls for practice, and had proudly pieced together the fact that the lady of the house was having an affair. As she became more fluent, she would backtrack their conversations to test a certain phrase in English. "If I wanted a gringa," he would say, "I'd get the real thing."

The more intimate moments had taken considerable doing on his part. She was a señorita, until he had convinced her that a twenty year-old virgin was an American anomaly.

They barely said a word during the half-hour drive to Mexico: he let the radio do his talking. Soon everything would be back to normal, three weeks to the day when she had given him the news. The announcement had hardly surprised him. The thorny part was that she had already decided against an abortion: "I'm going to have our baby."

They were almost at the border when he asked, "Why today?"

"Sunday is my day of rest."

"But what made you change your mind?"

She faced him as though appraising a stranger, with that same guarded look from the evening they had met. "We don't really love each other. How could we love our child?" Although he had never admitted it, he could not have expressed his own feelings better. What bothered him was that she felt the same way; the same Consuelo who only last week had hinted at taking her life. His first morbid thought had been that a suicide was the proverbial killing stone, until he realized an autopsy would follow. The rest of the day had turned into an emotional earthquake: first, guilt for even thinking such a cold-blooded thing; then, resentment at the thought he was bending over backwards, ending up an emotional wetnurse instead of tending to the business at hand. When he had finally gotten around to checking on the legality of abortions in Texas, it had dawned on him: Consuelo was an illegal alien.

At the international bridge the weekend traffic into Mexico slowed to a snail's crawl. Driving across the Río Grande he checked for his birth certificate almost instinctively. "Do you have your papers?" he asked.

"No."

The sight of an armed Mexican cop just ahead froze his insides. "What if they stop you?"

"Since when is being Mexican a crime in Mexico?"

Her answer made him feel like an idiot. "But how will you get back?"

"Don't worry," she said, which made him worry even more. He returned her assurance by pressing her hand, but his affection seemed as wooden as their lovemaking the past three weeks, when all he could fantasize was the fetus inside her. Were there already features? Probably not, he thought. He had seen one preserved in a biology lab, where a teaching assistant had idly compared it to a piglet. He had set a time bomb inside of her, a flesh-and-blood charge—pulsing, gestating. Now it came down to defusing it.

One afternoon, in a calculatingly offhand way, he had shaped his hand into a pistol and had centered Licha's belly in its imaginary sights. "Suppose you wanted to put out a contract on Junior . . ." She had shielded herself with crossed arms as though thoughts could kill. "Just pretend, Licha . . ."

"My best friend—you don't know her anyway—did just that. The public nurse who did the work had her clean her house afterwards. She said it was to help bring on the miscarriage. I think she just used her to get her housecleaning done."

"A public nurse. Are women born with that knowledge? Like a maternal instinct?"

"You go to any plaza in Mexico and ask for a public nurse, dummy."

Consuelo waited in the car while he squeezed through a human vice in the main plaza, lurching through the fluid rhythm of street life. He circled the zócalo to work up the nerve, then took a park bench facing his car. The reflections of passers-by dressed in every imaginable hue spattered vivid colors on his car's windshield and camouflaged Consuelo's face, but he could sense her watching him. Finally he walked up to a blind street musician, but had trouble expressing himself. His gestures fell on sightless eyes, and the old man's fixed, unblinking stare seemed rude. He continued strumming a battered guitar until a newsboy hawking a mafioso bloodbath told Esteban, "He's stone deaf, too!"

"You're what's making me deaf!" yelled the old man. He sought out Esteban in the same stern tone. "So you need a public nurse, eh?"

"This girl and I . . ."

"Aha! The wages of sin! Well, now get rid of it quick, hear?" For a moment Esteban thought he had read his mind, until he added, "No sense ending up blind and crippled like this poor beggar."

His directions to a nearby public nurse's house were accompanied by aimless head bobs that gave him a disoriented air. Esteban thanked him and tossed some coins in his cap.

After a few blocks Consuelo pointed to a water tower and broke her silence. "I know where we are now. My cousin Quita lives a kilometer away, in the other direction."

They found the nurse spading her garden, half-hidden among yellow flowers. He had not expected that, nor her good spirits and open smile. She welcomed them into a spacious living room with wicker furniture and ceramic flower pots that made the room feel cooler.

She made some mental calculations from Consuelo's last period, then escorted her into another room. He stood too, but she smiled faintly. "For this part we just need her." She glanced out at a large shade tree. "Give us until three."

From behind the closed door he heard heavy furniture dragged and half-expected his own chair pulled out next. Waiting would not help, so he left his birth certificate on the coffee table to let them know he would return.

He retraced his route to the zócalo through several flooded intersections. One avenue required extra caution: children flanking the street lay half-hidden like small alligators along a riverbank. The driver ahead of him, distracted by a girl crossing the street with her skirt lifted to her thighs, suddenly slammed his brakes on hearing a bloodcurdling scream. Several faces popped up laughing from the water. Esteban slowly passed the stalled car, blasting his horn to flush out the rest.

He climbed into a shoeshine stand overlooking the plaza. The bootblack squinted at the puddles that made the day annoyingly bright. "It's still a pigpen, jefe."

"That's okay. I'm just killing time."

"So's everyone else." He indicated a park bench where a couple embraced, oblivious to the world. Near them a man with the pampered, lazy expression of a macho used to having women wait on him hand and foot lay on the damp grass, his head cushioned on his partner's lap.

In a restaurant window across the street a row of kid goats, skinned and stretched on spits over an open fire, seemed to suffer public torture. The aroma of cabrito al pastor that wafted from the restaurant reminded him he had fasted all day, but the idea of eating was not the least bit appetizing.

When he returned, Consuelo was already waiting in the living room. She forced a smile to avoid talking and hurried to the car. Behind him the nurse cleared her throat and busied herself with a pair of figurines—a wood nymph and a Pan—which she was treating with the care of patron saints. She clasped her hands, as if embarrassed to bring up the matter of money, then quoted him a price in pesos. The wholeness of the price pleased him. Unlike Americans, who loved to complicate transactions—ninety-nine dollars and ninety-nine cents, plus tax—Mexicans preferred to round theirs out. "Here you are," he said. The thought of paying thousands in cash, even if only pesos, gave him a slight satisfaction, the only one in weeks.

In the porch chair, eating a pomegranate, sat a woman who appeared ripe for childbirth. The nurse explained, "I'm also a midwife."

"Then maybe we'll visit you when we're ready for children."

Consuelo gave him directions to her cousin's house then fell into a long silence until he asked, "What did she say?"

"Rest."

"What else?"

"If anything goes wrong, I don't know her." She cut off his next question. "It's over."

The rains had almost turned her cousin's barrio into a shallow lagoon. A rooster, perched on a crate, stood stranded in midstreet. "You can't go any farther," she said. "She lives down the block."

"Is there anything I can do?"

She handed him a sealed note. "Give this to Pepita, the girl who works across the street from where I did. She'll bring my things over."

"Aren't you going back?"

She pushed against the jammed door. Outside she seemed her old self, capable of surviving anywhere. "Who knows?" she finally answered. She greeted a girl outside a shanty as if she had known her for years.

"I'll be home in case you need me," he called out, but the gulf between them was already that of strangers. She waded away without a word, and he put his car in reverse.

He crossed the river, roiled by the rains, on a bridge that now seemed anchored by little more than pedestrian faith. He remembered his grandfather's tale of his first crossing. A pale, watercolor rainbow rose to Esteban's left, its arc not quite buried in U.S. soil. He felt certain he had followed it before, on a day like this, through his grandfather's eyes.

Back home he spread a fotonovela on the living room floor and scraped the mud from his shoes. His cousin Licha, pacing the floor and eating a mango, covered every square yard of the room like lava, then looked out the window at his car. "Where in heaven's name have you been? Hunting or making out in the mud?" She nibbled the last shreds of meat from the mango's pit. "Well?"

He was too exhausted to invent an alibi. "I went across, to the mother country."

"Why didn't you tell me?! I've needed new fotonovelas for weeks."

He picked up the magazine by the corners. "Here's something better. Soil from the homeland."

"How mean! And you know I've been craving cabrito." She closed her eyes and licked her lips at the image. "Mmm, drenched in blood sauce."

He dropped the muddy magazine in a straw waste basket and fell exhausted on the sofa. At that moment it seemed that the last few weeks of his life had happened to someone else. "Cabrito's out of season," he said.

Chapter 41

By the time Licha gave birth to a boy, don Heraclio's old bedroom had been converted to a nursery. The baby was already teething when a young man around Licha's age arrived at the house. She introduced him as her brother Quinto and said little more. He was wiry, the way don Heraclio had been, with the bare-bones spareness of someone raised in grinding poverty. That first evening, after Quinto accepted one of don Heraclio's old shirts, Esteban secretly bet Marina ten dollars that their new relative was another moocher. "Licha might as well have had twins," he said.

But Quinto made it clear he was there to discuss family matters with Licha and would leave at the end of the week. He won the family over as effortlessly as had Licha, but without her duplicity. Even Esteban took a liking to him. Unlike Licha, who saw Chicanos as neither here nor there—"ni aquí ni allá"—Quinto showed a genuine interest in them. "The problem with the raza here, though," he told Esteban, "is that most of them only worry about getting a slice of the—how do you call it?—American apple pie."

Licha forced a contained smile. "My brother doesn't even bring an extra shirt, but he never forgets his soap box."

"It's true, sister. How many Chicanos care if someone else in Latin America has to take their place at the bottom?"

But that line of reasoning went completely over the head of Gilberto, who assumed that the rest of the world was beating a path to America. He was even amused at the young man's attitude. "My father-in-law has come back to haunt me! Well, this time I'll put his soul on the right track." That said, he offered to put Quinto up and help him look for a job.

Quinto thanked him but added, "If I had a family to feed I'd take you up on the offer, tío. But right now it's just me and my amoebas." He half-turned in his chair. "Speaking of parasites . . ."

"I already told you," said Licha. "I'm staying."

He shrugged his acceptance. "Just remember, your mask is wearing thin." Although he meant the remark as a joke, he immediately realized he had touched a sore point; for after all was said and done, their blood bond was at bottom a matter of faith. "Anyway, why should family come first? Sometimes someone else deserves a hand more than a relative."

For Gilberto the lesson again fell on deaf ears. "Speaking of relatives," he told Esteban, "have him meet David. He knows important people in Mexico. If Quinto insists on going back, let's at least extend him a helping hand over there."

Imelda agreed. "It'll help bury the hatchet with Lalo's in-laws."

The next day, when David asked Quinto where he was from, Esteban answered for him, since it was one of the few things he knew about him.

"Really?" said David. "Then you must know the Aguilar family."

"I've heard of Onésimo and Martín."

"They're my compadres."

Quinto said little else the rest of the time. Later, on the way back, he asked Esteban, "So our cousin's a pusher, eh?"

"Is it that obvious?"

"Why else would he know the Aguilar pack? Back home they run the drug traffic. They also run over anyone who gets in their way. A while back a few of us took the law into our own hands. That was the only justice that town's ever known."

"Since they're still dealing, I guess the justice didn't last long."

"They brought in some gunmen."

"Hired guns?"

"Cops. Criminals. Same difference. At first the muchachos held them back with ambushes. They even aimed mirrors at a mountain curve and sent a jeepload of the bastards straight to hell."

"What finally happened?"

"What always happens. All hell broke out. People disappeared. But it's not over. Not by a long shot."

"You mentioned something about muchachos . . ."

"That's what they called the kids who fought back."

"Are they part of a group?"

He gazed out the window. "They're part of humanity."

Late that afternoon, while Quinto played catch in the front lawn with Armandito, Licha put her baby to bed. She returned to the living room and paced up and down until she worked up the nerve to break the news. "Forgive me for not telling you earlier: Quinto's running from the law."

Gilberto was the first who managed to speak: "You mean we've been sheltering a common criminal?"

She looked down and nodded. "He had to hide out for a while. Otherwise he'd never leave that two-dog town. That is, if they haven't eaten them both already."

"Why, he's the last person I'd suspect of stealing," said Imelda, "or whatever it is he's done." Her betrayed look turned to worry when Licha walked to the window and back, squeezing every ounce of suspense.

"He murdered a man. He and his friends."

Esteban immediately questioned her candor. "Why didn't you tell us before?"

"I was afraid."

"Of your own brother?"

"Of his enemies. They're probably tracking him down this minute. I have a son to think of. And you, of course. You're family, too."

Something slammed against the frame house, startling everyone. Marina ran to the window and saw Quinto shrug an apology and retrieve the hardball. "Maybe he's innocent," she said.

"Ay, mi vida," said Imelda. "Grow up. If he's innocent, why's he running?"

Gilberto was more pragmatic. "Innocent or not, they won't ask questions before barging into the house." He shook his head and shivered, as if the conversation were too chilling to continue.

Everyone stayed inside except Esteban. It was already dusk when he found the courage to confront his cousin.

Quinto took a deep breath, and Esteban braced himself for a complex alibi. But in the end his cousin simply dropped his arms. "Let's call it a day," he told Armandito, "before the monsters drag us into the night."

That evening at the dinner table Imelda and Gilberto covered up their anxiety with a trivial crisis: whether or not to landscape the front yard. Halfway through the meal Licha said she heard the baby crying, excused herself and did not return.

Afterwards Esteban lay awake under Armandito's night light and Marina's muffled stereo from the next room. A few feet away, sharing Armandito's bed, his cousin finally broke the silence with a deep sigh. "I don't expect you to understand, Esteban. Don't expect an apology either. It's something that simply happened."

Esteban braced himself on one elbow and asked point-blank: "Was it self-defense?" He waited, then asked again: "Was it?"

"Nothing's ever simple, not when you mix politics and poverty."

"But if you're innocent . . . Don't you have legal rights back home, like our Fifth Amendment?"

"Pardon? Fifth Amen . . .? The only way we can plead our case down there is with an M-16."

Both dropped the topic. They talked for a while about sports— Quinto had been an amateur boxer—but even that conversation came in hushed voices. "I had to give up fighting. In the ring, at least. What with a beat-up face and beat-up clothes, the only women I attracted were nuns and nurses."

Esteban offered him some slacks he no longer wore. "I've put on so much weight I look like a bullfighter with a beer belly in them."

"Thanks, but they're still too big. Licha says I already dress baggier than Cantinflas."

"What was your fighting weight? Fly?"

"Bantam. On bad nights I'd swell up to welter."

"Too bad you can't stay. You could put on some weight from tacos instead of knuckle sandwiches."

"Thanks. But you know what they say about house guests and the dead."

Esteban turned off his brother's night light and was on the borderline of sleep when Quinto's words filled the darkness, like the times Armandito was haunted by shadows in the night. "It's coming!"

Esteban asked in an urgent whisper, "What?!" He waited for an answer, then realized Quinto was having a nightmare.

The following morning he awoke earlier than usual, but his cousin had already left. It was only a vague sentiment, as opaque as their kinship, but the thought that they had not said goodbye saddened him.

Chapter 42

The international bridge was still a block away when David began applying the brakes. The distance to the toll lanes turned into an eternity, as though he had down-shifted in time, and an obscure voice from his memories explained how an arrow never reached its victim because the trajectory could be bisected forever. But before the voice could flesh out into a face, he and Mario had reached a toll booth.

The female attendant, shirt back plastered with sweat, said without turning around, "Can't recall a hotter day."

Mario was gazing idly towards the Mexican skyline when the feminine lilt brought him back. "Maybe it's cooler on the other side," he said.

She smiled and peeked at him through the driver's side, so close that David noticed sweat beads on her hairline. He glanced at his rearview mirror: the inspection lanes for cars returning from Mexico were full. Two customs men searched a van while a waiting gringa in a rainbow blouse fanned away the heat. He tried to get his cousin's attention, but just then a car honked behind them.

"Hurry," Mario told the attendant, "what's your phone number?"

She glanced at his wedding band and shook her head with a smile. "Some other time," she said and peeled the shirt from her back with a naked unsticking that made David's spine shiver.

They were barely across the bridge when he said, "Let's take a raincheck. They're putting a full court press at customs."

"So? It's not us they're looking for."

"No, but we'll still end up caught in the net."

"Camacho already has our word." Mario stressed this as though legally bound.

"Let's cross somewhere else, then."

"What's the problem, cousin? You like doing things the hard way?"

"I have this feeling . . ."

"A psychic pusher!" Mario made an extraterrestrial sound. "Leave that to your aunt Fela. Last month we almost lost out when you got this feeling about our Austin contact."

"What about when I refused to go with Torres?"

"Maybe he had second thoughts and went underground for a while. I'm sure he's lying low."

"They laid him low all right. Six feet under. Rumor has it that river pirates got him."

Mario shrugged. "Like dad says, 'One man's misfortune is another man's fortune.' If we don't snap this up there's a hundred other guys who'll step over us to get it. This is coke we're dealing with. The real thing!"

He had heard it all before. "Yes, yes. We're not part of the grass-eating herd anymore. We're meat-eaters."

"Cocodrilos!" Mario grinned and snapped his jaws like a crocodile.

While they waited behind a bus letting out passengers in mid-street, David settled into the same insulation from their first crossing. That time, after tricking Mario's married sister into driving them across and back, each had discovered his true mettle. For Mario, the edgier a situation, the more convincing his dissimulation. While refereeing a squabble among his nephews, he even joined the free-for-all and barely took note of the customs check. But inside the same station wagon, surrounded by screaming brats bent on quartering the goose piñata he had stuffed with downers, David had to tell himself the boys were not some captive species of cub. The customs official who asked, "Are the kids U.S. citizens?", would have been closer to the mark asking whether they were human. In the midst of the savagery, imagining the worst scenario, David had plotted his revenge in case they were busted: tearing open the piñata's paper gizzards and cramming an overdose of downers down the closest brat's throat.

But now, as he drove past Mexican curio shops closed for the lunch-hour, he looked back on that day with the ambivalent nostalgia of a survivor from an initiation rite. He turned off the tourist strip and drove down a narrow street full of pot-holes and patched cars on each side. "My God," he said, "Do people still drive these things?"

Mario yawned and raised his cowboy hat from his eyes. "No. Now they live in them."

Two transit cops sitting on the hood of their patrol car noticed their Texas plates and watched with unusual interest. David locked gazes with one, who glowered as though reacting to a telepathic insult.

"Careful," said Mario. "We don't want them sniffing around."

"We don't want them to smell fear either."

"They're good at that. Fear smells just like money."

David muttered through clenched teeth, "Give these bums khakis and a cap gun and they're lawmen."

Instead of a shared indignation, his cousin responded with a bemused, amoral air. "All God's children got to eat. Besides, you can always buy them off with a bribe." He pointed to a crudely painted Christ on a wide, red cross. "Park behind this drugstore and get lost for a few minutes. I'll pay Camacho and load the stuff."

David sought some shade in a dance hall where the women seemed to have spent the night on the benches. The clients at that early hour were three men in plaid shirts who picked partners and clamored for a polka. The band played a few bars, then abruptly stopped while a boy ran up to collect the money, handed the women tokens and ducked away as though the dance floor had become electrified with the music. David waited for the musicians to warm up, but their noise only got worse. By the fourth number the women clinched their partners like exhausted boxers, and the band's attempt to revive them with a faster beat only stunned them further. The largest of the women danced without a shred of grace, but with an unstoppable stubbornness, like a performing bear. Her partner, content at being engulfed by so much warm, shuddering flesh, seemed on his way to another world. He pressed harder against the woman, and his grin turned into a gravity-defying grimace.

David stepped outside, where a sun-crazed dog ran circles in the street and a shoeshine boy stoned it with a sadistic silence. Two girls under an awning suspended their chat to encourage him, even after David called out, "Careful or he'll turn on you."

If the boy heard, he gave no sign. Plotting the dog's orbit, he waited for it to slow a bit, then connected squarely on the snout. The animal went yelping down the street, and the girls applauded the heroics.

A moment later Mario gave an all-clear sign from across the street and pointed to a bar. "Let's have one for the road!" he hollered.

They entered the cantina, deserted but for the barmaids, and their timid groping in the dark prompted a slurred remark, "Look, two pansies holding hands."

The girl who brought their beer paused by an old juke box that beaconed like a squat lighthouse. Its light bathed her face and arms while she licked her mouth in a slippery ellipse and lip-synched an American song. She gave David a semi-interested glance. He held her gaze, but in a way that added distance rather than intimacy.

The front door opened with a violent mass of light. Quickly, without even pausing to adjust to the darkness, the shoeshine boy made a beeline for their table while David watched amazed. "That kid must have radar."

He pestered them for a shoeshine until Mario tucked his pant legs into his cowboy boots. "I can relate to these little bastards. Before papá got into the business I used to sell tamales in cantinas." He leaned over to tousle his hair, and in the smudged light David thought he saw the boy's face harden.

"Camacho almost went back on the deal," said Mario. David shushed him and glanced at the boy, but Mario added, "Relax. He doesn't understand English. As I was saying, everyone's nervous since Torres disappeared. The machines think he burned them, but the runners insist he was set up."

"All the more reason to wait."

"Where's your business sense? Now's the time! I even talked Camacho into giving us a better deal for the risk."

David looked at the boy's quiet, uncluttered rhythm with a vague yearning. "If they're not crossing, the customs boys aren't making their quota. So they're anxious for a bust."

"So? Camacho's already paid his man at the bridge. We just take the leftmost lane. Like following the yellow brick road, cousin."

"What if Camacho's as tight with his bribes as he is with our share? Remember what your dad always says: 'Two things where a man always feels cheated . . .' "

" 'His bribe and his prick.' " His father had repeated the advice so often that it had become unquestioned dogma. He flexed his fingertips on the table like twin ocutupi doing push-ups and said nothing. David thought he had dropped the matter when he suddenly banged his fist on the table, upsetting their beers. "We'll swim it across, then. Let's follow the road to Perros Prietos, up to that abandoned hacienda by the river. There's good camouflage there."

For the first time that day David smiled. "That's all you had to say."

Mario was about to add something when a second boy opened the door and yelled at the first, "The comandante wants to know what happened to his goddamn bottle of beer!"

"Tell him it's hanging right here!" He quickly added, "I'll be right there!"

He squeaked his cloth on Mario's boots, tossed his lids and bottles into his box and took his money. Mario tried to give him a tip, but he refused.

"These street kids can live under a rock," said David. "In Nam they'd just as soon sell you their sisters as poisoned dope."

"Poverty builds men. Hell, if I'm still shooting blanks by next year I'll come down and take one of these little bastards." He finished his beer and went to the restroom. David turned to say something to the boy, but he was gone.

Outside they followed a vendor's pushcart around the potholes until their eyes adjusted to the glare. Across the street the comandante removed his sunglasses long enough to press a cold bottle of beer to his forehead. David wondered whether they were being watched from behind the sunglasses, but just then Mario took his Saint Christopher's medallion from under his shirt. "Patron saint of the smuggler," he said.

David had heard the list of miracles countless times, but at that moment he was in the mood for a repeat. "Tell me again about the time you beat the rap, when the narcs discovered you'd only sold them alfalfa . . ."

The comandante met two young men inside a dust-covered sedan and guided their gaze towards the two cousins. "Our tickets . . . out of here," he said, as though he were either stuttering or running out of breath.

A young man with a full head of curls smiled, and the flash of his gold tooth instantly corrupted his angelic features. "Did the brat find out how much they're crossing, comandante?"

"Beggars can't be . . . choosy. Be grateful for . . ."

The impatient driver squirmed in his seat and finished the phrase for him . . . "our daily bread."

"So there you were, comandante, nursing the world's worst hangover when this kid brings your beer and a hot tip. That's better than winning the lottery."

"Damn right!" said his accomplice. "The minute you win a lottery there's relatives crawling out of the woodwork."

"Our Father remembers . . . all his children."

"Then play God and give the kid their stereo afterwards."

"Hell, no!" said the driver. "Even God's not that generous. I get first crack at the car." He gripped the steering knob embossed with a naked mermaid under glass and swung the wheel to and fro. "If the little bastard's lying, I swear . . ."

"The comandante cross-examined him in English."

"My, my, comandante! No wonder you wear sunglasses! To hide your baby blues, eh?"

"A man should know . . . a little of everything." He draped a sweat-stained tunic on his shoulders with the studied dignity of a don.

"Uh, comandante, the air conditioning's not working."

"By the end of the day you'll have one blasting like a hurricane."

"Let's go . . . prepare their welcome."

"With mariachis and fireworks!" said the driver.

Their ill-tuned car passed alongside David, drowning out his words: "And what about the time? . . ."

Chapter 43

The letter, postmarked from Mexico and addressed to the Menchaca family, told them of the death of one Gabriel Herrera in a traffic accident in northern Mexico. The hospital nurse who wrote the letter knew him and was present when he was brought dead on arrival. There the attendants had divided up the little money he had and had thrown his wallet into the trash, where she had fished it out and had found their address.

Gilberto read the letter aloud, but no one had a clue who the deceased was. "No doubt she got the wrong Menchacas."

"How do you explain the address?" asked Esteban.

His father shrugged, and his mother added, "What if it's David?"

"She said she'd known this Gabriel for almost a year," said his father. "Don't worry about David. He'll show up soon enough."

They passed the letter around in silence, trying to read between the lines, their eyes narrowing as if they were filing past a slab to identify the corpse. When Licha hastily passed the letter on to Esteban, he asked on a hunch, "Was Quinto your brother's real name?"

"Of course. Quinto Suárez." She clutched her boy and added, "Suárez, like my son and me."

His next lead was more personal, but he asked anyway. "And the boy's father?"

His father cleared his throat, but Licha seemed unconcerned. "He's still out there. Bad weed never dies."

"So did you know this Gabriel at all?"

His mother started to protest when Licha's answer took everyone by surprise: "It was Quinto's alias." She crossed herself and said nothing more.

"Well," said his father after a collective silence, "that's the end of that," as though an invaluable lesson had been learned.

The matter was resurrected that weekend, when Esteban received an unusual request. "Lalo asked if you'd make a quick trip into Mexico," said his mother. "He wants a cross placed where Quinto died."

"What's the use?" said his father. "The next day some mariachi will sell it for scrap."

"So?" she said. "It's his money. I still think it's a nice gesture."

Esteban agreed to it. "I'll talk to tío tonight and leave tomorrow morning." He turned to Licha. "Any words for the folks back home?"

"Tell them to stay on the other side."

Esteban's visit to his uncle that evening was his first since don Heraclio's funeral. "I had this cross made for papá," said Lalo. "I wanted to place it by your porch steps, but you know how superstitious your mother is."

He now understood why his mother had backed the trip, and soon his uncle revealed his own motives: "While you're over there, keep an ear to the ground for any word on the boys."

"Still no word?"

"I'm sure it's nothing serious. It's happened before. They get into hot water and head south to dry out. They have friends there." He gave him money for travel expenses. "In case you have to grease a few palms. And careful with trucks and turkey-class buses down there. Those cast-iron bumpers serve as emergency brakes."

The following morning he dropped by his aunt Fela's for her blessing and found her tending her garden. "I'm going south," he said. "Need anything from Mexico?"

"Samuel," she answered, "if you happen to run into him. He swam over three days ago for roots and herbs and hasn't come back."

"You mean he still swims across?! He could have amnesty by now. He's lived here since the days of tío Porfirio Díaz."

"You know the saying about old dogs. He says he'll never pay the bridge toll. He and Heraclio were two peas in a pod." She went to the porch to feed her ancient parrot, a gift Samuel had smuggled across the river decades ago.

"Lately Cuco sings nothing but love songs," she said. "Hears them on that blasted radio out there." She pointed to a trio of teenaged girls sitting on the hood of his car.

"Seems like you have a following, tía. Early risers, even."

"Early to bed too, I'm afraid. Every male in the barrio over ten is after them. They want to sell my love potion at school for a commission, like some cosmetic. That's all I need, for people to say I'm peddling stuff on playgrounds." She glanced at one of the girls as if they had made unspoken contact with each other. "That tomboy reminds me of myself at her age. She's been pestering me to teach her."

"How else will you pass on your love potions?"

"I doubt your generation even knows what love is."

"All the more reason to pass it on."

"Trying to trick me into it, eh?" She put his fingers in Cuco's cage, something that had terrified him as a boy. "Good thing you didn't study to be a crooked lawyer. What with one nephew smuggling dope and the other defending him . . ." Her smile lingered, but the feeling was lost. "Any news on David?"

He shook his head. "That's one reason I'm going."

"Lalito came and asked for help. But some days my powers seem like a thing of the past."

She gave him her blessing, then called out after he was in the car: "Get back as soon as possible. There's a storm brewing off the coast of Mexico." She dismissed his mystified stare. "I heard it on the news."

His route through the Mexican Sierra was shorter but with occasional surprises. On several hairpin turns livestock lounged along the asphalt or drivers worked under stalled trucks. Death was as visible as life itself: stark roadside crosses, rusted and nondescript, and roadside chapels sprouting bright plastic flowers. Even after he left the mountains behind, they cropped up along the flat highway and served notice that no spot was safe from sudden death.

The distance to the town appeared every few kilometers, but when he finally arrived there were no street signs to guide him. He waited outside the hospital for the first shift to let out. Around three o'clock a group of nurses crossed the street, and somehow he singled out the right one at a glance. She kept a slight distance from her more vocal friends without seeming aloof, and her efficient walk would have made her seem prim but for her healthy, outdoor complexion.

When he overtook the group and told her his surname, she introduced him as a cousin she had not seen since childhood. Later, as they drove to the accident site, she explained, "People here are suspicious of outsiders, especially after Gabriel's death."

"Couldn't you just say I was his cousin?"

"I had to be careful. A lot of people didn't like him."

For a moment he had the impression they were describing two different persons, then he remembered how his own family had emotionally disowned Quinto. "You said his death made them more suspicious . . ."

She searched his face for trust, then said, "He didn't die in an accident. He was murdered on a ranch then dumped on the highway. They covered it up to look like a hit-and-run, but their fingerprints were all over."

A part of him reasoned that the news should not have upset him; either way his cousin was dead. But another part had to know: "Who's they?"

She looked at him again, wondering whether his voice hid the threat of a vendetta. "Hired guns. Lately that's been our town's most popular profession." She indicated a hill up ahead. "That's where they left him."

By then they were outside the town limits. She pointed to a spot on the shoulder and he parked alongside. Taking a shovel from the trunk, he scraped off the brush and dug up plugs of hard, arid earth. Then he planted the cross while she braced it with a mound of stones. They were walking back to the car when she suddenly returned to the cross and stood rooted to the spot for several minutes.

Back in town they stopped at a modest restaurant whose sole

decor was the Christmas tinsel that remained year round. The clientele—a few bureaucrats who dressed beyond their means and dined there to cut corners, along with laborers who savored the luxury of eating out—gave the place a deceptively democratic air.

A young beggar entered and began making the rounds. Esteban dug into his pocket and set aside a small mound of coins, when the nurse said, "You'll only rot his teeth."

Her matter-of-fact response took him by surprise. "How's that?"

"I know this boy. He spends his money on junk food. Whatever's left he spends on video games."

"Maybe that's the only entertainment he has."

"Maybe. But Gabriel refused to give him a single peso. He said it was the only way to push people into action. Now you see why a lot of people didn't like him."

"Maybe if he had explained to the boy . . ."

"I tried once. I told him how important a balanced diet was, but he made it clear he wanted pesos, not sermons. He said if words could fill his stomach, he'd go listen to politicians."

He considered pocketing the change but felt emotionally blackmailed by the other customers who had already given. In the end he rationalized his charity: "Might as well give them away. I'm leaving in a while."

"I wouldn't advise driving at night. You can stay with my friends and leave tomorrow."

He shook his head. "There's a storm on the coast. If I don't get back, I'll get caught in the rains."

"We're too far inland."

"Not for this one."

"Is it true your country's working on ways to break up hurricanes?"

"That's right. Destroy a storm before it gains strength and you'll save lives and property. Not just in the U.S., but here too."

"Did it ever occur to you that some of us might not want that?"

"I don't understand."

"Did you notice the countryside on the way down? It's practically desert. The mountains stop the rain from the north. The only way we get coastal rains this far inland is from hurricanes. Take that away and you take away our crops."

He stared into his cup and stirred the coffee clockwise and then counter, a habit he had picked up from his grandfather. At that moment the boy reached their table, scooped the money and droned out his thanks. His t-shirt had a whale spouting a mushroom cloud, and he wore its English message in all bloody innocence: "Nuke the whales".

Esteban tried to mask his surprise, but she read his thoughts anyway. "We're a garbage dump for your country. When you tire of a fad it's sold over here." He noticed a sad nostalgia in her voice. "I sound like Gabriel now."

"You must have been very close."

Her reply seemed too difficult for even a single, simple word. Finally she managed to say, "It's strange, but the times I miss the most were the ones we never got to share." Her gaze wandered around the room as though she were searching among the faces. Twice she seemed about to say something, and he said nothing until she did. "Maybe we shouldn't have left that cross."

He remembered his father's warning. "You think someone might steal it?"

She shook her head. "I remember what Gabriel said in passing. He wanted no part of a God who allowed so much suffering."

"What did you tell him?"

"What could I? In my job that's all you see."

They finished their meal in silence, then he caught the attention of the first waiter who passed by.

He was already on the road back home when he saw his cousin's cross along the shoulder. He parked in front, found his camera and framed a snapshot for his uncle Lalo. It was while he took the photo that he noticed the dark mass of clouds closing in from the east. He had to work fast: grabbing the cross where the arms were welded, he pulled until it started to dislodge by degrees.

A freight truck zoomed by, all noise and festive colors and with a donkey-killer bumper that read, "The Disobedient Son." He caught the driver's alarmed honks until they grew faint, but he did not stop until he had uprooted the cross completely. Then he hurled it into the brush without bothering to see where it landed, because he had to cross the mountains by nightfall.

Chapter 44

Enough daylight remained for Fela to water her plants. She was untangling the garden hose and dragging it to a corner of the yard when her three teenaged companions took up their usual haunt on the other side of the fence. The tomgirl who wanted to become her apprentice stood among them, surrounded by a silence that drew as much attention as her friends' chattering.

"Oh, señora," said the noisiest one.

"Señorita," Fela corrected her. "Even though it's longer to pronounce."

The girl exaggerated each syllable: "Se-ño-ri-ta, then. One of the men at the casa asked us to give you a message."

She immediately thought of Samuel, and her heartbeat quickened as if she were their own awkward age again.

"A young man named Luis needs your help again."

Fela knelt by the herb patch to pick the young man's remedy and to hide her disappointment. She worked quickly then caught herself and smiled, remembering the days when, on the slightest pretext, she would rush to the casa hoping to see Samuel. She was snipping the healthiest leaves and rinsing them under the hose when the quiet girl offered her diagnosis. "That muchacho looked lovesick to me."

Fela looked up, impressed by her innate talent, and made room for her among the herbs. "In that case help me pick a remedy."

The words were barely out of her mouth when the girl vaulted over the hurricane fence and crouched beside her. The oldest of the three turned down her portable radio when the news came on. "Oh, señora . . . I mean señorita . . . about that guy who was here this morning . . ."

Fela needed no sorcery to intuit her thoughts. "He's my grand-nephew. And he's too old for you."

"No he's not."

"I'll put it so you can understand me, then. You're too young."

Esteban should be returning home by now, so she kept one ear on the radio for any news on the storm. Overhearing the assorted noise of the day's events, it amused her how everything sounded so predictable. "The more things change . . . ," she told herself.

Then, over the adolescent chatter, came: "One final item. The body of an elderly man, nationality unknown, was spotted in the Rio Grande this morning. No foul play is suspected. Authorities believe that despite his age, he may have been an undocumented worker. Rescue workers on both sides were unable to recover the body, which slipped from their nets and was lost downriver. One border patrolman cited the incident to underscore what he called an epidemic of illegal aliens currently . . ."

"Oh, please!" said the noisy girl. "Let's hear something more cheerful!" Taking the matter into her own hands, she tuned in a Mexican love ballad that brought a squeal of approval from her friend.

Fela barely felt her apprentice take her hand. Somehow, through senses that seemed more unreal than any of her trances, she man-aged to pass on her handful of herbs. She tried to stand, but her will was a thing of the past, and when the garden hose fell at her feet, her helpless eyes could only follow the puddle that swirled and encircled her. For a moment she stood lost at the crossroads of an eternal genesis, seeing everything else she might have been: the mother of the girl beside her, sharing unspoken intimacies; an ordi-nary woman with her commonplace happiness of hearth and hus-band; any of a hundred destinies but the very one she wanted desperately to erase.

A rivulet branched off from the small moat that surrounded her and cut an eccentric path along the patch of herbs. She watched the muddy artery flow from her faint shadow, searching the earth until it spread darkly at the girl's feet. Her eyes brimmed as she witnessed a world that glistened as if newly created. She rediscovered herself in those serene, adolescent eyes, as her thoughts took her back to a time, over forty years ago . . .

Rainbow's End is first an adventure novel that deals with dangerous border crossings, confrontations with a sorceress and drug smuggling. It is also the engrossing chronicle of three generations of a family from the Rio Grande Valley of Texas. The trials and tribulations of the protagonist, Heraclio Cavazos, and his offspring are representative of cultural evolution on the U.S.-Mexico border: the rich spectrum of cultural exchange alongside the wanton traffic in laborers, drugs and a myriad of illicit services.

Rainbow's End is a fascinating glimpse into the prism of intimate life and the rarely revealed social and financial networks which dominate this region that is so much a part of the folklore of both the United States and Mexico.

Rainbow's End is Genaro González's first novel. The author has previously published short stories in magazines throughout the Southwest.

A native of McAllen, González resides currently in Wichita, Kansas, where he teaches social psychology and minority studies at the state university.